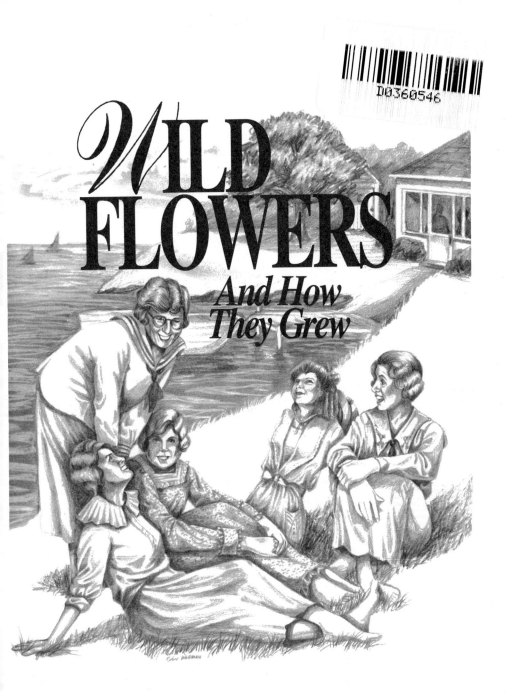

WILD FLOWERS
And How They Grew

A SOUTH DAKOTA HISTORICAL NOVEL
~.. *By Barbara Oaks* ..~
ILLUSTRATIONS BY ROBIN WOLLMAN

WILD FLOWERS AND
HOW THEY GREW

An Historical Novel
of South Dakota

Copyright © 1995 by
Barbara Oaks
4500 E. 33rd Street, Apt 58
Sioux Falls, South Dakota
57103

First Printing 1995

Visual Arts Copyright © 1995
by Robin Wollman

Illustrated by
Robin Wollman

Library of Congress
Catalogue No. 95-92150

ISBN 0-9618582-4-9

Printed in United States of America

PINE HILL PRESS, INC.
Freeman, S. Dak. 57029

ACKNOWLEDGMENTS

Marie Birks, Huron, South Dakota
Ellen Ebert, Huron, South Dakota
Harry Eisele, Frankfort, South Dakota
Evelyn Friese, Huron, South Dakota
Wanda Gardner, Huron, South Dakota
HURON REVISITED (1988) by Dorothy Huss,
Robert Kuni, William Lampe, Margaret Moxon
Gertrude Lampe, Huron, South Dakota
Jean Ohm, Huron, South Dakota
Barbara Wilkens, Huron, South Dakota

AND all the good people of Huron whom I have met and grown to know
and respect whose names are not listed.

SPECIAL THANKS to my sister, Alta Ford, whose assistance
was invaluable.

Violet

Daisy

Gloria

Lavrel

Holly

Sunny

Myrtle

Rose

Lilly

FLOWERS AND THEIR NAMESAKES

DAISY   White petals, yellow center: Clear visioned, bright.

GLORIA   Morning Glory, trumpet-shaped flowers: Exalting,
               honoring God.

HOLLY   Hollyhock, tall with hardy flowers: Sturdy
               and long lasting.

LAUREL   Foliage was woven into wreaths as a sign of fame
               and honor for one's accomplishments.

LILLY   White, waxy flower: Denotes delicacy and purity.

MYRTLE   A creeping evergreen, used as an edging.

ROSE   Flowers of many-colored blooms: Bold with prickly,
               thorny stems.

SUNNY   Sunflower, tall and sturdy with large daisy-like
               yellow flowers.

VIOLET   Small bluish-purple flower nestled in large dark green
               leaves. Needs care, hard to grow.

Dedicated to
"The Girls" Everywhere

PREFACE

Prairie women were as sturdy and strong as the wild flowers that grew and flourished, despite adversity.

Their friendships throughout their lifetimes are what this book is about. The joys and sorrows they shared and the men who loved them became the substance of what made those lives meaningful. The example they set is a testament to what they made of their abilities, perseverance and vision.

It is told through the eyes of Holly.

TABLE OF CONTENTS

South Dakota

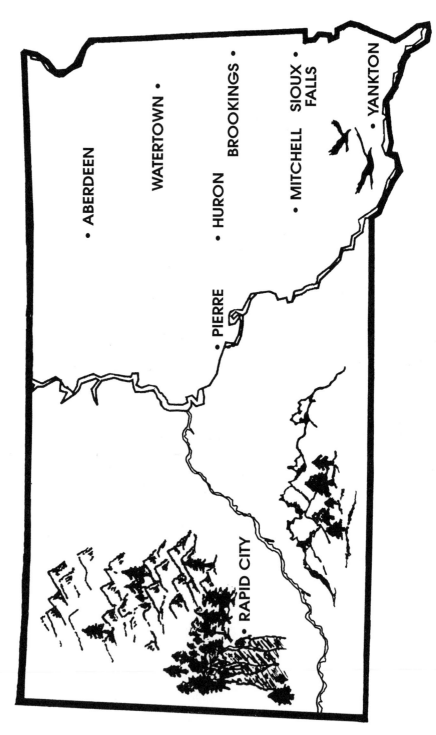

- ABERDEEN
- WATERTOWN
- HURON
- BROOKINGS
- PIERRE
- MITCHELL
- SIOUX FALLS
- YANKTON
- RAPID CITY

PART I
SEEDLINGS

Chapter 1

It was 2:15 and Karen was late. It was hot and the humidity hung in the air like a mist, a typical day in late August in South Dakota. It was already 97 degrees in the shade and was sure to get even hotter. She was in no mood for the assignment and she hoped the building was air conditioned.

She was to interview a woman who had just turned 100 years old to be included in the Sunday Supplement of the Huron Plainsman. She drove into the driveway of Sun Quest Village and continued on the curved driveway to The Huron Nursing Home, in front of which stood a flag pole with the American flag and the flag of the State of South Dakota hanging limply from it. The parking lot was full and she had to park a distance from the double-door entrance of the one-story brick building. Even the handi-capped parking spaces were occupied and, she noted with some irritation, by cars with no handicapped identification. She shut off her car, grabbed her briefcase and purse and walked resignedly toward the nursing home. Perspiration dotted her forehead and her hot feet squished inside her shoes.

She entered the building and noted that corridors extended, spoke-like from a central circular admittance desk, behind which several young women were occupied. It was somewhat cooler inside, but not with the icy temperature she was used to. Several elderly men and women were seated in the lobby to her right. It was a pleasant area with comfortable chairs, a large television and a clock with big numbers over it, and colorful pictures on the walls. There was a beauty shop behind the desk and nearby shelves of crafts done by the residents.

She stopped at the desk and asked for Mrs. Hoekstra's room. One of the young women in white pointed and said, "Third door on the left down that hall." As she walked down the hall Karen's senses were assailed with an occasional sour smell long associated with nursing homes and decided then and there that she would make it fast. The interview would be brief. She would take a photograph and leave quickly. She had other assign-ments.

1

At the designated room she paused, took a deep breath, and told herself it wasn't Mrs. Hoekstra's fault that she was hot and tired and didn't want to be there. She also told herself that she, Karen Williams, news reporter, would not ever get old and end up in a place where only feeble old people lived. She tugged at her blouse to get some cool air circulating, put a fixed smile on her pretty face and, although the door was open, knocked softly and said politely, "Hello."

There was no response. She remembered that often old people don't hear very well and stepped quietly into the room and said, "Hello?" once more. She was greeted with a loud snore.

Oh no, I hope that isn't her.

She soon realized that it was not her. There was a curtain separating the small room and on the other side of it she heard a firm voice say, "Yes, who is it?"

"It's Karen Williams from The Plainsman," she said, raising her voice slightly.

The woman in the first bed continued snoring loudly.

Karen moved to the middle of the room and pulled back the curtain. She was relieved to see a tall, gaunt woman, slightly stooped with age, sitting on the bed. She was fully dressed and her small area was neat. Her white hair was thin and was twisted into a bun on top of her head. She wore no glasses, permitting a clear view of her bright blue eyes. Her bed was near the only window and on the sill sat several pots of blooming plants that appeared to be thriving. Also on the broad sill was a quantity of greeting cards neatly aligned , undoubtedly for her recent birthday.

The old woman smiled and said, "Come in, Miss Williams. They told me someone was coming to see me."

"Yes. The Plainsman asked me to interview you for the Sunday paper."

Mrs. Hoekstra expressed surprise. "My goodness, whatever for?"

"We want to run an article about your life, considering that you just celebrated your 100th birthday."

"Oh that. Others have lived as long and longer," she replied.

"That's true. But from what I have learned, you were instrumental in forming a women's club and have led an interesting life."

"Yes, but I was only one of several of the girls who belonged and that was long ago." She smiled at the word 'girls.' "Goodness, that club is very different now, but the name is the same, the Huron Fortnightly."

Karen felt a slightly cool breeze from a fan set on the sill and shifted her weight. She wiped her brow with a tissue. "Are you too warm, Miss Williams? I can boost the fan up to high if you like."

"I'm fine, but the fan feels good. It is really hot today."

"These old folks in here like it warmer than you younger folks. This place does have air conditioning, but it's not kept too cold. When it's on we can't open the windows. I'm always glad when the windows are open and the breeze comes in and we can hear the birds. There is a nice big tree outside my window and the birds .... "

"Mrs. Hoekstra, do you mind if I sit down?" Karen found a metal folding chair leaning against the foot of the bed.

"Please do sit down. I'm afraid that uncomfortable chair is all I can offer you. I never use it myself. It's too slippery and hard to get up from. Whoever invented that torturous device never had to sit in it for any length of time. When I need a change of scene I walk to the lobby and sit in one of the comfy chairs in there and watch the people come and go. The television is usually on but I can tune it out and work on my needlework or read the paper. Television has certainly changed. Goodness, I remember when it first came out with just a couple of programs for a few hours a day. Such a novelty it was." Karen unfolded the chair and literally sat at the feet of her subject seated on the high hospital bed. The chair was not comfortable and she would make her interview brief and fast. She looked up at Mrs. Hoekstra who was gazing at her with interest and, she noted with some discomfort, considerable piercing insight. Her face was thin and wrinkled, but her clear eyes told Karen that somebody was assuredly at home. And, much to her surprise, Mrs. Hoekstra had already had much to say.

The snoring in the other bed continued. Mrs. Hoekstra said, "You'll have to forgive Ula. She needs her afternoon nap. Gets cranky if she misses it. She can't even enjoy any company she might have. As for me, I never take naps, never did even as a child. My mother would get completely out of patience with me because of my stubbornness. Poor woman, she needed her rest with ten children to tend to. I was the youngest, you see. Now I'm the only one left. All of them gone, but me. Even all my friends — Sunny,Laurel, Myrtle, and the others."

She looked out the wide window, seeing things Karen couldn't even guess at.

"Mrs. Hoekstra," she said hesitantly. "I don't wish to bother you. If you are tired, I can come another time."

"Oh no, Miss Williams. I'm fine, just fine. I get to day dreaming now and then. Sorry. Just what was it you wanted to ask?"

"Well," she said as she pulled out her notepad and pencil. "You've just reached the age of 100. That is a very long time and you must have some interesting memories, some remembrances you'd like to have in the paper."

Mrs. Hoekstra's bright blue eyes crinkled at the corners as she observed her young guest.

"Gracious, I wouldn't know where to start."

"Let's start at the beginning. Where were you born?"

"Right here in Huron at the south edge of town. That is, it used to be the edge of town. Right now it would be close to where the bandshell stands in Campbell Park. I am a born and bred South Dakotan. It was the last day of July, 1893. Mama said it was the hottest day she could remember. She would never forget how hot it was."

Karen was making notes. If it was as hot as it was that day she could imagine the discomfort. No modern medical care, no air conditioning, not even an oscillating fan. She wiped her neck with a tissue. Mrs. Hoekstra turned up the speed on the fan. "All of us children were born at home. Doctors made house calls and babies were born at home. Mama said it was the way it was supposed to be. And there was always someone to help out until the mother was back on her feet again. In those days new mothers often spent many days in bed with someone on hand to help her with the baby and to make sure she was fully recovered before she resumed her duties."

Karen thought of her friends who had babies one day and went home the next, only to become frazzled and worn out, with no one to help. Maybe she wouldn't have children was the thought that occurred in her warm brain. The fan was cooling her down and she began to relax and enjoy Mrs. Hoekstra's good nature, a plus she had not expected.

"As I said, I was the youngest of ten children. Big families were the norm, as they say, back then. Actually, large families were a necessity. Life was hard and many hands and backs were needed to do all the work that was necessary to survive in those days. Not like it is now with both parents working and the little ones left in the care of a sitter or, worse, all alone. I suppose it's progress, but something has been lost." She sighed.

"Really, Mrs. Hoekstra, if I am tiring you I can do this later."

"Land sakes, child, you are not tiring me. What do I do to get tired these days? I walk up and down the halls every day for exercise and to keep my stiff joints working. Can't just sit. I don't know how some of these old people can just sit and nod."

A loud snort interrupted her. "See what I mean? I do like Ula, but her snoring gets on my nerves. That's when I go for a walk."

Karen continued. "Coming from a big family you must have some great stories to tell."

"Yes, some fun times. Lots of laughter as well as lots of hard work. We all had chores to do, even the younger ones. My job was to wipe dishes. I really hated doing the silverware. There were five boys and five girls. Mama and Papa said they couldn't have done it better if they had planned it." She chuckled. "Planning a family was unheard of back then, not like it is now. Then, with mischief in her eyes, she said, "Although I do believe that when the Holy Edict of 'Go forth and multiply' was issued, folks had no idea of the consequences, of what it would mean centuries later when that command was more than fulfilled — too often by irresponsible people. There

4

are so many poor souls in the world with so much poverty and needless suffering."

Her words gained in fervor as she spoke and she looked at Karen apologetically. "But that is just my opinion, Miss Williams. I really don't care how many children folks have, but they had better be able to take care of them. During the Great Depression they had better sense."

Karen was amazed at Mrs. Hoekstra's unconstrained comments.

"Please, call me Karen. I find your remarks quite candid for a woman so ...."

Another chuckle and Mrs. Hoekstra finished her sentence. "Old? Out of touch? I do a lot of reading."

"No, nothing like that," Karen said hastily, as she fumbled to extricate herself from a poorly expressed thought.

Mrs. Hoekstra smiled. "No need to explain, dear. I understand. I am opinionated, and when there is someone to talk to I talk too much sometimes. Now let's see, where were we? Oh yes, my family. Papa worked on the railroad, the Dakota Central. He was an engineer and was paid well. We were so lucky to know the security of a closeknit family. Mama never let us forget how well Papa supported the family and how much better off we were than some unfortunates in town. We realized eventually that the conductor probably had an easier and more interesting job with all the people he came in contact with, but Papa had to guide the train along the track in all kinds of weather. More than once he had to act fast and bring the train to an abrupt stop, if he could, considering the tons of train he was controlling, because of an errant cow standing on the tracks, chewing its cud, calmly watching the engine bear down upon it .

"Huron was the headquarters of the railroad in Dakota Territory. Everyone depended on trains to bring essential goods to settlers in the territory and later to the State of South Dakota. Suppertime was lively back then, with the family seated around the table, and Papa always told us how important the railroads were and how essential his job was. He'd be gone a lot, but when he came home at last he had such stories to tell, and sometimes he'd bring us something, maybe a special treat like a sack of hard candy. His run often extended clear to the Missouri River, the Mighty Mo it was called. Have you ever been to the river?"

Karen admitted she had not.

"You should see it. It's mighty impressive. Good fishing, too."

They were interrupted by an aide who brought in glasses of juice on a tray.

"Here you are, Holly. Be sure to drink all of it," the young woman said in a loud voice.

When she had left the room Mrs. Hoekstra said, "That one always shouts at us. Thinks just because we have white hair we can't hear. They

5

call us old folks by our first names, which is not very respectful, but I suppose they think it puts us at ease."

Ula, now awake, asked in a confused voice, "Who was that? Did you get some juice, Holly? Where's mine? I want my juice."

"It's right there on your table, Ula. See? Right beside you," Mrs. Hoekstra answered, slightly raising her voice.

A mumble came through the curtain separating the two beds and she said, "Poor Ula. She gets a bit addled at times. She came a few years after I did. I lived alone in my home for years after Mr. Hoekstra died, but eventually had to give it up and come here. We never had children. It was the Lord's will, I guess. I don't have as much company as I used to. Most everyone I knew has passed on. And now I am living with old folks."

Time was passing and the hour Karen had allotted herself was almost gone. She had not gotten all she came for.

"Tell me about your brothers and sisters, Mrs. Hoekstra."

"As I said, there were ten of us, five boys and five girls. Bernard was the oldest and he worked on the railroad with Papa and for years after Papa died. It pleased Papa to have him continue in the profession. Howard was a teacher. George was killed in World War I. Carl went to Chicago to make his fortune, he said, and just disappeared. No one ever knew what happened to him. It devastated Mama and Papa not knowing. That, along with Oliver, the youngest of the boys, almost did them in. Oliver and Rachel died during a diphtheria epidemic when I was just a toddler, so I never really knew them. There were old photographs in fancy frames that Mama kept on the piano. They were forever young and Mama could not look at them without tears coming to her eyes. Diphtheria, scarlet fever, smallpox and even typhoid were deadly back then and took many lives for several years. Folks didn't have the know-how to treat such diseases, nor how to prevent them. In those early days the Welter Hospital was where those contagious people were sent. It was called the 'pest house' just like some awful institution in medieval times. Mama and Papa refused to put Oliver and Rachel there. Caring for them wore her out. Mama nursed them the best she could, but they died.

"Madge was the oldest of us girls. She seemed more like an aunt than a sister. The older ones tended the youngsters back then, so I had lots of attention. Madge never married. She stayed on at the house with Mama and Papa after the others had left until our parents passed on. She was completely used up, practically gave her life for the rest of us. I think she just gave up after Mama and Papa were gone, as she felt she was no longer useful. She looked ages older than she was. Then there was Hazel, along with Opal, who were close together in age, and of course Rachel, who died young. I came along last. Except for me, Opal was the only one left until 30 years ago when she died at the age of only 85. I sometimes wonder why I'm still here."

Karen couldn't imagine living that long. She was still coping with a boyfriend who couldn't seem to commit himself to her. The sun had moved past the window in the room and long shadows of the trees in the yard would remain in the late afternoon until the warm evening would gradually erase them, without noticeably lessening the heat that lay heavily on the land. Ula had turned on her radio and the sound of religious music filled the room as she valiantly sang along. Karen could see that she was finished for the day, but far from the end of her project. She folded her notebook and said, "I have to go now, but may I come again? I'd like to hear more."

"Of course, but I don't see what all the fuss is about. I'd love to visit with you again. I don't have much company anymore. Come as often as you like."

Karen smiled and shook Mrs. Hoekstra's hand. "Thank you. I've enjoyed talking to you, too, and look forward to hearing more of what you have to tell."

Back at the office she told her boss, Ralph Stern, "I'm afraid I won't have the article on Mrs. Hoekstra done in time for Sunday's edition. I'd like to do an in-depth interview and it will take more than an afternoon to do it. She is talkative and interesting and I think the result will be worth the extra time it takes."

"That's OK. Take your time. Something else has come up. I just sent Bob out to check on reports of animal cruelty and take some pictures. What makes anyone be cruel to dogs? It's beyond me."

The Interview

Chapter 2

Karen pulled into the parking lot of the Huron Nursing Home and emerged with more enthusiasm than she had the day before. She was on time. She gave the young woman at the desk a friendly wave and went directly to Mrs. Hoekstra's room. Ula was taking her nap, snoring contentedly. The curtain separating the small room was partially open and her subject appeared to have been waiting for her. She brightened when she saw Karen. The fan was set on high.

"Hello, Karen."

Mrs. Hoekstra was fully dressed, as she had been the day before, but it was a different dress and she had applied a spot of rouge and a touch of lipstick. Karen could see that she had once been a striking woman.

"Hello, how are you today?" Karen asked.

"Just as I felt yesterday and the day before that. Just fine. I am really a healthy person. I'm just old, with the aches and pains of old people. You are looking very pretty."

Karen was a pretty young woman in her twenties, slim and well groomed, neatly dressed in a pastel sun dress. Her blond hair and brown eyes made a pleasant combination. She set up the folding chair and took her notebook from her briefcase, prepared to continue the interview, and to finish as quickly as possible.

"It sounds like you had a happy childhood, Mrs. Hoekstra."

"I did, for the most part. There were lots of children in the neighborhood to play with and we played together harmoniously most of the time. Of course, there was that nasty boy, Butch. We didn't know him very well and didn't want to. He was called just Butch. He was a few years older than the rest of us and he was a bully. He took a strange kind of pleasure in knocking us girls down and making us cry and in picking fights with the boys. We hated to see him come because there was always trouble. But Randolph acted as our protector. Dear, gallant Randolph. He was taller than the other boys, but he was no match for Butch. He would always try, but Butch would call him a sissy and then punch him and knock him down, too. Then he'd walk away with a swagger, as though his mission had been accomplished, and laugh his husky laugh at us. We could never figure out why he was so disagreeable until we were older and wiser."

She looked out the window at the trees, standing motionless in the shimmering heat, their leaves wilted and faded. Karen didn't know if she should interrupt her reverie or not.

Holly was seven again with her young friends in the vacant lot. It was a bright warm day. Holly and her best friend, Sunny, were standing close together crying. Randolph lay on the ground, his nose bloodied and his clothes covered with dust. He was crumpled in the dirt, humiliated again in front of the girls, to say nothing of the boys, futilely glaring in anger at Butch as he swaggered away, his cap set at a cocky angle, his hands in his pockets.

That Butch! Why was he so mean? None of them ever did anything to provoke him, and he seemed to enjoy it so. Besides, he was bigger and stronger. It wasn't fair. The boys stood around Randolph. The girls had struggled to their feet and were clustered together, apart from them.

"Come on, Randy," said one of the boys. "Don't let that dummy bother you."

"Yeah, come on, get up," said Clarence. "That dumb old Butch is so big he has to wear his pop's underwear."

That made the girls giggle. Butch in his pop's underwear. What a picture. Sunny's crying stopped and she joined in the laughter. Soon they were all laughing at Butch, chiding him, hoping he would hear them, but knowing they were safe, and he didn't turn around at the end of the path.

The neighborhood vacant lot served as a play area. There were bare spots where the grass had been worn away from all the traffic. No weeds grew except around the perimeter, and there was plenty of dust. A large tree on one side served several purposes. It was the central point of any gathering. It served as a lookout for imagined danger. It was the headquarters for meetings, mainly among the boys, who assumed leadership and who, though they accepted the girls, made it plain they were in charge. Girls didn't attempt to climb the stick ladder that had been pounded into the huge, gnarled trunk to get to the rickety platform, because girls weren't supposed to climb trees. Holly and Sunny did so one night when no one was around, but they were punished by their parents when they got home too late with torn, muddy blouses.

Sunny was Holly's best friend. They had much in common and were both tall for their age of seven. Holly envied Sunny her long, blond curls and colorful ribbons in her soft tresses. Holly had darker hair and she had been called plain too many times to suit her. It was hard to take comfort in her mother's oft-repeated remark that to never mind; she had good bone structure. Holly really didn't understand the phrase, but thought it must be a compliment.

Mrs. Hoekstra stirred and turned from the window. "Back then, if a nice boy was put in an embarrassing situation, no one teased or set upon him, except in good fun. It was the bullies who were really hurtful."

Karen wondered what had been going on in her head, but only said, "What about the town? What was Huron like then?"

"It was a busy, active community and it was the railroads that brought settlers west. Like many established communities that were begun at that time they had advertised in papers back east and even in Europe, where conditions were pretty bad, to try to get people to come to the midwest. And it worked, because thousands of people from all over came to get free farm land. That was before I was born, of course, but Mama and Papa made sure we knew about our beginnings and our heritage, and also our responsibilities. Nothing was free, he insisted, but had to be worked for. He planted trees around our house. It's hard to believe it to look around Huron now, but there were very few trees at first. There was just flat prairie with a few buildings here and there. Folks got trees down by the James River, the Jim River we called it, and transplanted them all over town. They looked real pretty and, over the years, they grew tall and gave us shade as well as beauty in the hot summers.

"It was a time when big houses were built to accommodate the big families. Porches ran around half of those Victorian homes and many evenings were spent on those porches, cooling off after a hard day's work. Papa bought our house for under $1,000. It was three stories with a full basement, where Mama did the wash in cast iron tubs and a washboard, hanging things on lines strung across the basement in the winter when she couldn't hang them on the long lines in the back yard. The older girls would help and bring in the baskets of dried linens and clothes, sprinkle them for ironing — you know, dampen them so they could be ironed with a very heavy iron that had to be heated on the cook stove. It took two days each week to do the washing and ironing and it was tiring. Poor Mama's hands were so red and rough all the time.

"Of course, the winters were just as cold as the summers were hot. I remember Papa telling us of the blizzard of 1881-1882 when so many died. It happened again in the famous blizzard of 1888. Snow drifts reached to the rooftops, they said. We were told of how we had to stay home for weeks because schools were closed. Trains became stuck in the mountains of snow and it was spring before they could run again. Mama said she loved that time when the whole family was safe at home and we were all together, snug and warm. We never were bored.

"Then Dakota Territory became North and South Dakota, and Huron began to grow. It became the county seat. Papa said Huron was supposed to be the state capital, but Pierre got it instead. Prosperity caused wages to go up to $2.50 a day. Of course, a work day would often be twelve hours long, and plenty of men worked all day Saturday, too. But you probably know all of this. It's a matter of record and in the history books."

11

"Tell me, Mrs. Hoekstra, about the Women's Club. I'm sure our readers would like to know about this contribution to Huron."

"To set the record straight, Karen, our group joined the General Federation of Women's Clubs, which was formed nationally in 1899. Our club was called the Huron Fortnightly. It still has that name. I haven't been a member for many years, but it is still going strong. We joined way back when World War I ended. So many changes had occurred and women were beginning to 'feel their oats' as the old saying goes." Her eyes twinkled at Karen's puzzled expression. "You know, as when a horse is full of ginger when his belly is full; he gets a bit frisky."

Karen nodded, but it was clear she didn't understand.

"There were nine of us in the club at first. We were young and full of hope and idealism. The Great War had ended and the future looked bright. Little did we realize. Do you know, my dear, how many wars I have lived through? I don't remember the Spanish-American War, of course. But after the First World War there was the Second World War a generation later. A dreadful time. A few years later there was the Korean War and then Viet Nam, for which no logical reason has ever been given for our being over there. Perhaps you can tell me, Karen. What was Viet Nam all about? To say nothing of our meddling in the affairs of other countries in between wars right up to the present time. When will the foolishness end? So many innocent lives have been lost."

Mrs. Hoekstra was clearly upset but she could see that Karen was at a loss as to how to answer.

"I'm sorry, but I do get all het up about the stupidity in the world and the helplessness of those of us who have seen it happen over and over. Please ignore the ramblings of an old woman."

She was breathing heavily and waved her tissue before her face in the closeness of the small room.

Mrs. Hoekstra was certainly not the senile person she had expected and dreaded.

"You needn't apologize. I, too, think wars are stupid and archaic. When I attended Huron College my major was in the liberal arts and I loved it. I only wish the third world countries would enter the twentieth century."

"We old folks still call them backward. But we can't solve the world's problems, can we?"

"Perhaps we should get back to the Huron Fortnightly Club."

"Let's see. There were nine of us at first, as I said, and we were all so different. I suppose that is what made us so effective. We were in our twenties and were the generation that would make a difference. We had so much to contribute in the changing world. We had been out of school for awhile. Only two of the group had gone on to Huron College when we graduated from high school, Laurel and Violet. Talk about differences! Laurel was so smart and graduated Valedictorian and also graduated from college with honors. She needed glasses so strong and thick that they took away from her good looks. Violet was smart, too, and came from a wealthy family. She was tiny with black hair and deep blue eyes the color of dark lilacs. She was an adorable child. Why she ever enjoyed being with such a rambunctious bunch as the rest of us were as children I never understood, or why her family permitted it, being of a different class of people and all. Maybe it was because she was an only child with a background so different that her folks figured she should know how others lived. I'm sure they didn't like the way she went home all dusty and dirty, but she had fun and we accepted her after we learned that she wouldn't break if she fell down."

She smiled at the memory and gazed out the window. She was a child once more back in the vacant lot.

Violet wasn't crying but her small heart-shaped face was full of rage as she watched Butch swagger away. She uttered a disgusted sound and shook her tiny fist at his receeding back.

"Dumb Butch." Then louder, "Damn Butch!"

Her eyes grew large and she quickly covered her mouth as the offending word spewed out. The others looked at their small companion in astonishment. In their tender years none of them had ever said such a thing and most of them had never heard such a thing, especially from one more refined than they. And they couldn't help but wonder where she had heard it. Then they giggled and began to chant, "Dumb Butch. Damn Butch!" and jumped up and down, secure in the knowledge that Butch was long gone and couldn't hear them.

Then Holly spoke, "I think that must be a naughty word. My brother, Bernard, said it once and Papa told him to never say it again, 'specially when Mama was around. I think we oughtn't to tell about what we said. We can tell about dumb old Butch though."

All were in agreement, and that night at the supper table, after grace, parents in the vicinity were again regaled with a story about Butch, who would not stop bullying their children. Holly's father said he would speak to Butch's father, but he didn't seem very eager to do it. They lived on the north end of town, across the tracks, and folks over there had a tendency to be rough and tough. But the children were pacified, at least until Butch showed up again. They thought it odd that he always showed up by himself, never with buddies. Maybe he didn't have any buddies. But, they rationalized, it served him right not to have any, being so mean. When he was twelve, Butch dropped out of school and went to work with his pop at Blume's Brewery.

Mrs. Hoekstra sighed and once again Karen worried about tiring her, but Holly shook her head and replied, "I'm sorry, Karen. I do tend to go off now and then, just remembering. Where was I?"

"You were talking about Laurel and Violet."

"Oh yes. Then there was Myrtle, Daisy, Rose, Gloria, Lilly and Sunny, of course. Violet and Lilly were close, being small, just as Sunny and I were close being so tall. Myrtle was on the edge of everything we did. She never took any initiative, but was willing to follow us on any of our adventures. Daisy had such a clear view of everything. She could get to the crux of any situation and would get out of patience with the rest of us who took too long to see her point which she considered to be obvious. Rose was very outspoken, sometimes too much so, and there were hurt feelings. She often spoke before she thought, but that is a failing many of us have. We understood and forgave her. Maybe it was her red hair. Gloria had an excuse for anyone's behavior, even Butch's. She said maybe he didn't have a mother; maybe he was an orphan; maybe his pop was mean too. Besides, we were all Christians, weren't we, she'd ask. We were supposed to forgive. Dear little Lilly was always so pale and suffered from asthma. We were friends from childhood and remained so all our lives. Now they are all gone, except for me." She smiled. "Those close friendships were our strength as we traveled the bumpy roads of our lives. Young people nowadays — do they have such ties? If they don't, they are missing more than they know."

Karen thought of her small circle of friends and wondered. Some had not lived in any one place for very long and seldom kept in touch.

"We formed our own chapter of the Huron Fortnightly eventually but began our own Women's Club as a lofty experiment in self-improvement. We'd get together and read deep books and then try to analyze them, to have discussions and improve our knowledge and expression. Eventually, over the years, others joined us and we ultimately became a part of the General Federation of Women's Clubs. We made mistakes to be sure. We began with the hardest books we could find, The 'Iliad' and the 'Odyssey', which we thought would be a snap and show how intelligent we thought we were. Only Laurel could make any sense from them, and that wasn't much, so we decided to lower our sights a bit and get to the more difficult books later. We tackled Shakespeare and especially liked 'The Taming of the Shrew.' It pleased us to read about a woman who could be independent and a bit wild. Of course, we all had a certain amount of knowledge of the Bible because every child we knew went to Sunday School and church. Gloria was the only Catholic in our original group and, as children, didn't know the difference until we got older and certain comments she said made us curious enough to ask her questions. The answers she gave seemed a little odd, almost by rote the way you learn multiplication tables. But as we grew up we paid no attention to any differences in denomination. We were as one in our group from childhood to adulthood. I hope I haven't offended you, Karen. What church do you attend?"

Karen had to admit that she was not a churchgoer, but Mrs. Hoekstra paid no attention. She was looking out the window at gathering clouds.

14

"Looks like it's clouding up." She turned back to Karen. "I always hated it when it rained, because that meant I had to stay inside. I argued with Mama that it was only sprinkling and it would cool me off if I could go outside and play. But we all had to stay inside, except for Bernard and Carl, who had jobs on the farm of an uncle. I sulked for awhile and then gave up and picked up a book and was soon lost in 'Alice's Adventures in Wonderland.' How I longed for such an adventure, especially on such a dark, dreary day. Later, when we were in the fourth grade, the class read 'Rip Van Winkle' and I marveled that anyone could fall asleep for so many years and not even have to go to the bathroom. Mama patiently reminded me that it was just a story and to not spend time thinking about such things. My interest in reading grew and never left me. I read some of the boys' books: Daniel Defoe's 'Robinson Crusoe,' Jonathan Swift's 'Gulliver's Travels,' and Robert Lewis Stevenson's 'Treasure Island.' I could escape into another world anytime. I never understood why everyone didn't read as avidly as I did."

A loud clap of thunder made her jump. "That was a loud one. It's going to rain all right. Do you like to read, Karen? I would think you do if you write for the paper."

"Yes, it's one of the reasons I took a job in journalism. It was college that increased my curiosity about the world and my interest in people. I like expressing what I learn. Actually, I plan to write a book some day."

"How exciting. I was not good at such things. How would one begin? The Women's Club progressed from reading aloud as many books as we could to reading by ourselves and then discussing them at the next meeting. It went faster. Previously, we never finished a book. We would laugh at Laurel, the smartest one. When it was her turn to read aloud she would become so engrossed in the text that her voice would trail off and she would be reading to herself.

"I loved adventure stories, such as 'Robin Hood' and anything by Mark Twain. He had such a marvelous sense of humor. I understand that nowadays some of the classics are in danger of being forbidden. How can that be? They have stood the test of time for generations and they give us an idea of what life was like years ago. But there I go off on a tangent again. Anyway, we met once a week at first because we had the time. We took turns meeting at each other's houses. Of course, we had refreshments and took pride in preparing something special. We would dress up, complete with white gloves, and put on our best manners with lots of 'pleases' and 'thank yous'. Over our tea cups we attempted to have an intellectual discussion. We must have looked pretty silly." She smiled at the memory.

"All nine of you were in the club?"

"Yes. We had known one another all our lives so there were no surprises. We were comfortable with each other. I think our moral upbringing

15

sustained us all those years. Even in the schoolroom the other children knew we were inseparable and the best of friends.

"Laurel was the smartest and she looked smart with her thick glasses, which she really hated. But Violet could sing, too. How she could sing. I remember on Friday afternoons before being dismissed we had a half hour of 'expression' as the teacher called it. She would lead off with reciting or reading something from a book she kept in her desk, a book she apparently really took a fancy to and from which she read exerpts of literature not in our regular books. I loved those Friday afternoons. Then anyone could give an 'expression' in a creative way. That was the key.

"It had to be creative. The girls were better at it than the boys. The boys were a little embarrassed, although they could act up at times when they were supposed to behave. One of the boys, Clarence, was such a show-off. He loved to recite, and he memorized several comical poems, some of which he made up, much to the teacher's consternation and the other boys' amusement. The trouble was he often couldn't remember all the words and he turned into a comic, attempting to cover up, but he did it in such a fashion that the room was full of laughter at his antics. Even the teacher couldn't help but smile. He would stride back and forth in front of the room reciting verses of 'Casey at the Bat,' only the verses weren't in sequence, but he did know the last verse, which he would finish with a flourish." She gave her soft laugh. "We hoped he would learn something new, but we enjoyed his specialty anyway.

"As I said, Violet could sing. She had a lovely soprano voice. She could sing hymns of course, but she loved to sing the first two verses of 'Mighty Like a Rose.' Are you familiar with it?"

Karen had no idea and was pleasantly surprised to hear Mrs. Hoekstra's thin voice as she sang.

"'Sweetest little fella, everybody knows; don't know what to call him, but he's mighty like a rose.' Even the boys would hush when Violet sang. Our fourth grade talents were not suited for long memorizations or attentions, but how we enjoyed those Friday afternoons. Miss Brown, our teacher, was homely as a mud fence, the boys would say, but we loved her and she won't be forgotten, at least as long as my memory serves me.

"Violet later took singing lessons. Her father was a banker and, as I said, she came from a wealthy family, so she had all the advantages. Miss Moselle gave singing lessons, as well as piano lessons. She didn't have many pupils, but she did the best she could, considering the times and the lack of employment opportunities for her profession. She recognized Violet's God-given talent and encouraged her. Violet aspired to be an operatic soprano, her goal."

She paused a moment, then said, "Randall took piano lessons. He had long fingers and was very good, but the boys teased him about taking piano

16

lessons sometimes. Later, they enjoyed the tunes he played and came to admire him even more. Dear Randall." She grew pensive.

Karen decided it was time to leave. She had much to do at the office. She was beginning to like her assignment, but wondered if it would ever be finished.

"Mrs. Hoekstra, I have to go. But I would like to continue tomorrow. Would you mind?"

"I'd like to very much. It is nice visiting with you, Karen. I do enjoy young people."

As she left the nursing home and got into her car, she turned on the air as high as it would go and considered the possibility that she might have to spend a good deal of time on the life of Mrs. Holly Hoekstra.

It started to rain and she gratefully switched on the windshield wipers.

At the State Fair

Chapter 3

After a noisy night when rain came down in torrents, Karen returned to the nursing home. It was clouded over and a drizzle was still falling. She was tired from opening and closing the windows in her apartment, finally getting a semblance of sound sleep around 4:00 o'clock. It was imperative that she get on with her interview. When she entered Mrs. Hoekstra's room the overhead light was on and a small lamp on her bedside table was lit. As usual, Mrs. Hoekstra was seated on the bed, ready to greet her young friend.

She smiled in greeting, "Hello, Karen."

Karen was touched by the eager welcome in the old woman's face. How lonely it must be to be the last person in the world in which you once lived.

"Hello. You are looking very well, Mrs. Hoekstra."

"It's good to have it cool off, but it is so dark. Do you have enough light?"

"Yes, this is fine." She unfolded the chair as she spoke. "Mrs. Hoekstra, it appears I am not going to meet the deadline for my article ...."

"Oh dear, I am sorry. I have gone off in all directions, haven't I?"

"It's quite all right. I'm really enjoying talking to you; and I've spoken to my boss, Mr. Stern, about it and he told me to go ahead and take all the time I need, that we can condense it later. Actually, I would like to make a feature article of it on a full page with your picture."

"My goodness; that is flattering. But my life was ordinary and I am not photogenic. I know that is true."

"You are far too hard on yourself. Your life was so different from life today and you have so many experiences to relate. Everything has changed so much in 100 years, such as the Huron Mall, Huron College, the State Fair, the ...."

"The Fair!" Mrs. Hoekstra's face lit up. "The State Fair was so important to everyone, to folks in town where it brought in business, and to folks from the country, who brought in livestock, baked goods and home canned goods and handiwork. Folks wanted to kick up their heels a little after working on the land so hard all summer long and before cold weather set in. I guess this is still true, isn't it? Huron wanted to be the state capital, you

19

see, but it didn't happen, so we got the State Fair. Huron has been home to the Fair almost my entire life. Before that, it was held in various towns about, but Huron is pretty centrally located and it turned out to be an ideal location. I'll never forget the time some of us girls went to the Fair."

Karen got out her notebook and this time took out a small tape recorder as well to get her exact words down, she explained when Mrs. Hoekstra looked at in suspicion.

"Well, we were there with our folks, of course, but we had a little money to spend and were permitted to be on our own for a few hours as long as we stayed together and provided that we were back at the entrance by 6:00 o'clock.

"Our families took picnic lunches and spent the entire day, ending with sitting in the grandstand, craning our necks to see the marvelous fireworks display. It was September and the weather was perfect. There were four of us that day and we were going to enjoy one last holiday before school started. We were in high spirits and feeling independent and free of parental restraints. We were in our early teens with heads full of romantic notions and adventure. Of course, we were interested in boys, but boys that age considered girls foolish, so our coy looks were rewarded with taunts and crude noises. We finally considered their immaturity and hoped that some day they would grow up. We turned our attentions to the older boys, although with much timidity to hide our daring and excitement. We were entering forbidden territory and were brought up properly, so we had to be careful. You know how it is at that age."

Karen couldn't imagine such innocence as she considered her own teen-age years.

"Our mothers went to the Women's Building for some sort of function and the men and older boys took in horse shows and livestock exhibits, which we considered boring. Anyway, we rode the carousel, then rode the huge ferris wheel, which had terrified us, but that was why we rode it, to be terrified." She laughed her soft laugh. "Sunny and I were in one car and Myrtle and Rose were in the one behind us. I think the operator of that ride made it stop on purpose while we were way up on top, making the seats wiggle precariously. We had thought it such fun to go way up high and to see out over the fair grounds and to point out our various homes, but the ferris wheel jerked to a stop and swung back and forth for what seemed like an eternity. We screamed and hung onto the bar for dear life. When we finally reached the ground we decided to forget the rides and take in some of the side shows and keep our equilibrium. Poor Myrtle was pale as a ghost. She felt whoozy after desperately trying to not get sick up there as we swung back and forth.

"We watched some boys throwing balls at bottles to knock them over and hoped they would notice us as we stood by, giving them admiring glances. We were totally ignored. Then we spotted Butch. He was creating a commotion as he threw those balls with deadly aim, knocking some of the bottles down so hard he broke the mechanism. The man behind the booth threatened him with bodily harm if he didn't pay for the damage, but Butch was not intimidated. He grabbed the man by his shirt and glared at him as he shook his fist in the poor man's face and shouted that it was all rigged anyway. Then he collected his prize, some fuzzy toy animal that he gave to the woman at his side. I say 'woman' because she was older than he was, not a school girl, and she was all made up. We hid around a corner and whispered so Butch couldn't hear us. 'A painted woman' we giggled, because we figured we knew what that meant. We were so innocent.

"Butch draped his arm across the woman's shoulders and swaggered off, with his cap set at a jaunty angle. We thought he must be really grown up, being in the company of such a woman. He had grown so much bigger and taller and he looked even meaner. We were glad he hadn't seen us.

"We had to be frugal with our money, so we passed up some of the more tempting booths, only stopping to watch others spend their money to show off their skills at pitching pennies, shooting ducks, that sort of thing, just to win a cheap prize. I really wanted to win a Kewpie doll. Have you ever seen a Kewpie doll, Karen?"

"Afraid not. I don't know what kind of doll that is."

"It's a small doll made out of celluloid, which was a material used to make lots of cheap, disposable items. The doll looked like a cherub, only its hair came to a curly point and the face had such a sweet, innocent smile. It had no clothes, sort of what you'd call a unisex doll nowadays."

Her subject's knowledge continued to surprise Karen. How had she come to know the modern word 'unisex'?

"We came to the end of the row of booths and stopped across the dirt path from one that looked intriguing. There was a black curtain in front of it and a strange looking woman was sitting there. She was fat and dark with a colorful bandana tied around her thick black hair. I remember her hair because it looked sort of greasy. Big, hooped, dangly earrings hung beneath the bandana and a tattered fringed cape was around her shoulders, which seemed strange to us, as it was far too hot to wear a cape. Best of all, we spied a clear ball, a crystal ball, in her hands. On the black curtain behind her, written in yellow letters that had been sewn on — I suppose to make folks think they were sewn with gold thread — were the words 'Zelda, Fortune Teller Deluxe from Europe. Sees all, Tells all. 25¢.' From Europe, no less. We were so gullible and impressed. She smiled at us, staring at her, and beckoned. 'Tell your fortuncs, only a quarter.' We hesitated, but there was a fascinating air of mystery about her that appealed to us impressionable girls. I can see it just as plain as when it happened."

She paused, lost in thought. "She was a gypsy, you know, a real gypsy and she had our interest despite warnings from our folks about staying clear of them." Her attention waned, so Karen switched off the tape recorder and waited for her to speak.

Sunny spoke in a low voice, "Do you think we should? Would it be terribly wicked?"

"I don't know," Holly replied. "She looks sort of different. Besides no one can tell fortunes can they?"

"Let's just ask her," declared Rose, and she walked toward the woman, her small figure defiant.

"Rose, come back here!" said Holly in a loud whisper but Rose would not stop.

Looking the woman in the eyes she asked, "Can you really tell fortunes?"

The woman's smile revealed crooked yellow teeth. She replied sweetly and in a curious accent, "Of course, my child. I can see the past, present and future in my crystal ball, only 25¢, a special price for you and your friends ."

As the price indicated on the black curtain said 25¢ Rose didn't consider it much of a bargain and said as much. The others stood close together behind her, shocked at Rose's boldness. They were beginning to reconsider their decision and were becoming somewhat nervous as Rose persisted, "How do we know that? You could just be making it all up."

The woman only looked more mysterious and said, "I can tell you at this very moment that at the present time you are in some trouble, perhaps you are being punished?"

Rose gasped and the others looked at the woman in amazement.

"But it was so unfair," said Rose defensively. "I just got back at him. He deserved it and it was no reason to punish me so bad." She tossed her red curls.

They could not imagine how she had known about Rose's punishment, not only by her teacher, but by her parents, as well. Tom, a good looking boy who liked to tease the girls and then charm them into accepting his oftentimes unwelcome remarks, had caught a mouse and put it into Rose's desk on Friday. By Monday it had expired, but not before it had left remnants of himself during the time he had vainly tried to escape, destroying Rose's spelling book with her last assignment, in the process.

Rose knew it was Tom because he sat behind her and liked to torment her. He denied doing it, but she knew he lied as he mocked her with his teasing eyes. In retaliation, Rose had poured ink from his inkwell over his arithmetic book, destroying it and causing the teacher to make her stay after school on that last day. Her parents scolded her severely when she obediently handed them the note from the teacher and they confined her inside the house for two days while the rest of the children played outside in the sunshine with the balance of the summer to enjoy.

How did this woman know all that? Of course she didn't know. She was only proficient in the art of defrauding the gullible. She knew human nature and could tell by Rose's impertinent manner and her outspoken ways that she was often in hot water. The fact that the incident Rose got into trouble for happened many weeks before did not occur to them. And with her offered information the woman could put together a fortune.

"How about you girls? Do you want to know your fortunes? Only a quarter. No charge for what I just told this young lady."

Up close they could see that she was not very clean and had an unfamiliar odor about her, but she was most beguiling and her voice mesmerizing, and they were curious, so they each gave her a quarter and followed her inside the booth. She placed a sign on the ragged curtain indicating that it was occupied.

The interior was dimly lit with a kerosene lamp hanging from a pole next to a round table on which she placed her crystal ball, after first laying a worn piece of dark cloth of what appeared to be velvet and motioning for them to take seats around the table. The lamp cast strange shadows on their faces and gave the woman's face a sinister appearance. The seats were nothing but upended small barrels, but they didn't care. They were eager and excited. What would she tell them?

She began with Sunny. "First, give me your palm. Palms reveal much."

Sunny held out her hand, palm up. The woman took it in her rough hand and slowly traced her forefinger with a dirty nail along the creases in Sunny's white hand. The woman said, "Hmmm, a long lifeline. You have authority. You command respect. Your life will present many responsibilities. You will marry and be happy. Now let us look into the crystal ball."

She passed her hand over the ball a few times as though summoning up something inside. They leaned forward expectantly and peered intently into the ball, trying to see something, a vapor, a vision, anything. Later Myrtle said she thought she saw a green mist. Rose said emphatically that she saw nothing. Holly and Sunny's rapt attention indicated that they would accept anything the gypsy would tell them.

"You are a good friend to one of those present here." Sunny nodded enthusiastically. "You have been good friends for many years and that friendship is returned."

Sunny looked happily at Holly and nodded, which was duly noted.

"I see that you will be a leader in your life."

"Who will I marry?" Sunny asked in anticipation.

"You will marry a man with money and have many children. Hmmm. The vision is fading. Who is next?"

Sunny was disappointed, wanting more, but Holly said, "Do me next," and held out her hand.

The woman held her long hand, palm up and expressed surprise. "You have a very long lifeline with many roads to travel. I do not necessarily mean actual roads, but that you will be needed in many areas of your life. Now what will the crystal ball tell us?"

She released Holly's hand and Holly quickly wiped it with her handkerchief under the table, hoping it wasn't noticed, but she was passing her rough hands over the ball, then inquired, "You have a boyfriend?"

Holly thought of Randolph and flushed.

"Ah yes, of course. I am getting a name ..."

"Is it Randolph?" she asked eagerly.

"Yes, that's it. Randolph is his name. A nice young man who returns your affection."

The girls squealed in delight.

"Will I marry Randolph?" asked Holly hopefully.

"You will marry and have many children. Who will be next?"

Rose said firmly, "Me."

The woman and her outspoken adversary faced each other. Rose extended her palm. The woman took it and when she finally released her fixed gaze at Rose, gave a slight jump at the small hand in her own.

"What do you see?" asked Rose, suddenly alarmed.

"It is nothing."

But they didn't believe her.

"You have an interesting palm, a lifeline that indicates surprises in your life." She quickly released her hand.

"Is that it? Is that all?" demanded Rose.

"I'm afraid so. Let's see what the crystal ball reveals."

"But that's not fair," objected Rose.

The woman was already passing her hands over the ball. She stated matter of factly, "I see that your recent punishment was well deserved."

Rose let out a loud, "Wait a minute!"

But she continued, "So was the punishment you gave the young man. A word of caution. You have a sharp tongue. Learn to master it. Otherwise, your future could be not so bright."

Rose was angry and didn't like the piercing look she got, but the woman turned to Myrtle. "You are next and the last. Let me see your hand."

Myrtle held back, but extended her hand. The woman said, "Hmmm, puzzling. You, too, have a long lifeline, but it is faint. You are timid and pull back. You enjoy being with these friends, but do not contribute much. You are too shy."

Myrtle said faintly, "I just like to be with them."

"You are afraid?"

"Of what? No need to be afraid if I am with them. I'm just careful, that's all."

"Yes, careful. These are nice girls?"

"The best," said Myrtle, looking to them for approval. "I just don't have a lot to say."

"I can see that in the crystal ball." In answer to her unspoken question she added, "You will marry and have many children."

With that she covered the crystal ball with the thin cloth and the session was over. Reluctantly, they left, thanking the woman, who had made an easy dollar in a few minutes.

Once outside, they squinted in the sunshine. They were disappointed, yet they agreed that much of what she had told them made sense.

"Maybe if we had paid her another quarter she would have told us more," said Sunny.

"Oh sure, she'd like that. Did you notice she said nothing about me getting married and having any children," said Rose in disgust. "I still don't believe anyone can tell fortunes. Come on, let's get some ice cream."

They were at the end of the dirt path that was lined with carnival booths on each side so they prepared to turn back, but stopped when they saw a queer looking wagon behind the fortune teller's booth.

"That sure isn't a hay wagon," said Holly.

"Let's go look," said Rose.

"I don't know. Do you think we ought?" asked Myrtle, hanging back.

"What's the harm? We're just going to look. We won't touch anything," said Holly.

"As if we'd want to," said Rose. "That woman was really dirty; didn't you think so?"

They looked back at the booth and saw that the 'Occupied' sign was displayed, so she couldn't watch them. Looking as nonchalant as possible they turned and walked slowly toward the wagon.

It was a rickety wagon with a high boxed enclosure with windows. Two mangy horses were loosely tethered to a tree. The girls jumped when a young man stood up on the other side of the horses. He was lazily using a curry comb to groom them as they stood idly, flicking flies with their tails. The lad was swarthy with tousled black hair. He was bare chested and they noticed with some consternation his fine build and tawny color. His trousers were ragged and he was barefoot. They were surprised to see that he wore earrings, too.

"I think we should go," said Myrtle, hanging back.

"Come on; we're here, aren't we?" replied Rose, walking toward the wagon, looking intensely interested.

The young man never took his eyes off them, all the while smiling a broad smile, showing discolored teeth between thick lips. The girls followed Rose protectively.

"Hello, pretty ladies," he said. His grin remained fixed. "What are you doing here? You lost?" He threw down the curry comb and walked around the horses. Myrtle stepped back behind the others. Holly swallowed hard and opened her mouth to say something, but Rose beat her to it.

"No, we're not lost. We just wanted to look at your wagon. You don't haul hay in it do you." She said it as a fact, not a question.

He laughed a low, seductive laugh and said, "No, pretty ladies, not for hauling hay. We live in it. This is the wagon of the family of the Warnoskis. We travel with the carnival. Perhaps you have seen my mother, Zelda, the one who sees all?"

"We just came from there," said Rose smartly. "She wasn't very good. What are you doing?"

"Tending to the horses. It is my important job to keep everything in good working condition."

The flies were thick around the animals and Rose wanted to snap that he didn't do a very good job either, but thought better of it as he came closer. They stepped back at his purposeful stride. His manner made them uneasy, not at all what they might have expected from an adventurous encounter with a handsome stranger.

He stopped before Sunny and touched her long blond curls, stroking them lightly with his dirty hands. She cringed.

"You have beautiful hair, Miss. You sell it? We give you good price."

"No!" exclaimed Sunny in revulsion as she stepped back. They were eager to leave the sun drenched yard that had suddenly turned menacing.

"Manuel, what you think you're doing? Leave those girls alone — right now!"

They were startled and relieved to see an old man in strange clothes, pants tied at the knees and a colorful vest. He stepped down the narrow steps of the wagon to the ground. Manuel moved away from them swiftly and his demeanor turned submissive in a flash.

He said sullenly, "I've seen better hair anyway." The old man walked toward them and they continued to back away.

"You. Leave! You girls get out of here if you know what's good for you."

They turned and scurried away, glad to have gotten out of a tricky situation, their romantic illusions shattered. They walked quickly, looking back now and then, getting through the noisy carnival, not hearing the gay sounds of the carousel. They kept on going till they reached the entrance, where they waited for the protective arms of their parents. They were out of breath.

"Well," said Holly. "I don't think we should mention this to our folks, not even about getting our fortunes told. They sure talked funny, didn't they? I wonder where they came from."

Upon their parents' arrival and words of approval about their girls' showing up on time they asked if they had a good time. They all talked at once, describing what they had done, except about the gypsies.

The events Holly remembered had taken but a moment to travel through her head, but Karen was glad to hear her speak again. Her wandering thoughts were unpredictable, but she was patient.

"We really had fun at the Fair every year, but we never forgot that one and our run-in with the gypsies. Our folks repeatedly warned us about gypsies, said to stay away from them because they were sly and could be dangerous. There were periodic reports of a group of gypsies around the midwest every summer. They would camp outside of town until they were eventually run off. Wild rumors scared most people with stories of how they would kidnap babies. I really don't think they did, but they were a race apart, not like anyone we'd ever seen. Later, before the Fair was over that year, the authorities ran them out of Huron. Manuel had gotten too friendly with one of the young visitors at the Fair and Zelda was turned in and reported as being a charlatan. Nevertheless, we didn't forget what she told us."

Karen offered, "I think gypsies are rare nowadays. There are psychics now who claim to be able to predict the future."

"Really? You know what they say: things change and they remain the same." She thought a minute, then added, "Do you know — that Manuel stole the blue ribbons right out of Sunny's hair without any of us knowing what he was doing? Sunny was so upset that he even dared to touch her that she washed her beautiful hair as soon as she got home."

Chapter 4

Karen kept on trying to get information about the Women's Club, although she had enjoyed hearing about Mrs. Hoekstra's early life. She had much on her tape recorder and much in her notebook and she was certain she could piece it all together with a few more questions. She tried a different approach.

"Mrs. Hoekstra, it's clear that the strong friendships among you nine girls must have contributed to forming the Women's Club. Can you fill me in?"

"Yes, of course. I keep meandering away from that, don't I? I get to reminiscing and wander off. Well, the idea came from long hours spent at the Red Cross rolling bandages and putting together comfort kits for servicemen during World War I. Young ladies lived at home until they married, so we had plenty of time to donate to the war effort and spent hours doing our part for the boys 'over there' . Naturally, we did a lot of talking to pass the time doing such repetitive work, even though we were constantly admonished by the director to not visit so much, that our work would suffer. None of us could roll tighter bandages than Rose. Maybe it was just her nature. She was wound up so much of the time." She chuckled at her remark.

"All nine of us volunteered and did our part, along with other young and not so young ladies of Huron. The older women knitted sweaters and socks and tolerated us. We talked about everything under the sun, even our lack of formal education, except for Laurel and Violet and they never put on airs because of it. We all said that our children would get all the education we could provide and some of us did."

"Were any of you employed in those days?" asked Karen.

"Some of us were. In those days young ladies were expected to marry and raise children. There were plenty of young men to choose from. The early settlers were mostly men and they produced more of them. But there were not many employment opportunities for young women, not like it is today. Goodness! They weren't even permitted to vote or to serve on a jury. That was for men only. Women were teachers or nurses and some did secretarial work. Often only a rudimentary education was all that was necessary to get a teaching certificate. We had three teachers in my family,

Howard, Hazel and Opal. Mama and Papa encouraged us to read and improve ourselves. As a matter of fact, I took a nursing course at the Sprague School of Nursing, took my training at Sprague Hospital. I was so proud of my certificate. I loved nursing and, in time, became Randolph's nurse. That's right. He became Dr. Randolph Thorne, M.D., and I gladly took my place beside him."

Karen considered Mrs. Hoekstra's name and wondered why she had not married Randolph, as she had given every indication that she regarded him with affection, but she said nothing.

"Myrtle became a telephone operator and worked until she was married. We had crank telephones then; you know, the kind with a handle on the side of a wall telephone that you had to give a whirl to get the operator. Then she would ring the number you wanted. You've seen old pictures of those switchboards, haven't you?"

Karen nodded. "It must have been a tedious process."

"I suppose it was, but for the times it was a marvelous way to communicate. Too much sitting for my taste. But lots of women worked for the telephone company and it suited Myrtle. She didn't have to make decisions, just plug the cords into the proper jacks. She told us in confidence that operators could listen in on people's conversations, at least when the supervisor wasn't hovering over you. It was right up her alley. Close to World War I Huron had dial telephones, but that didn't eliminate the need for telephone operators."

"So, it was volunteering at the Red Cross that led to the formation of the Women's club?"

"That's right. We considered ourselves to be bright and intelligent with so much more to offer than the repetitive, but necessary chores of our volunteer work. After all, the war would not last forever and we needed to find something else to occupy our time. When we organized we talked about the books, newspaper articles or magazines like *The Saturday Evening Post* and *Colliers*, and surprised ourselves with what we knew and also at our various opinions, each in some way different.

"The war ended and it had changed everyone, especially the ones who had served in the war. Even Randolph — I told you about Randolph, didn't I?"

"Yes, you said he took piano lessons and often came to the rescue of you girls and eventually became a doctor. He sounds like a nice man."

"He was a nice boy, a gentle man and a good doctor. It was his nature to want to help people. He had always been studious and had to wear spectacles — glasses. He was tall and handsome with deepset blue eyes and wavy brown hair." She sighed. "I was quite smitten, I confess. In fact, I don't remember ever not loving Randolph. So when he volunteered for the Army I was crestfallen. But they wouldn't take him even though he was a doctor, because of his eyes and, they said, his flat feet. Imagine. He was very angry and said it was just one more reflection on his manhood, but I was thrilled about not having to see him go overseas, I can tell you.

"Then in 1917 Butch was drafted and was he ever mad! He ranted and raved about the injustice of it all, but he couldn't get out of it and was shipped over to France. In no time at all he was made a Sergeant, just a plain Sergeant, but it was a rank that suited him to a T. Some of the men in Huron who served under him sent word back that he was just as big and mean as ever. But his infantry unit got commendations for being rated the bravest with the highest honors. They saw action in some of the bloodiest fighting in the Argonne Forest and there were casualties, but the ones who came home grudgingly gave Butch credit for keeping the loss of life to a minimum. Folks around hoped that his experiences in the war had changed him. But it only made him worse.

"Butch never let up bragging about his accomplishments, completely ignoring the men who returned with him, those same men who told of his leadership. He was even bigger, strong and burly with the swagger that the war had only intensified and which he had perfected. He was quite proud of that swagger, but it was a mannerism that was evidence of a huge ego. He wore his uniform until he got too big for it and went back to work at Blume's Brewery. He became a big shot there, whether by his ability or his threatening manner. His pop had long since died. Butch called himself 'a man of property' and loved to brag about how he had come up in the world, at least until Prohibition. Then he just went underground and made boot-leg liquor, while the brewery converted to making an orange drink and rootbeer. He took to wearing loose fitting clothes to cover his beer belly.

He didn't come into town much and folks were grateful for that. Everyone was afraid of him. He got his way with anything he wanted — even murder, some folks said. But there I go again.

"The nine of us concentrated on our goal of improving ourselves. We knew that education and the thirst for knowledge were keys to a better, more rounded and useful life. We met at each other's homes, taking turns and meeting every week at first. We had been in all the houses many times, but Violet's was the exception. Her parents made us welcome, but not as often. They had so many social obligations and couldn't be bothered with us. But we understood. We knew our place.

"Violet had become a vital part of our group. She not only had an education, but she had social graces which the rest of us were eager to learn. Oh we had proper manners. Our folks saw to that. But Violet was from the upper class, if you want to call it that. She was an only child and closely watched over by the Cranes. That was Violet's last name — Crane. The rest of us came from large families. She had culture and we learned a lot by observing the way she did things. She was so dainty and correct in every-

30

thing. But she was intensely loyal to us, her friends, and she let her hair down a bit when she was away from home." She paused and said, "It seems that too often nowadays young people seem to have no goals and their values have sunk to a very low common denominator. I'm glad I grew up when I did."

Karen thought of her circle of friends who were so mobile and of Jack, whom she wanted to marry. He was urging her to move in with him and she was resisting.

"Anyway, we met in the afternoon and read aloud for awhile, taking turns. But as I said, that took too long and we found it impossible to finish a book, so we each read a different book and reported on it at the next meeting. We had spirited discussions, as our interests and opinions as a result of what we read were so varied. We certainly impressed Miss Eberley, the librarian. We attempted more difficult books, but gave up on 'Beowulf,' finding epic poetry difficult, and we agreed that the value of trudging through it was not apparent. At least, that's the excuse we used for having failed.

"But we read all of Louisa Mae Alcott's books, probably because they dealt with different children who grew up together. I particularly liked Jo. 'King Arthur and the Round Table' held a fascination for some of us. It appealed to our romantic natures and the adventures of a long ago time. Naturally, Rose read 'Frankenstein' and gloried in telling us the horrific details. Did you know that 'Frankenstein' was written by Mary Shelley? A woman wrote that, just think of it! She was the wife of the poet, Percy Bysshe Shelley. Such an imagination from a woman in a time when she would not be permitted to express such thoughts, to say nothing of having it published. I did enjoy the poetry, especially Elizabeth Barrett Browning. What a romantic story her life was. You have probably guessed that beneath this gawky, plain exterior lies the heart of a romantic.

"After our meeting we would have tea. After all, that is what the cultured ladies of the Victorian era had done. We drank tea from china cups. Even the poorest families had cups and saucers that matched. At Violet's house we were served tea by the Crane's maid from a fancy pot that Mrs. Crane had purchased in France. Her beautiful china cups were delightful, but I was terrified I'd break one. I stuck out above the others, along with Sunny, and I felt clumsy, but Sunny assured me I looked elegant and proper. Maybe so, but at least Sunny was pretty. We were also served tiny bread and butter sandwiches and pretty petit-fours. Throughout all that fuss Violet never put on airs."

Karen could not imagine not working and in having afternoons to drink tea from real china cups in a beautiful old house, having conversations in well modulated tones and in English that was not totally fractured. She

31

was lucky enough to have time to grab something at McDonald's to eat in her car before hurrying back to work.

"As years went by we got jobs and got married and our time together was limited to meeting after supper. We also added to our group, eventually joining the General Federation of Women's Clubs and calling ourselves The Huron Fortnightly.

We put our abilities to use by doing good works and sponsoring worthy projects. We continued this way for many years until our original members became too old, we no longer worked, and we met once again in the afternoons; we took our time, while a younger generation took over the more time consuming activities. Time does fly, and the older you get the faster it goes. Such times we had and how innocent we were."

She grew pensive again.

It was 1918 and the war would soon be over. Holly was 25. The meeting of the Huron Women's Club was at Lilly's house. It was 8:00 o'clock in the evening and they had just finished their evaluation of Edgar Allan Poe's 'The Raven'. Halloween was a few days away and they had a good time scaring themselves with Poe's dark writing and applying it to their time.

Daisy's face shone pale in the light of the table lamp with its fringed shade. She got right to the point, as was her nature, cutting right down to the cob, as the expression went.

"Well, I think Poe was a drug addict. Who could write so consistently about such weird topics unless he took dope?"

Gloria, ever ready to rise to a defense, responded, "We don't know that. Some people are naturally moody."

Rose interjected, "But look at 'The Telltale Heart'. I really like that one: thumpety thump, thumpety thump under the floorboards."

"You would," laughed Lilly as she gave a slight wheeze which happened whenever she laughed too hard or exerted herself. Her asthma was worse in the fall. It wouldn't take long before her breathing was normal again but they were concerned for her when her small frame would be wracked with the severity of an attack. She would always reassure them that it was nothing, she was used to it, that she was all right, The doctor had told her that it was just asthma and not tuberculosis, which was contagious and which killed the patient. She would be fine until the next asthma attack.

"Guess what I heard and saw today," said Rose with a toss of her red hair. "You'll never guess."

All eyes turned to her and the sly smirk on her face indicated they were in for a spot of gossip, although they endeavored not to indulge in it.

"Well, spit it out. What is it?" demanded Laurel. The night was warm and she pushed her heavy glasses onto her nose. What a nuisance they were but she couldn't manage without them.

Restrictions on gossip were forgotten and they all clamored, "Come on, Rose, tell us."

"Well," she said in a low voice. "I heard something today at Perriton's Drug. You'll just never, ever guess." She covered her offending mouth that persistently got her into trouble to stifle a naughty giggle, then said, "All right, all right, I'll tell you. I found out that Miss Moselle has a standing order for a box of something. I couldn't see what it was called, but it was plain that it was used to keep from having a baby."

She paused to assess the effect of her announcement and was pleased to see the shock and disbelief on their faces.

"You mean — so she wouldn't have a baby?" asked Myrtle, not sure of what she had heard.

"Of course, that's what I mean, silly. It's true. She came in while I was there. I wanted some hand lotion, and I overheard her ask Mr. Jones for it. As a matter of fact, he asked her, 'The usual, Janet?' Did you know that Miss Moselle's first name is Janet? She's always been just Miss Moselle to everyone."

"Rose!" they exclaimed in unison.

"All right. Well, they didn't see me, but I peeked around the magazine rack and overheard. I had to see what the 'usual' was. He handed her a box of something and said he'd put it on her account. She has an account! Mr. Jones was smiling as he handed it to her and she put it in her purse, and I can tell you the smile he gave her wasn't the smile we've gotten from him for a bottle of hand lotion or a prescription for pink eye. She smiled at him, too, a very familiar smile. They were both completely different, not at all the way we know them.

"And then she said, 'Haven't seen you for some time, Joe.' She called Mr. Jones 'Joe'. He said to her, 'How about tonight after I close up. I could give you a gent's name, too, if you like. He's made inquiries.' Then they spoke in low voices and she gave him that smile again. 'I'll look forward to it Joe', she said. And you should have seen the look on that nice Mr. Jones's face. After she walked out — and you should have seen that walk — he turned to the man behind the next counter and they snickered. You should have heard. He said, 'Doin' it tonight, Joe?' And Mr. Jones said, 'What do you think?' I was so afraid they'd see me, but I tiptoed out of there while their backs were turned."

Stunned silence was the reaction to Rose's recital. Then Lilly asked, "It? My Lord, you don't mean ...."

Rose was enjoying the bombshell she had dropped into the group and laughed loudly as she nodded.

They all talked at once. "No, not Miss Moselle. I don't believe it."

"She's the music teacher. She is so cultured and refined."

"Maybe you didn't hear it right. Are you sure?"

"It's true and you should have seen Mr. Jones' face," replied Rose. "It was simply lustful."

Lustful was not a word they used in their vocabulary except from a book report, and they had tittered about it. Now in their very own community were people they knew who embodied that very word.

Violet said, "But Miss Moselle is so plain."

"It must not make any difference," replied Daisy. "Men are like that — so I've heard."

33

Holly offered, "What about Miss Moselle? That's not ladylike, what she's doing. Why would she do it?"

Gloria made an excuse for the woman she had long admired, who had coached her in singing to more aptly express praise for The Lord in her church. She was keenly disappointed, but said, "Maybe she needs the money."

"She takes money for it?" asked Myrtle.

"Oh grow up," sputtered Rose. "How can she possibly live on giving music lessons?"

"But it really is wrong," Gloria said sadly.

"So is starving to death," snapped Rose. "Have you ever been hungry? I mean really hungry?"

Holly's thoughts were of Randolph. He had taken several years of piano lessons from Miss Moselle and he played beautifully. But he was very young at the time and Miss Moselle had to be years older. Why she must be at least 40 by now, an old woman. Still, she wondered if he knew.

"I don't think we should continue like this. We have an agreement about gossiping, remember," cautioned Holly. "And we must never, ever mention this to another soul."

They solmenly vowed to never breathe a word to anyone, but they wondered how many in town knew about Miss Moselle.

Mrs. Hoekstra stirred and looked at Karen. "Did you know there used to be a brothel north of town across the tracks?"

Karen didn't know how to respond. What had been going on in her head?

Chapter 5

Karen had persuaded Mr. Stern to give her extra time to continue working on her article on Mrs. Hoekstra and to make it into a full page feature for the Plainsman's section about interesting people in the town of Huron. She had been leaving her tape recorder in Holly's room and she promised to talk into it whenever she recalled something that might be of interest. With her reminiscences to Karen and from the recorder Karen was able to piece together a chronological series of events of Holly's life and of the lives of those who interacted with her. Her daily lapses in concentration had left some gaps that Karen eventually was able to fill in, after a fashion, along with tidbits offered by Ula whose voice was often audible on the tape. Karen found herself looking forward to the daily afternoon visits. She was not there one day and Mrs. Hoekstra appeared upset when she appeared on Tuesday.

She greeted her with a relieved smile. "There you are, Karen. I missed you yesterday and became quite worried when you failed to come to see me. I did talk into your tape recorder though. Were you sick?"

"No, nothing like that. I took the day off. I had some time coming and the weather was perfect at last, so my boyfriend and I decided to enjoy it before the summer is completely gone."

"You have a boyfriend, how nice. I'm sure he must be a fine young man."

"He is. His name is Jack, Jack Littleton. We drove to Lake Byron for the day. Jack's family has a cabin there."

"Lake Byron is lovely. At least that's the way I remember it. It's been many years since I've been there. Cabins used to be really rustic and there were not many of them."

"The cabin is more like a big cottage with many comforts, and there is a dock and a fancy motorboat."

Karen looked up from her notepad and saw a sudden sadness come over Mrs. Hoekstra. She asked in some concern, "Is something wrong?"

Mrs. Hoekstra stirred herself. "I'm all right. I was just remembering something."

"If I am bringing up unpleasant memories I am sorry. Shall we continue this another time?"

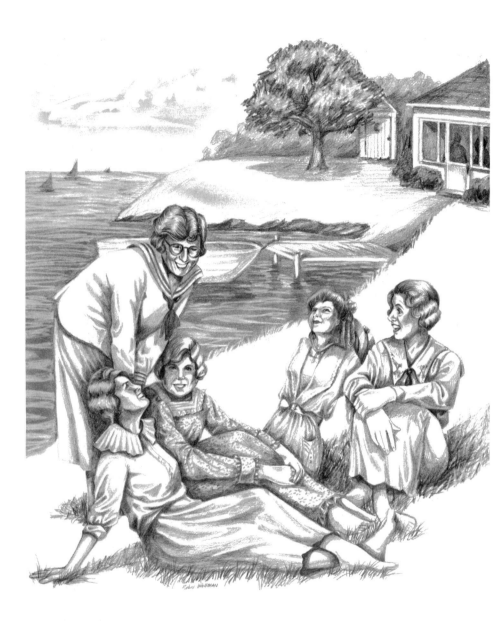

At Lake Byron

"No, no. It happened so long ago. It's just that in talking about things with you I remember what I thought was long forgotten. It was just after the war, World War I, that is; it must have been the summer of 1919. We all needed a lift from the sadness of that war. As I said, my brother, George, was killed in the war; my brother, Carl, had disappeared; and my brother, Howard, settled in Brookings to teach, with his wife and two sons. Bernard lived at home with Mama and Papa but was gone a lot, since he continued to work on the railroad. And my baby brother, Oliver, died in infancy. Coming from such a large family, I often wondered why there were so few descendants. Anyway, we girls were in our twenties and some of us were invited to go to Lake Byron to celebrate the 4th of July. Violet's folks had a cabin there and the Cranes would ask a few of us at a time to come up. They had a summer place that rivaled any other on the lake. It might still be there. It was up to date at the time in every way, except for the outhouse, of course. But we considered ourselves to be living in a modern age. We were so young and innocent in the ways of the world, in spite of all the newly found freedom the end of the war had brought.

"We rode to the lake in the Cranes' big touring car. It had been purchased new at the beginning of the war and was in excellent condition. It had lots of room, with a top that folded back. Four of us rode in the wide back seat, but Violet had to ride in front with her parents. They said they were afraid she'd catch cold — on the 4th of July — imagine! According to them Violet was delicate, but we didn't really believe it because she had always joined us in our activities back in our rough and tumble games as children. She certainly wasn't delicate to us. We thought they were overly protective and it was obvious that Violet was embarrassed. She did sunburn, though, and always had to wear a broad-brimmed hat in the summer.

"So, Laurel, Daisy, Sunny and I sat in the back seat. We thought we'd never get to the lake because of Mr. Crane's slow driving. The road was bumpy and unsurfaced, so it was for the best, but we were impatient to get there for the fun that lay ahead. We whispered and giggled back there, figuring we should have traveled on horseback, but they didn't hear us because of the noise of the car. We were glad that Mr. Crane put the top back and we laughed as the wind blew our hair all to pieces and Laurel's glasses got fogged up. But we didn't care about our hair because we had gotten the short cuts which were all the fashion, being free of the care of long hair, ribbons, even corsets. We gladly adopted the new loose fitting clothes. But Mrs. Crane refused to acknowledge the new styles and sat up front with her cinched-in waist, long sleeves and fancy hat. Mr. Crane was more comfortable, having shucked off his coat. Oh dear, am I boring you?"

"No, not at all. Please go on."

"We finally got to the lake and we all piled out of the car, ready for fun. We had brought swim suits and hoped to cool off in the water before the picnic lunch. We had been to the Crane's cabin only once before and eagerly ran up the steps to the wide porch. Mrs. Crane took off her hat and led us inside where it was somewhat cooler. She pulled up the long green shades and opened the windows. There were a lot of them and soon there was a nice breeze blowing through, bringing in the smell of the lake. It was quite exhilarating."

She smiled. "Such a lovely day it started out to be."

She became lost in thought and Karen turned on the tape recorder to capture the few words Mrs. Hoekstra said during those times. Various expressions flitted across her face and she wished she knew just what was going on in Holly's head.

The girls took off their shoes and stockings and ran down a slight incline to the dock. Mrs. Crane's admonitions to be careful and to not go in the water until later were acknowledged with waves of their hands. Mrs. Crane sighed at the exuberance of youth and turned to the task of setting out lunch. The girls paused at the shoreline and wiggled their toes in the warm sand. Violet's hat had slipped off and hung on her shoulders. They stepped into the gently lapping water and felt the soft sand beneath their feet and the cool water rippling around their ankles.

"Scrumptious!" exclaimed Laurel as she bent over to inspect what lay beneath the water. Her glasses got spattered as Daisy playfully kicked. A water shower ensued as they splashed merrily, getting thoroughly soaked.

"Look at us," laughed Holly, looking at their drenched clothes. "I think we should dry off; we'll be going in soon."

"Oh Holly, you're such a mother hen."

"We're guests and must look nice at the table."

"You're right, as usual," said Daisy. "If we sit here on the grass for a few minutes the sun will dry us in a jiffy."

They plopped themselves down on the grass up the slope beneath the shade of leafy cottonwood trees. The breeze rustled through the shiny leaves soothingly.

Violet said, "Look at all the boats. There are lots of people out here today. I think Mum and Daddy plan on taking us out in the sailboat later."

Their happy exclamations pleased her. She loved the time she had with her friends and was glad when she could return their hospitality, no matter how infrequently.

"It's a good thing Myrtle isn't here. She'd never leave the shore, not even in a sailboat," commented Sunny.

They laughed, knowing Myrtle's timid nature. She had to stay in Huron because they were having company for the day. Besides, she didn't want to miss the fireworks. They had considered that they were missing the fireworks, but decided they would rather be at the lake. Maybe the Cranes would have fireworks, but they secretly doubted it, due to the caution with which they did everything. They looked at Violet, turning pink.

"Violet, you'd better put your hat back on or you'll get red as a beet and we'll get blamed."

Violet reluctantly replaced her hat. Sunny was right, but she had loved the feel of the sun on her pale skin and the breeze blowing her long black hair. One of those days she was going to defy her parents, much as she loved them, and get her curls cut off. She didn't share her mother's rejection of modern fashion. She said that to the others more than once. The hat did shade her eyes from the glare of the sun on the water. Some of the occupants of the boats were fishing; some were paddling lazily in the warm air; a few had noisy motors. There were a few sailboats.

"Look at that boat over there. Isn't it going awfully fast?" asked Holly.

They watched as a motorboat zig-zagged on the lake, coming dangerously close to the other boaters. They could hear the loud guffaws of the big man who was operating the boat as he swung out and off across the water, creating waves that rocked the crafts, missing the other boats in the nick of time.

They sat up in alarm.

"Why would anyone be so foolish?" asked Daisy. He's endangering the others."

"Yoo hoo, girls, dinner is ready," came from Mrs. Crane standing on the porch, looking like an elegant gentlewoman from Victorian England. They scrambled up the incline to the cottage, the boaters forgotten, smoothing their rumpled dresses, but they were dry. Their short hair needed only a shake of their heads and a quick pat.

Their dinner turned out to be picnic fare, but it was served in the dining room on a linen cloth. The sun streamed into the room from the tall windows and the breeze from the lake wafted inside, giving the feeling of a picnic without the discomfort of the outdoors with its bugs and, as Violet put it, without the creepy crawly things. They were ravenous and devoured the fried chicken, potato salad, corn on the cob, bread and butter, with chocolate cake for dessert. Iced tea was served with the meal, a beverage they were not much acquainted with. They wondered about the origin of the ice, but enjoyed the cool drink, which they assumed was upper class.

Mrs. Hoekstra's reminiscences were broken with a loud snort from Ula, to whom they had become accustomed in their daily talks.

"Mrs. Crane, God rest her soul, was very particular, but she certainly knew how to entertain. We felt we were in pretty fancy company. I think she invited us girls for Violet's sake. It wasn't always the same ones who got to be their guests. She had only a few at a time, especially at the lake, because that is all she could manage comfortably, so some of us got left out from time to time, but we each got a turn and we understood. At the lake Mrs. Crane took pride in doing all the work herself; the maid had the day off and Mrs. Crane waited on us, but we did clear the table and wanted to help with the dishes, but she wouldn't permit it. I think she was afraid we might break something, and she was probably right in that. I was so clumsy. Violet had friends from her family's circle and we were never with that group, but Violet was relaxed and herself when she was with us. She lived in two worlds, a sophisticated one in which she was born and raised, and ours with its rough edges, and she flourished with the best of both.

"Well, to continue. After our 'picnic' we had to sit on the porch and let our dinner settle. We sat sipping our iced tea, feeling quite important up above the lake watching the panorama below — the swimmers, the boats and the sun shimmering on the water. When Mrs. Crane decided it was all right to go in we made a trip to the outhouse." She chuckled. "Even that was not your run of the mill outhouse. Even the seats had covers and were painted white. There was room for two inside, but we preferred the privacy of one at a time. We still had our modesty. But the occupant was harangued with a steady stream of urgent requests to hurry up. How impatient the young are.

"We quickly put on our swim suits in the cabin while Mr. Crane was getting the sailboat ready. I'm sure you have seen pictures of what was considered stylish back then, to say nothing of daring, but which was really very modest. One piece, dark wool suits with legs that came almost to the knees were the fashion. Still, they brought admiring glances from the men and boys. I suppose it was because of the contrast with the former yards of material we had been clothed in for years.

"We ran down to the dock and stopped, not knowing how deep the water was. So we sat on the end and dangled our feet for a few minutes. It felt so refreshing. Then Sunny stepped in carefully. The water came only to her waist so I went next, followed by the others. Violet was the shortest, so she got in on the side where it was more shallow. We had to wear ugly rubber bathing caps to keep our hair dry and the water out of our ears so we ducked beneath the water, holding our noses, and came up gasping and sputtering. None of us could really swim, so we splashed around for awhile having a great time. After awhile we waded to shore and sat on our towels, soaking up the sun. We removed the confining rubber caps and basked in the freedom from the cares of the world, at least for the day. We told Violet to put her hat back on to keep the sun off.

"She began to sing 'By the sea, by the sea, by the beautiful sea; You and I, you and I, oh how happy we'll be' in that sweet voice of hers and we joined in. Then we started on 'Oh Johnny, Oh Johnny, How you can love' and harmonized after a fashion, and collapsed on our towels in gales of laughter, because Laurel, for all of her smarts, couldn't carry a tune and our songfest sounded like we had a bass part. It must have carried out across the water because some of the boaters waved to us.

"Then Daisy said in alarm, 'Look, there's that crazy boat again. Just look at that man. Someone is going to get hurt if he doesn't look out. '

"We could see him more clearly as he swung closer to shore, making people in the water shout at him to look out.

"Daisy gasped, 'Oh no, it's that awful Butch.'

"It was Butch all right. He had a woman in the motorboat and they were shouting back, laughing and drinking from beer bottles. Then they suddenly swerved and took off across the lake.

"We didn't see Butch again for some time. Sunny said she didn't think he was finished with fooling around and in a low voice told us what she was sure he and that woman were doing, at which we expressed shock, although by then we were knowledgeable about what ' IT' was and repulsed with the thought. But Butch did come back."

Mrs. Hoekstra looked as if she were about to cry. She looked out the window.

Mr. Crane walked over to where they were sitting.

"Did you see Butch, Mr. Crane?" asked Laurel. "Even I saw him. He came in real close with his motorboat and scared everybody."

"He appears to be gone now," he replied. "How'd you girls like to go out in the sailboat? There's plenty of room and the wind has picked up. Mrs. Crane has declined and is lying down, but I'm ready to get out on that water. Let's get to the dock now."

Their eager acceptance banished any apprehension they might have had about Butch and his woman friend. They were helped into the boat as it rocked a bit, sending them into shrieks as they hung onto his hand. Violet sat beside her father with her hat squarely in place. The others sat on cushions placed around the sides.

"Ready?" inquired Mr. Crane.

A chorus of yeses greeted him and he hoisted the single sail which filled with wind and they slowly began to move. They followed the shore carefully until they cleared others in the water. He headed the sailboat to the middle of the lake and the wind sent it on at a brisker pace. Violet's hat fell to her shoulders but she didn't bother to put it on, as she hung on to her father's arm and the side of the boat. The girls hung on and squealed in delight at the smooth glide over the sparkling water. Spray sprinkled their faces and their hair blew around their heads and into their eyes.

After several turns in expansive, wide sweeps, maneuvering the boat expertly and enjoying the laughter of his passengers Mr. Crane turned toward the shore when, seemingly out of nowhere came the errant motorboat with Butch at the controls, unmindful of anything but taking the last swig from his bottle.

Mr. Crane shouted, "Look out, you maniac!" and frantically worked the tiller attempting to steer away from the speeding path of the drunken man's motorboat. But it was too late. Violet was flung from the sailboat as she lost her desperate grip on her father's arm.

41

A soft sob came from Mrs. Hoekstra. She looked sorrowfully at Karen. "She died. She drowned. Dear sweet Violet was knocked overboard and the deep water claimed her."

"Oh no."

"The other boaters saw what happened and rushed to help, shouting and cursing at Butch. But they were no match for his fast boat and he was gone with that woman, who had sat there and just laughed at the whole thing."

She wiped her eyes with a tissue and said disgustedly, between her sobs, "We used to have nice soft handkerchiefs. These darn tissues aren't worth a toot."

Karen was alarmed at how the memory she had evoked had affected Mrs. Hoekstra. She passed the box of tissues to her as tears rolled down Mrs. Hoekstra's wrinkled face.

"The rest of us girls were hanging onto the side of the sailboat for dear life as it rocked back and forth. Mr. Crane was calling for Violet, reaching into the water, finally slipping over the side, floundering around looking for her. He was pulled into one of the boats and had to be restrained from going back in. All the time he was shouting and became hysterical. The men dived into the deep water again and again and finally took us all in to shore. Mr. Crane was limp as a kitten and whimpering and we were crying."

She blew her nose and took a deep breath.

"Violet's body was recovered, but she was past reviving. They did try. Back on shore we stood together in shock, huddled together for comfort and feeling chilled in the hot sun. They carried Violet up to the cottage and placed her gently on the wicker setee on the porch. She was so pale, except for her pink face which the sun had got to. Mrs. Crane, obviously awakened from her nap, came bustling out to see what was going on and let out a scream. I'll never forget her anguished scream. She went completely to pieces and collapsed."

She dabbed at her eyes and wiped her nose. "I tell you, Karen, it was one of the saddest days in our young lives. It put a damper on the others at the lake, too. We were taken home. The poor Cranes. Their beautiful, talented only child was dead. How they had doted on her. Our hearts went out to them and ours were broken too. There weren't any telephones out there, of course, and no way to get Violet back to Huron, so they took her back in their car."

Karen was shocked and surprised.

"How else? Besides, they wouldn't let her out of their sight. Mrs. Crane insisted on putting her up front with them — just held her in her arms with Violet's head on her shoulder all the way back. We were frozen in silence. None of us said a word. Mr. Crane stared straight ahead, looking grim .

"The funeral was in the Methodist Church where most of us had gone to Sunday School. It was full to the balcony. Violet lay there in her casket, so beautiful, looking like she was only asleep, those deep blue eyes closed forever. Her long black curls she had wanted to cut off laid on the gorgeous white gown they had dressed her in. The organist played 'Mighty Like A Rose'. We couldn't bear it."

"Mrs. Hoekstra, please don't think about it anymore. I am so sorry to have upset you." She hesitated. "Do you know what happened to Butch?"

"He dropped out of sight. No one ever saw him again; at least that is the story. Some said otherwise."

She was silent for a moment and Karen did not intrude. Mrs. Hoekstra finally said softly, "Our innocence was lost forever that awful 4th of July. We never forgot the sight of Violet's hat bobbing up against the shore."

Chapter 6

Karen was going to try to make the next day's visit more upbeat. She'd not mention their previous day's conversation. She would not bring on more tears. Karen liked the old lady and didn't wish to cause her distress. Mrs. Hoekstra was seated on the bed as usual in anticipation of her arrival. What was not usual was Ula, who had seated herself in a wheelchair and was stationed next to the curtain which separated the room. She greeted Karen with a toothless grin. Her teeth were soaking in a container on her bedside table.

"Hello, Ula," Karen said pleasantly.

Ula's grin never wavered as she remained close beside the partially open curtain, attentive to what would be said.

"Don't mind her, Karen. She is only curious. I think our voices woke her one day and she became interested in what we said. I don't mind. At least she is awake and the snoring has stopped."

Karen had her notebook and tape recorder ready. She noted with satisfaction that there was a quantity of tape wound, indicating that Mrs. Hoekstra had been speaking into it.

"I did put some thoughts on the tape. I even played it back, once I figured it out. A person's voice sounds so strange when it is heard for the first time. I would never have recognized it. I sound like an old woman."

"I'll enjoy listening to what you said when I get back to the office. Don't worry about it; it will be just fine. Now, I think this would be a good time to take your picture," she said as she took the camera from its case. She looked at her subject and smiled as she said, "You look so pretty today."

Mrs. Hoekstra did indeed look nice. She had taken pains to look her very best since her young visitor had been calling. Her dress was dated, but neat, and her white hair combed and fastened into a bun on top of her head with some large odd-shaped hair pins. Her wrinkled face brightened with her ready smile. She had applied a touch of makeup which heightened her fine appearance. She straightened herself on the bed to be as straight as she could be, explaining that she would stand, but that she had become quite stooped in the last five years or so and it wouldn't look good in the paper. Karen calmed her concern and took several poses. Mrs. Hoekstra's lined face looked younger than her 100 years with her smile and the excitement of having her picture taken. At last, Karen was finished and Holly sighed and relaxed.

"Well, that wasn't so bad," she said, obviously pleased.

"Thank you. I think I got some excellent shots. I'll make sure you get one."

She sat down again on the folding chair and opened her notebook. "Now then, you said the period after World War I was an interesting time, that there was a surge of optimism."

"That's true, but there was disappointment too, with lots of unemployment, hard times and the influenza epidemic of 1918 and 1919. It spread like wildfire and Huron didn't escape."

"I remember that," spoke Ula from beside the curtain.

"I remember it well, too," said Mrs. Hoekstra politely. "I was taking my nurse's training and our class got hands-on experience that turned us into first class nurses in no time. There were 185 deaths in Huron, far too many for the town of Huron, and that didn't include those who got very sick and eventually recovered. I think Huron numbered around 9,000 people at that time. Sprague Hospital was overrun with sick folks and there was no more room, so some patients had to be cared for in the Episcopal Parish House. Facilities were even set up on the second floor of the Elks Lodge. Every nurse was called into service and we accompanied the doctors everywhere. It was heart-breaking to watch so many die and to stand by so helplessly. We did our best, but it was futile. All we could do was to make patients as comfortable as possible. We became exhausted, to say nothing of the doctors, who tended to the sick until they were walking automatons. The entire town closed down to keep the infection from spreading. Everyone was frightened."

"You didn't catch it?"

"I was lucky. Of course, doctors and nurses were well taught about cleanliness and were scrupulous in sanitary measures. But poor Papa ...."

Karen's heart sank. This would upset Mrs. Hoekstra, but she was composed as she continued.

"Papa was one of those who died. Randall did everything he could for him and hardly left his side at night, because he was my father. I was there with him, too, when he died and Randall was so comforting. I needed his comfort, losing Papa, being so tired and having shared so much with Randall, plus being head over heels in love with him. It meant so much to me, more than ...."

"My little sister died," offered Ula, peeking around the curtain.

"Ula dear, please don't. Karen and I are having a private conversation," said Mrs. Hoekstra kindly.

45

Ula retreated further behind the curtain where she thought she was invisible, but her shadow betrayed her presence as she sulked, her chin in her hand.

"Poor Ula," said Mrs. Hoekstra in a confidential tone, "she's getting a bit senile and pouts whenever someone speaks crossly to her. "

"But you didn't speak crossly."

"I know, but Ula thinks I did."

Karen went on, "By this time in your lives some of you must have married and had families."

Mrs. Hoekstra brightened. "After the epidemic was over people settled down to a normal life and we entered the roaring twenties. Perhaps you have heard of the roaring twenties?"

She nodded but it seemed like another age to Karen, totally incomprehensible.

"The enthusiasm when the war was over was expressed in different ways. Hope for a better life was the motivating force for most, but there was poverty for many, while others went on to true prosperity. Others, changed abruptly by the actuality of what the war had done and at how quickly lives had been turned upside down, became reckless and wild and lost themselves in parties and dances. Even fashions were completely different with shorter skirts, silk stockings, swinging beads, high heels. There were regular dances at the Elks Club and the Marvin Hughitt Hotel on that beautiful marble floor. Many returning veterans proposed at those dances."

Mrs. Hoekstra laughed. "I remember the dance pavilion at Ruskin Park, outside of Huron. There were Saturday night dances and they were well attended. In those days these affairs had matrons to sort of chaperone the young people. One Saturday night the young folks were particularly unruly and the matron was vainly trying to keep order. She was shouting so loudly at them as they frolicked at the river's edge that her false teeth came loose and fell into the river. The young men thought it a lark to dive in to retrieve them and one did come up with some uppers, but ...." and Mrs. Hoekstra's shoulders shook with mirth, "they weren't hers!"

Karen couldn't help but join in and Ula emitted a raukous hoot. "That happened to me once."

"There were dances at Daum's auditorium, too. Schumacher Liquor was across the alley, making it convenient in later years for the young lads to keep spirits up — so to speak. And some of the more affluent neighborhoods had houses large enough to contain a ballroom, where more sedate dances were held. There was a group called the Merry Patriarchs which held fancy affairs, but by invitation only. Huron was a mighty social town for a good number of years right through Prohibition.

"The years of Prohibition — let's see. I think it was from 1919 to December, 1933 — a long time, but it didn't work very well. Butch went right to work bootlegging and Huron never ran out of liquor. Of course, he couldn't call it Blume's Beer, but people who wanted it could get it. In the 1930s the brewery was sold and once again produced beer, Schooner's Beer. As I said, the brewery kept in operation during prohibition making an orange drink and root beer. I was not a drinker, but I did enjoy the orange drink and especially the root beer. The stuff they call root beer nowadays doesn't have the zing it had then.

"We didn't see much of Butch. He seldom showed his face in town, at least during the daytime. He had a group of questionable companions and they all prospered from the liquor trade. Ever since that terrible accident when Violet was drowned her parents were so grief stricken they could hardly think straight. Then when he showed up when everyone thought he had left the area Mr. Crane was said to have sworn revenge. Nothing was ever proved about what happened to Butch, but the Cranes' lives were ruined. Mr. Crane retired from the bank and devoted the rest of his life to taking care of Mrs. Crane, who never recovered from the loss of Violet. Anyway, Butch made a lot of money and finally built himself a big ugly house north of town where he had a certain element of women who frequented the place."

She shook her head in disgust.

"But the rest of us went on with our lives. I eventually became Randy's nurse. Dr. Randall Thorne was one of the best doctors in the area and I was mighty proud that he chose me to be his nurse, because there were others who had skill and compassion. But we knew each other well and I understood him. We were comfortable with each other, but he was always most professional. I was thrilled to go to work every day to be with him and to work side by side, and never gave up hope that he would love me as I loved him.

"He had a good general practice for years and tended to the needs of patients from delivering babies to caring for the aged. Some of the girls went to him for their ailments, a couple even for pregnancies, but some felt ill at ease with a man they had played with as children in the vacant lot, plus my presence there probably made them uncomfortable.

"We all married and the first of us married was Rose, who married Clarence Koning, the class clown. We were all totally surprised but it was a successful marriage. Clarence began work at the Marvin Hughitt Hotel when it opened in September, 1921 . He was there for years, eventually managing the place. Imagine! He loved working with those who came to the hotel, whether it was the staff, who respected him, or someone who was just passing through or regulars like salesmen who made that fine hotel their home away from home. His friendly wit appealed to people and the hotel prospered, right up to the 1970s when it closed. He retired at 65 and continued to enjoy life with Rose and entertaining his grandchildren, who adored him. Now the Marvin Hughitt is called Dakota Plaza with apartments on the upper floors, small businesses on the lower floor and basement parking — but of course you know all that. Rose and Clarence had four children, all redheads with freckles. She was a wonderful mother and had such fun with them, sort of growing up together — until she died.

"Lilly was engaged to be married but was having increased trouble with her asthma, so she became one of Randy's patients. Her asthma became worse as she got older, especially in the summer and the fall when pollen filled the air and dust blew down the streets. Most streets were paved except for those on the edge of Huron, but side streets were graveled and the dust rose up in clouds from the traffic when it didn't rain for weeks and weeds were the only things that seemed to grow. One September while she was in the office she had a real bad attack. She had become so thin and pale over the years from the severity of the illness and she was doubled over, just wracked with coughing and then flung back wheezing and trying to breathe. We were so alarmed that Lilly was admitted to the hospital. Randy stood by her bed and did everything he could to relieve her suffering. A steamer at her bedside that sent warm, moist air into the tent-like contraption that was placed over her did little to help. Her poor lungs were strained to the limit and she was further weakened by the last spell which finally laid her low. Her folks were so afraid for her and her intended was distraught to see her so sick. Randy told them that her heart had been damaged and they could only watch and wait. Lilly, too, was an only child.

"Some nights Randy would sit up by the bed to keep watch when Lilly's breathing was particularly labored. She was his friend, too. The slightest movement would wake him if he nodded off. One morning he awoke with a start. The sun was red on the horizon and I had just come into the room. I had a strong feeling that I should get to the hospital to check on Lilly. But she was gone. She had died in the night. The anguish on Randy's face was painful to see. He railed against his ineptitude, said it was his fault. He had fallen asleep, shirked his duty, totally unforgivable. I tried to calm him down, tried in vain to comfort him. I pointed out there was no sign of a difficult death. Lilly looked so serene and peaceful with no ravages of the pain that had plagued her for so long. She had obviously simply died in her sleep. But he would have none of it. He had failed to save her and he blamed himself for a long time. He couldn't bring himself to tell Lilly's folks, so I did it. Poor Randy. He had been strained to the limit with all that had been required of him from the beginning of his practice.

"Later, in his office, he poured out his feelings to me, told me of his guilt in not having been able to heal the sick who had been in his care during the influenza epidemic and in seeing too many people he knew succumb since then. I suspect that his boyhood years and his encounters with

Butch and his torments about Randy's lack of measuring up had made a deeper impression on him than we realized. I was overcome seeing him like that and in losing another dear friend. Tears came; I went to him and put my arms around him. He held me close and we cried together. He fairly trembled in his sorrow and I thanked God I was there for him. Then he kissed me tenderly, his lips still salty from his tears. I just melted."

"I got kissed once in the park," came from the other side of the curtain. They ignored Ula.

"My heart soared with that kiss. I was so in love with him and that kiss told me he loved me, too. And he did, as a familiar, comfortable friend. I was naive, but never stopped loving him. Do you love your Jack, Karen?"

Caught off guard she stammered, "I ... I don't know."

"If you are in love you will know." She sighed and continued. "So now two of the original nine of us were gone and it was a thoroughly devastated group that attended another funeral."

"But enough sad talk. Gloria married an insurance agent who stopped regularly at the Marvin Hughitt. That's where they met, at one of the dances. He turned Catholic for her and moved to Huron to stay and she was ecstatic. At the wedding she fairly glowed with happiness; she looked like an angel. It was a fancy affair, very colorful. Her folks and her nine brothers and sisters were happy for her, because she was the youngest and the last of them to get married. She had dozens of nieces and nephews. She and — Neville Jones, that was his name — she and Neville had eight children and it eventually killed her, but they were married almost 20 years."

"Those dances were such fun. The Marvin Hughitt was a grand hotel, built by the Elks Club and they held their meetings there. There was an elevator because there were seven floors and on the third floor was a beautiful ballroom with a marble floor. That floor cost $4,000 which most folks thought terribly extravagant, but the dancing was so smooth and the dances were well attended, in large part because of that marvelous floor. The waltzes, the two-step, even the naughty black bottom were all danced with enthusiasm. There were few wall flowers, believe me, especially during the roaring twenties.

"But to get back to the girls. Myrtle even got married to an odd fellow by the name of Elmer Black. We thought his name was appropriate because he seemed to be forever in the need of a good scrubbing." Mrs. Hoekstra's eyes twinkled. "He worked at Armour's packing plant. What a pair those two were. It was too bad, though, that they lost a baby shortly after he was born and Myrtle was unable to have more children, so she took in stray cats. She seemed content, but with Myrtle it was hard to tell. We thought Elmer could have provided for her better than he did. They lived in a small house on the west edge of town, just off the fairgrounds. She never moved from there and her lackluster life didn't change. To each his own, as they say. She remained a club member, though. I think it was the only social life she had. Poor Myrtle became absentminded as she aged. She was such an enigma to the rest of us, but she was our friend.

"Daisy married an intelligent man of few words, a professor at the college, Melvin Moberly. He wore glasses and his hair never seemed to take a good combing. But Daisy was happy and the two of them knew what the other was thinking and wasted few words in conversation, unless it was of a controversial bent, when Daisy could see things so clearly and deemed it her purpose to try to get others to see. They had a circle of friends outside our club with whom they associated, all bookish types who enjoyed each other's company and their intellectual wit, which none of the rest of us understood at all. Their vision was clear, but I think they often overlooked human nature. I've always disliked the term 'egg head' because it denotes knowledge as an object of scorn. What do you think?"

Karen was amazed at the insight Holly had for her friends of so long ago and was taken aback at the question.

"I do know that a smart student in school is often looked down upon and made fun of, which is unfortunate, because the future surely doesn't depend on the lowest mentality."

"Karen, you are so smart yourself. Who was it who said: The disadvantaged were not meant to lead us?"

Karen's pencil was filling the pages of her notebook. Her subject was in rare form, appearing so alert and sharp. Mrs. Hoekstra smiled and continued.

"Laurel married Wendell Swanson, a man who barely got through high school, but who treated her like a queen and deferred to her every wish. He didn't mind being instructed by her on things he didn't quite comprehend. Laurel was so smart and she was patient with him. The rest of us said she made a man out of him. I should have said that she brought him to his full potential — and he let her 'have her head' as the saying goes."

At Karen's perplexed look she said, "You know, as when a farmer lets his trusty horse proceed without having to guide him or use the reins. He let him have his head, and the horse would trot to wherever they were going from habit."

Karen nodded. She was learning all sorts of strange expressions from Mrs. Hoekstra.

"Laurel and Wendell were very happy. He took good care of her — and forgave much — all the years they were married. It takes all kinds and life has a way of confounding us all."

Karen was pondering how to ask the next question and looked up to see Mrs. Hoekstra smiling kindly at her.

"You are wondering about Sunny and me, aren't you?"

Karen replied, "I don't wish to get too personal."

"It's all right. Sunny and Randall were married and I married Jonathan Hoekstra. It broke my heart to lose Randall, but I probably never had him to lose after all. I cried for weeks, but eventually rationalized that if I truly loved him I should want only the best for him, I would want him to be happy. The fact that it was Sunny, my very best friend, who was the one making him happy started the tears all over again. Mama thought I was sick and wanted to call Randy to come see me. Of course, that would never do and I snapped out of it, although I wore a sad face for a long time. I thought I managed to fool the girls but of course they knew and they were very kind. We didn't talk about it. What a long time ago it was."

She stared out the open window into the September sunshine. A light breeze stirred the curtain and the sound of chirping birds floated into the room.

The last patient had left and Dr. Randall Thorne sat wearily in the chair at his desk. He was bone tired. Holly laid the last of the patients' files before him.

"Just leave them there, Holly. I'll go over them tomorrow. A busy day, wasn't it?"

He looked up at her in fondness. What would he do without Holly's devoted assistance, without her loyalty? How long had they known one another? He had lost track. His grateful smile in appreciation for her crisp efficiency swept over her.

She was a handsome woman. Her neat brown hair beneath her nurse's cap shone above deep blue eyes. She returned his smile with the smile she had bestowed on him for years.

"Sit down, Holly. You must be exhausted, too, from all you have done today. I want to tell you something." She listened to him hopefully as she sat opposite him on the other side of the desk.

"We've known each other for a good many years now, ever since we were kids. Did you ever wonder why most of us are still living in Huron? So many leave their home towns for greener pastures."

She replied, "I suppose most of us found our opportunities here. This is our home. Our families and friends are here."

"Perhaps so. It is comforting to have lifelong companions around us, to establish roots with those we love. Holly, I want to get married."

Her heart gave a leap and she moved to the edge of the chair in anticipation.

"I'm in love for the first time, truly in love, and she feels the same way."

His words were not what she had hoped for.

"Sunny and I have known each other as long as you and I have. We are all good friends. It just happened like a bolt out of the blue at one of the dances we all enjoy so much. You and Sunny have always been the best of friends. She must have told you."

He didn't notice her crestfallen look. He didn't appear to wonder that, of course, she hadn't mentioned it, that Holly would have brought it up if she had. She slumped back into the chair and tried to keep her

51

composure as he said, "We are to be married in June and I know Sunny has lots of things for you to do to make it perfect. You are so good at such matters. In fact, you are so splendid at everything you do."

He stood and gazed at her with affection, the affection she had long misunderstood, which she had read more into than he meant. She kept a fixed smile on her face, but did not dare speak, lest she weep. He must not see her despair.

"She'll be here soon, meeting me to go to see the pastor to make arrangements. Would you like to come with us?"

Why was he torturing her this way? Holly declined, trying not to cry. He put on his topcoat and walked to the door. He paused and turned and went back to her. He took her hands and lifted her from the chair, took her into his arms and kissed her.

"Holly, you're the best friend I ever had."

He didn't hear her stiffled sob or see the tears begin as he left the office. She walked to the outer door and watched, her heart growing heavy from the deep hurt expanding within it. She watched as he waved to Sunny coming across the street. Love shone on his face, love for Sunny, the love she had yearned for all her life, but which she would never know. He was lost to her forever and she was lost in a void without him. Her sobbing increased as she stood alone at the door, unchecked tears streaming down her face. Her vision blurred as they walked away from her, absorbed in their mutual love. She turned and went back inside.

Mrs. Hoekstra stirred and said as she turned to Karen, her eyes moist, "I survived, as you can see, but Randall was the love of my life. He never knew. To him, I remained a good friend. My heart was broken. Perhaps it's a good thing that the sound of a breaking heart cannot be heard; we keep it hidden, invisible so others can't see. Now they're all gone, everyone's gone, except me. It's so hard to understand why sometimes."

Karen was glad she had taken Mrs. Hoekstra's photograph when she had, because she looked very sad at that moment. She vowed to herself to end the interview the next day. She must stop bringing up unhappy memories in the woman she had come to enjoy and admire.

Chapter 7

The next day Karen entered the Huron Nursing Home with purpose, determined to bring her protracted interview to an end. She had enjoyed Mrs. Hoekstra, but she had spent far too much time on her assignment and Mr. Stern was becoming insistent on seeing the finished product on his desk.

She had plenty of material to work with from her notes and on the tapes in which Mrs. Hoestra spoke sporadically. She had lamented the absence of offspring from such a large family. The only one who had children was Howard, who taught in Brookings. He doted on two sons who were cherished nephews of the others. Now she was the last of the line with no one to follow her. Her aging brother, Bernard, and sisters, Hazel and Opal, spinster school teachers, had been reunited for a few years in the family home, with Madge managing it despite her infirmities. Soon their meager pensions were not enough to keep it going so, reluctantly, they turned it into a boarding house which soon filled with teachers, working or retired, and their reluctance vanished as their home once again became a vital, thriving household filled with active people and good conversation. One by one they died and upon Madge's death at the age of 72 Holly learned that the old house had been left to her. It was too large for Holly and her husband and Howard didn't want it, so it was sold, providing Holly with money of her own. It tore her heart to see the family home fall into disrepair and eventually torn down to make way for new, smaller homes.

Karen walked briskly into the familiar room and smiled at Ula. She was startled to find Mrs. Hoekstra in her robe and slippers lying on top of the bed. Her hair was uncombed and it lay loosely around her thin face. She looked suddenly 100 years old. Karen slowed her stride and said in alarm, "Mrs. Hoekstra, are you all right?"

"Hello, Karen dear. Yes, I'm fine, just fine. A little tired, that's all. Oh now, don't you go. I do look forward to your visits. Old folks get to feeling poorly now and then. Please sit down."

Ula spoke from the other side of the room. "Holly don't feel so good."

She would make it brief and leave, just get a little more information about the Women's Club, return to the office and write her article that very

**Club meeting at
Myrtle's humble home**

day and be done with it. She was glad she had the foresight to take Holly's photograph when she did, because it had turned out so well.

"If you are sure it will not tire you I will ask a few final questions. Then I really must leave."

"Oh dear; I'm sorry to hear that. Whatever will I do with my afternoons if you don't come anymore?"

Ula said, "We could go down and watch television. You oughta feel better by then. Holly had to have a nurse last night." She directed this last statement to Karen.

"Hush, Ula. It was nothing. I'm fine now. I just get a little dizzy when I sit up. It will pass; it always does."

"I want to watch television. You used to push me down to watch television," Ula pouted.

"Yes, and we'll go again. Now please, be quiet and let Karen and me talk."

Ula's grumble let them know that she didn't like it, but she didn't bother them again.

Karen sat in the metal folding chair, looked at Mrs. Hoekstra apologetically and asked, "Did you continue with the Women's Club even though you were all occupied with marriages and children?"

"Oh my, yes. We had so much more to talk about; we wanted to put our energies and convictions to work; and, of course, we had to replace Violet and Lilly. Then a Mrs. Sylvia Wallace moved to town. She was a wealthy widow from a farm a few miles away with some pretty uppity ideas. We were in our thirties by then and she was somewhat older, something she tried to deny in her appearance, but she deemed it all an advantage which gave her an edge in guiding the club's activities."

She gave a thin smile. "Our first glimpse of her was quite by chance. Some of us were shopping one afternoon and we saw her coming out of Eiler's Furs with a big box tied with a fancy satin bow. She got into her brand new black Chrysler and drove off without looking right or left, her nose in the air. We stared at her in wonder. Except for Mrs. Crane, we didn't know anyone who had a real fur coat. Rose had it all figured out and said she must have inherited a wad of money from her late husband who, it was rumored, had been quite a few years older than she was and who had worked himself into an early grave. Nowadays he'd be called a workaholic.

"She was the one who got in touch with us and at first we were flattered and excited that the fancy Mrs. Wallace wanted to have anything to do with a few ordinary women who were trying to better themselves and contribute to the community. Daisy was president then and she told us that this Sylvia Wallace had called her and inquired in a low, cultured voice that she was new in town and wanted to get better acquainted and what better way than to join the Women's Club, The Fortnightly. Well, what could we do? It was our first new member and we couldn't just refuse her, tell her no, that she couldn't join, that we were somewhat intimidated by her, her money and expensive car. Mrs. Crane never put on airs like that. But since we had no regular procedure for accepting or rejecting members just then and we felt we must change with the times, we invited her to our next meeting."

Mrs. Hoekstra paused to catch her breath and waved aside Karen's protestations. She took a sip of water and leaned back into her pillow.

"We took turns meeting in each others' homes and, as luck would have it, it was Myrtle's turn. None of us said it, but we were all thinking that Myrtle's place was not the best place to induct a new member, especially one like Mrs. Wallace. Myrtle took some getting used to if you hadn't grown up with her as we had. But we couldn't just change the meeting place. We wouldn't hurt Myrtle's feelings.

"You see, there were many times when we forgave her for — how shall I put it? — lack of social etiquette. We knew Myrtle and overlooked things others might find inexcusable. But she was our friend and she was so happy when it was her turn to be the hostess. She would send Elmer out to play cards or horseshoes with his buddies and then she'd sweep and dust to make her poor house as neat as possible. Myrtle sort of heaped things in the corners, but we got used to it and didn't notice. She even put all the cats out before we arrived. As I said before, to each her own. Mrs. Wallace might not be as kind.

"Myrtle's house was small and on the west edge of town. The wood steps were in need of repair and Elmer never got around to fixing them, said he didn't have any tools. Of course, he did, but we suspected he was not very handy with them. Myrtle would borrow some mismatched chairs and they were set in a semi-circle inside the edge of curled up linoleum. Linoleum was the common floor covering back then, decorated with bright squares or flowers imprinted, with a border around the 9x12 size. In time, the border frayed and curled, especially in extremes of temperature and no amount of effort could straighten it out, not without breaking off a piece anyway. Not many could afford a wool rug and even wool rugs rarely extended to the baseboards. But, as I said, we were used to Myrtle's entertaining, and she was so eager to please."

Although she was breathing faster from talking, the memory of what she remembered made her laugh softly.

"At one of our meetings, after the discussion of the latest books, magazines, and of possible good works the club might perform, it was time for refreshments. We balanced our plates and cups on wooden trays on our laps as the dining room was too small for us to sit around the table. Those wooden trays were some of the few items of any value that Myrtle had fallen heir to from her mother and were very nice with a leafy design around the edges beneath layers of varnish. We passed around the table and filled our trays. Myrtle always set her table with her best china on the only linen cloth she possessed, a wedding gift from us girls, genuine linen it was with matching napkins. We took our sandwich. Myrtle cut off the crusts as she had seen the rest of us do to make them look fancy and she would save the crusts and make bread pudding with them. We all did, and mighty tasty pudding it was. We learned economics with actual practice. She stood at the end of the small table and poured coffee into the cups and we moved on to where she had salad set out in dishes. It was a gelatine salad with bananas in it. There were six individual molded mounds of gelatine, each with a little gouge scooped out of it. Myrtle's dish, which she had set aside for herself, had exactly six little scoops of gelatine with bits of bananas. Poor Myrtle, it never occurred to her that she might some day need additional molds. So you see, we were apprehensive about having Mrs. Wallace's first impression of our group to come from Myrtle's house. We were frustrated, to suddenly have it all matter just because of Mrs. Wallace. We felt guilty feeling the way we did, but we knew a first impression was important.

"So we let it stand as planned and met at Myrtle's house. Laurel picked up Mrs. Wallace in her clean, but old Chevrolet. We decided it would be best to have our smartest member pick her up and not have to give her directions to a part of town that could discourage her. They arrived after the rest of us were already there. We were fixed on the door when she knocked and Myrtle went to answer it. There stood Laurel in her neat frock and white gloves and small hat with Mrs. Wallace standing beside her with a prim smile on her made up face, all decked out in pumps and her new fur coat, with a hat trimmed in matching fur. After all, it was October and a lovely evening, but she did look mighty foxy. Laurel had a pained look on her face, but she politely introduced Mrs. Wallace to each of us. 'And this is our hostess, Myrtle Black,' she said.

"Myrtle had two nice dresses and she alternated them for each meeting. She was presentable. Her light hair was combed and held in place with dime store clips. Her house was neat and tidy and dimly lit by the low watt bulbs in each outlet, and every single one of them was turned on in an attempt to make as cheery a look as possible. Mrs. Wallace's reaction was obvious. It was doubtful she had ever been in such a poor home, but she rose to the occasion, brought her upbringing and breeding to the fore and extended her gloved hand with great composure and said, with her nose slightly elevated, 'How do you do, Mrs. Black. Thank you ever so much for inviting me.' We let out a collective silent sigh of relief. Myrtle offered to hang up her coat, but Mrs. Wallace said no, she would just put it over her shoulders. And she did just that. I think she got mighty warm, but she looked like something out of the *Ladies Home Journal*, and she knew it.

She sat gingerly on one of the chairs, crossed her long legs and, as Laurel said later, it was a shame there was no one there for her to impress, because she was a sight to see. The conversation was strained that night I can tell you.

"We explained to Mrs. Wallace what our small club was about, how we wished to expand it to include charitable work, how we got started — all of it. She listened politely, looking down her nose at us, and said it sounded intriguing, that she would think about it. She was so different from the rest of us, but perhaps she was just what we needed. We could be in a rut and change was inevitable if we were to grow. Daisy spoke in her capacity as president and said it would be an asset to the club to have Mrs. Wallace as a member. We had lost two members and should replace them and she hoped Mrs. Wallace would seriously consider becoming a member. Mrs. Wallace continued to smile that superior smile of hers and we stared at Daisy, thinking she must be out of her mind. Daisy gave us all a look that as much as said: Well, what would you do?

"When we adjourned to the dining room for refreshments we were relieved to note that there were no gelatine molds. Instead, there was a delicious spice cake set out on her linen cloth, a cake so light and tasty that Mrs. Wallace asked if it had been obtained at the local bakery. Myrtle just looked her right in the eye and told her that she had baked it herself, that it was an old family recipe, and that she had never given it out to anybody. Her unusually spirited response surprised us, as we had expected her to retreat into her shell. Even our guest was at a loss for words, but managed to say that it was most delectable. Myrtle beamed.

"We added members steadily over the years, by invitation only, and became a force for constructive works in Huron. As I have said, we became a part of the General Federation of Women's Clubs, a prestigious organization. The Fortnightly is still a member."

Her breathing was more labored from her long dissertation and her animation from telling of the evening so long ago had given her pleasure, but she was tired. She closed her eyes. Karen made up her mind. She could not cause Mrs. Hoekstra anymore undue stress. She folded her notebook and stood up.

Mrs. Hoekstra stirred and said, "Are you going so soon? Did I drop off? I never nap, as I told you once. Sorry, Karen. But you don't have to go. Please stay."

"I'm afraid I must go, but I'll leave my tape recorder for you in case you think of something you'd like to say. I'll pick it up tomorrow, and then I'll have to say goodbye. But I will bring you a copy of the photograph we'll be using in the paper. It's really very good."

Mrs. Hoekstra looked sad. Her eyes were heavy with dark circles under them. Karen moved close to the bed. Holly looked very old and tired and

Karen was strangely moved. She took Mrs. Hoekstra's hand, so thin and wrinkled, the knuckles bent with arthritis, but so light to the touch as to have no weight at all.

"Mrs. Hoekstra, I have enjoyed these visits with you more than you know. You are a grand lady with so much to show for your long life. It's been a privilege to know you."

She stooped and kissed the old woman's cheek. She smelled of lavender, of a different time. Mrs. Hoekstra smiled wanly, her eyes grew moist and she squeezed Karen's hand.

"Bless you, Karen," she said in a small voice.

Karen patted her hand, gave her a big smile and said cheerfully, "See you tomorrow," and left the room before she got all misty herself. Ula was asleep and snoring peacefully.

Holly watched her until she was out the door. A feeling of urgency was uppermost in her mind. Thoughts and images began to swirl and tumble in her brain. Intense emotions and sharp impressions of events long past demanded telling. I must put this on Karen's machine was the thought foremost in her mind. She reached to the bedside table to speak.

PART II
BLOSSOMS

Chapter 8

It was a Saturday afternoon in May, 1920. Holly was seated in one of the several wicker chairs on the wide expanse of porch that circled the house she had lived in her entire life. She could scarcely appreciate the glow of the afternoon sun on the greening grass and thick shrubbery and the vines twining around the lattice work.

She was waiting for Sunny and their inevitable talk, and her heart wasn't in it. But it had to be done. She couldn't, just wouldn't spoil the happiness Randall and Sunny had found in one another. She loved them both too much to do that. Sunny had called her and said she needed to speak to her. They both knew what needed to be said. Holly wondered if Sunny was as uncomfortable about the meeting as she was.

The day was warm and pleasant, perfect for making plans for a wedding, and she wished with all her heart that she was the one making those happy plans. She was twenty-seven years old and she should have been married long ago. All the others were and she had been a part of each of their weddings. Her wounded spirit would not cease reminding her: Always a bridesmaid, never a bride. She knew that thought must be in each of the girls' minds, too, as she was politely asked again and again if she would be the maid of honor. At first, she did enjoy the role, but it made her resentful, if not somewhat embarrassed, to show up as the maid of honor at so many weddings. But they were all close friends and her participation was expected and they would never not ask her. Now it was Sunny's turn and Holly must put on an agreeable face. She would force herself to be congenial and to give the impression of being happy for her best friend.

As Sunny turned onto the walk leading to the house Holly felt a twinge of jealousy, like a knife turning in her aching heart. She chastised herself for such an unworthy emotion, ignoring the fact that it was a very real, human emotion. She had always admired Sunny. She was tall and slim, graceful and beautiful. The sun shining on her short blond wavy hair gave off highlights that Holly's hair would never have. Sunny smiled broadly as she approached the porch and Holly bravely returned it as she rose from the chair. The women stood for a moment, looking into each other's eyes, searching for a solution to their mutual problem. Sunny spoke first.

"Holly, I — I don't know how to begin — but thanks for seeing me. This is so hard."

"I know. Please sit down. We have to talk about it. We've been friends for too long to not be able to talk about anything."

Sunny sat beside her in a chair apart.

"Yes, about anything." She burst into effusive explanation before she lost her courage. "Holly, it just happened. I know how you feel about Randy, how you have always felt. Don't I remember how we used to talk and moon about the boys we knew and how it always ended with your sighing and dreaming of Randy. And I figured he felt the same way about you."

So did I, was Holly's wry reflection.

Sunny continued in a rush, leaning forward in her chair.

"You know how all of us have grown up together. We know each other so well, sort of like brothers and sisters. I think in Randy's case he just got so caught up in being a good doctor and in working so hard that he didn't think of any of us girls as — special — at least until he had the time. And it was the dance. You know, the Valentine's Day dance when it was so cold. Remember how it snowed and everybody piled into Daum's Auditorium stomping off the snow before we hit the dance floor? And none of us girls was dressed for the weather. We had to be in style with the short skirts and about froze our legs off. Randy danced with all of us, even Myrtle, and she did have a good time. She was going with Elmer, remember?"

Holly remembered it vividly. She had waited for Randall to ask her to dance as he moved each of them around the smooth dance floor. She had been hurt when he failed to confine his dancing with her alone, but she had dismissed it as being obsessive on her part. She was glad to see him finally relaxing and enjoying himself.

"Well," continued Sunny, smiling at her and looking earnestly at her friend's face for forgiveness, "during the dance something happened between us. Maybe it was the music, maybe it was because it was Valentine's Day. I don't know, but something clicked and we fell in love — just like that. I didn't know it could happen so fast, like a bolt out of the blue."

Holly kept her composure, and her faint smile didn't waver .

"I can't give him up, Holly, I can't, even for you. Please say you forgive me. I didn't do it on purpose." Her eyes pleaded.

Holly took a deep breath and replied, "There is nothing to forgive. It is you Randolph loves, not me. I can't make him love me; he loves you. Even if I could it wouldn't work. Things like this happen. Does he know you're here?"

"Yes, but he thinks I'm only going to ask you to help in the wedding."

The hurt was deepening in Holly's heart and Sunny's hopeful expression wasn't helping.

She said, "I'll be glad to do anything I can. But, you mustn't tell Randolph about our talk. He must never know how I feel. I want to continue as his nurse and if he knew, it wouldn't be possible. I have no illusions, and I vow there will be nothing but a professional relationship, but he needs me in that capacity and we work so well together. Please don't tell him. Promise me."

"Of course, I promise. It will be our secret."

Their secret and that of Laurel, Daisy, Gloria, Rose and Myrtle. But she trusted their discretion.

Sunny reached over and touched her hand in love and friendship. Holly placed hers over it. The stone in her engagement ring was cool to the touch. Sunny had the good grace to not display it under Holly's nose.

"Now, what do you want me to do?"

"You must be my maid of honor, of course. No one else will do. Actually, you will be my only attendant. A friend of Randy's is going to be the best man. I haven't met him but he is with a pharmaceutical company and calls on Randy for medical supplies and such. Randy is quite fond of him, says he's a real peach. It will be a very simple ceremony and will be held at the new Methodist Church, the first wedding since it was built. Oh, it will be so exciting! It's the first Sunday next month at 2:00 o'clock. You'll need a blue chiffon dress. Can you manage it?"

Holly assured her that she could find an appropriate dress, but did not voice the feeling that she would be adding the blue chiffon to other bridesmaid dresses in the back of her closet. She stood, needing to end their talk before she broke down. Sunny had hoped for a longer chat and a visit about the happy preparations, but when she mentioned that Gloria was having a bridal shower and realized the pain she was putting her friend through she checked her chatter and knew she had to leave. They stood, looking at each other, hesitant, unsure.

"I'm so glad we could talk about this, Holly."

Sunny looked so forlorn that Holly held out her arms. She couldn't bear to send her friend away feeling unhappy and guilty. They hugged and Sunny left swiftly. Holly waved as Sunny turned with a bright smile when she reached the end of the walk. She hoped her wistfulness didn't show.

On a bright Sunday in June at the new Methodist Church Sunny and Dr. Randall Thorne were married. Although she felt too tall and plain and awkward, Holly looked very pretty in the blue chiffon dress she had purchased at Geyerman's. The scooped neckline and wide ruffled collar set off her long neck. With a matching blue hat with a wide, floppy brim she was striking and was complimented often. She didn't feel pretty. It was the most difficult day she had endured and she was positive she would never get over it.

When the wedding march sounded and she preceded Sunny down the aisle she was rigid in her control. She tried not to look at Randall waiting at the altar, so handsome in his new suit. She did not glance at the man standing at his side. Randall looked at her briefly and smiled, then focused his attention on his bride following behind her. Sunny was radiant, tall and elegant in her white gown and long veil, led by her father to the man she loved. Holly forced herself to not think, to just perform her role as maid of honor, standing at her friend's side, holding her bouquet, adjusting her veil. She repeated to herself over and over: Don't think, just keep smiling and do what is expected of you.

The vows were said, the wedding ring was placed on the bride's finger and Randall took her into his arms and kissed her. Holly couldn't watch, bowed her head, the brim of her hat concealing her expression. She didn't hear the pleased and happy laughter of the congregation as the recessional began and Randall and Sunny led them back up the aisle.

She joined them in the receiving line. Sunny hugged her tightly and whispered, "Thanks, Holly, you're the best." Then Randall took her hands and kissed her lightly on the cheek. His happy smile took in both of the women. He was about to say something but they were interrupted by the guests who were talking, hugging and kissing Sunny and heartily shaking Randall's hand. She stood beside Jonathan Hoekstra, Randall's friend, and smiled and shook hands automatically with the guests. She hardly looked at Mr. Hoekstra, except to note that when they had been introduced the night before he was quiet, polite and did not intrude into her isolation. He was a tall, gaunt man with a shock of sandy colored hair and piercing brown eyes that took in Holly's attractiveness .

At the reception Holly mingled with the guests, stayed clear of the bride and groom and was almost too animated. She talked cheerfully to her friends who were all participating. Gloria was at the guest book because she needed to be seated. She was pregnant again. Rose was at the punch bowl, talking to everyone. Myrtle was helping in the kitchen with the members of her circle. Laurel was queenly in her position as the pourer of the coffee, and Daisy was cutting the wedding cake after the bridal couple had cut the first piece. The gathering was much larger than planned, but the size had increased due to Dr. Randall Thorne's popularity in the town of Huron.

When they prepared to leave the church Holly joined the crowd that waved them on their way. Sunny turned, waved to Holly and gazed at her with affection and they were off in a shower of rice.

Holly was driven home by the considerate Jonathan Hoekstra. She sat with her hat in her lap, trying to make conversation as he offered an occasional comment. He stopped his old Ford automobile, swiftly walked to the passenger side and took her hand, aiding her from the car so she wouldn't dirty her dress. He showed her up onto the porch and stopped at the door. Holly felt dazed.

"May I call you, Holly? I get to Huron every month and I'd like to see you again," said the gallant Mr. Hoekstra.

"What? Oh yes, if you like. Thank you for bringing me home."

She went slowly inside to get out of her offending costume and threw her hat on her bed. She evaded the questions asked by her mother about the wedding. It was only later that she considered the fact that she had been rude to Mr. Hoekstra, so wrapped up in her misery had she been.

She changed into a loose, cool white linen dress and sat in the shade on the porch behind the vines on the lattice, and indulged in a massive session of self-pity. She was entitled to it she told herself as she curled up on the wicker setee. I have been brave and sweet and nice all I can manage today.

She sat quietly, feeling the welcome breeze on her hot face, listening to the birds chirp their incessantly cheery songs. She was too sad to cry. She didn't know how long she sat there, just that she couldn't bring herself to move. Maybe she would never move, just sit there until she turned to dust like a character in a Dickens novel. The smell of suppers cooking permeated the air, of fried potatoes, cabbage and onions, taking the taste of wedding cake from her senses. The aromas hung in the air, settling into the quiet of the evening. The fading, late afternoon sunshine cast narrow shadows on the porch from the slats of the railing. She stared at them, lost in thought, until the cool dusk made them disappear.

Chapter 9

The annual meeting of the Fortnightly Club was held at Rose's house on a warm spring night in 1924. All members were expected to attend to assess the events of the fiscal year and to formulate plans for the next one.

Holly looked forward to meetings at Rose's house. The hum of activity and the exuberance there was uplifting and fun. She and Clarence had been married for four years and already had their first child with another on the way. In fact, a number of the members of the club were expecting babies and Holly felt quite out of place, being one of just a few who were not married. She doted on the children of her friends and, while it was unlikely, she could still marry and have children of her own, but she had little interest since she had lost Randolph, the love of her life, forever. She even still lived at home, but she felt it was her duty to help out with her mother and Madge, who were getting on in years. Her sisters were now living in the family home and Bernard was thinking about retiring from the railroad and moving back.

She didn't hurry, strolling along, enjoying the spring air and the sounds of the birds. She never tired of the chirping of the birds. Their melodic songs filled the evening. She didn't even mind the squawks of the noisy sparrows. She recalled the old hymn and its comforting words: His eye is on the sparrow, so I know He watches me. Myrtle didn't have birds in her trees with all the stray cats she adopted. Holly supposed the cats gave her some sort of comfort. Everyone needed the love of a living creature .

Rose's house was a recently built bungalow with a wide porch open to the east. A few cars were parked in front. She hoped she was not the last to arrive. As she climbed the steps she took note of flowering geraniums set out in pots on the porch railing. Rose had an eye for color and their red blooms stood out against the brown painted wood. She could see members already seated in the large living room through the big window with a border of leaded glass. She had barely crossed to the open door when she heard Rose's voice mingled with a child's contagious laughter. She knocked on the screen door which was thrust wide by Teddy, Rose's three-year old, naked as the day he was born.

"It's Aunt Holly!" Teddy exclaimed as he flung himself at her, grabbing her around her legs. Rose hurried to snatch him away from the assembled women who were trying not to laugh too hard at his cherubic, energetic body. Teddy escaped her grasp and ran giggling from the room with Rose in pursuit as fast as her condition would allow.

"Come on in, Holly. I'll be right with you as soon as I put this kid to bed," she shouted over her shoulder.

A yowl of protest indicated that Teddy had been captured, but his voice would not be stilled.

"Aunt Holly put Teddy to bed. Want Aunt Holly!"

"Teddy, behave. I don't have time for this. Mama is having a meeting. Aunt Holly doesn't have to put you to bed. Now come on, hold still!"

Teddy would have none of it and ran back into the living room and flung his bare body against Holly's legs.

"What am I going to do with you? Come here this instant," said his mother in exasperation.

He clung to Holly. She picked him up and he grabbed her around the neck, looking at his mother defiantly.

"Rose, take care of your guests. I'll put him to bed. I don't mind, really," said Holly as she hugged the little boy to her. His bright red hair smelled clean and sweet.

Rose sat down wearily in a straight chair, panting from the exertion and holding her swollen abdomen, as the others commented in amused voices about her 'darling little boy'.

"I apologize for that display, but he is a handful. I hope this next one is a girl."

It grew quieter in the bedroom and they could hear Holly's steady voice reading a story.

"Holly is a natural with children," said Gloria.

"Too bad she doesn't have some of her own," replied Laurel.

It wasn't long before Holly returned with a contented smile.

"How do you do it, Holly? You can always calm him down," said Rose, "Thanks."

"He's a darling and I love children."

She looked around the room at the expectant mothers and fought down the envy that rose in her. Except for Myrtle, whose baby had died, her childhood friends each had a child and were expecting another in the summer or fall, even Sunny. Sunny's firstborn was especially dear to her because little Randy was the image of his father. She happily cared for him when Sunny and Randall had a social event to attend. She was 'Aunt Holly' to the children and she loved them as if they were her own.

Mrs. Wallace was in attendance. She was also childless, but did not share Holly's enthusiasm for children, and expressed some irritation at their interruptions. The room was filled with members of the club. Many new members had been added, by invitation, over the years, fine women with values, culture and integrity. The club had greatly expanded from its original nine members.

Since the Fortnightly had become a member of the General Federation of Women's Clubs the reputation of the original club had been enhanced and, although their original objective had been an interest in literature and attendant culture, they increased their efforts to include good works. Their motto: "Each for the joy of the working", a quotation from Kipling, fittingly described the worthwhile work they did.

It was their 25th year and Mrs. Sylvia Wallace, the President, was the delegate to the annual convention in Watertown. She had proved to be an efficient and beneficial member, if somewhat overbearing. She had influence and could get things done. She could organize special events with important speakers or bring presentations of foreign places by those who had been fortunate enough to travel. The uncomfortable, expectant mothers were only too glad to turn many responsibilities over to Mrs. Wallace, who viewed each accomplishment as a feather in her cap on her steady road upward from only a member to President and eventually to her goal of holding a national office.

Rose turned on a few lights to brighten the gathering dusk and the meeting was called to order. The members stood and recited the Collect*

> Keep us, oh God, from pettiness;
> Let us be large in thought, in word, in deed.
> Let us be done with fault-finding
> And leave off self-seeking.
> May we put away all pretense
> And meet each other face to face,
> without self-pity and without prejudice.
> May we never be hasty in judgement
> And always generous.
> Let us take time for all things;
> Make us to grow calm, serene, gentle.
> Teach us to put into action our better impulses,
> Straightforward and unafraid.
> Grant that we may realize it is
> The little things that create differences,
> That in the big things of life we are at one.
> And may we strive to touch and to know
> The great, common human heart of us all.
> And, oh Lord God, let us forget not
> To be kind!

*Collect: Käl'ekt, special petition, prayer
Mary Stewart, April, 1904
General Federation of Women's Clubs

When they were again seated Holly noticed that Gladys Pyle was not among them. She presumed she was busy with her political activities. They were all so proud to have her as a member. Her accomplishments were many, having served in the South Dakota Legislature with ambitions for further political office, Secretary of State, perhaps even Governor — unheard of for a woman! She took her convictions to other women's groups, urging them to exercise their freedom to vote since the 19th Amendment to the United States Constitution had been passed in 1920. She was continuing her fight to allow women to serve on juries, a basic right in the minds of many.

The business meeting progressed and Mrs. Wallace was officially made the delegate, as President of the Fortnightly Club, to the annual meeting in Watertown. She made her acceptance speech, assuring them that she would bring back a complete report when their meetings resumed in September. As usual, she was dressed to the nines in a silk dress printed with water lillies splashed against the green material. She always wore a matching hat over her short, marcelled hair, gloves and shiny patent leather high-heeled shoes. She made quite a fashion plate and all the mothers-to-be gave sighs of envy and admiration. Someday, when they were through with child bearing and were older maybe they could make such a stiking statement of style.

Light refreshments were served and, as was their custom when the meeting had adjourned, the original members were the last to leave, enjoying another coffee or iced tea and a more thorough visit. Gloria was due any day. She already had two children and was exhausted. The others were worried about her, because she was also a very social person and was hostess at many functions, further depleting her energies. But she put them off with the courage of her convictions, said it was God's will. He would provide and He would give her strength.

But Rose gave her usual sharp rebuttal. "That may well be, Gloria, but you have to help a little. You don't have to have the children so close together."

But they knew their concern fell on deaf ears. She would undoubtedly have more children. The Catholic dogma was her life. Gloria was the most devout of them and they would never try to change that.

Daisy was expecting her first child, as was Laurel. Poor Myrtle had lost her baby and, although they didn't know it at the time, she would never conceive again. Laconic, as usual, Myrtle said little, but her obvious contentment while at the club's meetings was evidence of her enjoyment, away from her drab environment and lackluster life.

Their conversation got around to another esteemed woman in Huron, Mrs. Lydia Larsen, who had gone from Beadle County's jailer to its sheriff, defeating two men in the election. She had become an effective officer, despite strong opposition from the men and a considerable number of women, who thought women should remain at home and take care of the family. But she proved to be most capable and pursued criminals with dogged determination. She and her husband, A. J. Larsen, served consecutive terms as sheriff for more than a decade and left their mark on bootlegging and crime during the 1920s.

The most wanted man was Butch who had literally thumbed his nose at authorities and who ignored Prohibition, running a profitable bootlegging business. The Larsens were undeterred in their pursuit, but fought a losing battle where Butch was concerned. There were few in Huron who would lament the demise of the man who had been a thorn in the side of the town ever since he was a child. Those who aided Butch in his disreputable pursuits made a living at it, kept him out of the arms of the law, and never crossed him for fear of his terrible reprisals. He had grown even more dissipated and unsightly with a beer belly, unshaven and a smelly cigar clamped in his mouth.

As they prepared to leave Rose said, "Why does that awful man still hang around Huron and why can't they catch him? You'd think he'd be off to a bigger place or another state. He thinks he's such a big shot."

"Maybe it's because he's comfortable here; he feels safe," said Daisy with her usual insight. "He knows this town inside and out. Remember, it's easier for him to carry on his disgusting business here than to begin all over in a new, unfamiliar place."

"Is it true that he has — well, 'ladies of the evening' at that ugly house of his?" asked Gloria, blushing slightly.

"Ladies! I wouldn't call them ladies," sputtered Rose. "They are whores, that's what they are."

"Rose, such language," cautioned Holly.

They laughed. Holly, the mother hen, kept them in line. And when Laurel inquired about the whereabouts of their old music teacher, Miss Janet Moselle, in the same breath as Butch's house of ill repute, she became adamant about ceasing to speak of such things. Maybe if she had married, her prudishness would lessen somewhat. As if she could read their thoughts, Holly countered,

"I know, I know. Actually, what do I know? But, we are ladies of the club and we should act like ladies."

"You are absolutely right," said Sunny, ever defensive of her friend.

The two of them smiled with affection and the girls were gratified to see that whatever animosity might have existed between them had been resolved. What they did not see was Holly's determination to not be the cause of a rift between Sunny and herself, or any of them, for that matter. Her love for them was that of family. Her childhood friends and their children had become her family; and her life, while not like theirs, was filled with love and friendship. She was not bereft of those things, she told herself firmly.

The meeting was long over and dark shadows were lengthening when they finally said their goodnights. They walked out onto the porch and were silent for a moment, surveying the peaceful scene. The sounds of children laughing and of birds settling down for the night rested easy on their ears.

"It is a good place to raise a family," Gloria murmured.

Myrtle said nothing, but the contented look softened her face. She accepted a ride home with Daisy.

They went their separate ways. Holly declined offers of a ride. She walked home in the gathering dusk, serene, yet with fragments of sadness in her heart.

Chapter 10

Holly grew tired of playing cards or checkers with her mother and older sisters and watching her brother, Bernard, play horseshoes with his cronies, so when Jonathan Hoekstra came to Huron on his monthly sales trips to doctors and hospitals she finally accepted his invitations to go to supper at the Marvin Hughitt or to see a movie at the Bijou. Anything would be better than the boredom she was beginning to experience. Clarence, Rose's husband, would give her a naughty wink if he caught her eye when they would arrive and pass the reservation counter on their way to the hotel's fabled dining room for one of the exceptional meals. The girls were teasing her about her regular dates with the tall, rugged salesman who traveled the entire state of South Dakota and the surrounding area .

But in late summer of 1924 she was looking forward to his visits and enjoying his never-flagging efforts to please her. She was sure he had lady friends in many towns but, nevertheless, she was anticipating an outing at Lake Byron for a picnic. Jonathan was taking care of every detail. Just be ready, was his request.

None of the girls had returned to the lake since Violet had drowned. It had become a dreadful reminder of what had happened. The Cranes boarded up the cabin shortly after their daughter's death and hardly anyone saw them after that. Eventually Mrs. Crane refused to leave her home and those who did see her told of how pathetic she had become, didn't care about anything — her appearance, her magnificent house, her husband. Mr. Crane was beside himself with grief, anger and frustration. His close friends told of his sacred vow to get revenge, and how he raged about Butch's having gotten away with murder, and the seeming impotence of law enforcement to bring to justice the man who had killed his daughter. His frustration ate away at him and he was further overwhelmed with the burden of dealing with things he had never given credence to, in dealing with his distraught wife who had taken care of everything in his smooth-running household. He eventually left his position at the bank and devoted himself to Mrs. Crane. They virtually became hermits in an unkempt house surrounded with an overgrown yard in which they had no interest.

But Lake Byron was still a pleasant place to escape to on a Saturday or Sunday, and Jonathan had promised that they would not be at the popu-

**Holly and Jonathan
at Lake Byron getting engaged**

lated part of the shore where the cabins were. She would not even have to see the Cranes' former summer place. They would be in a more secluded area apart from the rest.

He picked her up in his new Chrysler. He was doing very well in the pharmaceutical business and had just bought it in Pierre. According to his pleased description, "It purred all the way to Huron." He added, "It's important to make a good impression. A successful businessman has to keep up appearances."

The trip to Lake Byron was accomplished in far less time than when she had ridden in the Cranes' touring car, and she didn't get blown to pieces in Jonathan's enclosed smooth-running vehicle. She sat back and relaxed in his confident presence. They drove past the throngs of swimmers and boaters and stopped at a stretch of deserted beach. Tall uncut grasses and wild flowers erupted in the dirt of a sheltered cove. The water lapped against the shore and birds swooped and called in the blue sky. Puffy clouds seemed close enough to touch them.

"Jonathan, how perfectly lovely," she said as they got out of the car. She exclaimed over the pink Meadow Beauty and Snow on the Mountain scattered about, surrounding a solitary yellow wild rose shrub.

His face was wreathed in a big grin at her pleasure. Her good humor erased the former sorrowful expression that occasionally flitted across her face, a face which he considered very attractive. He took a basket from the back seat and handed her the old blanket she had brought along. She stood, shielding her eyes with her hand as she gazed out at the sun-dappled water and long, sandy beach, so primitively beautiful.

She turned to him with a mischievous look and said, "Well, come on. I'm hungry!"

She ran down the short incline, her skirt billowing in the breeze, displaying her long legs. Jonathan followed and they spread the blanket and sat down, drinking in the freshness of the day. Holly tipped her head back and shook her brown hair in the breeze, reveling in the sun on her face. Impulsively, she removed her flat shoes and short lisle stockings and wiggled her toes. Jonathan took his off, too, and Holly could not help but notice his long, bony feet.

"Big, aren't they?" he said as he waggled them back and forth as Holly tried to retain some composure.

He laughed aloud at Holly's newly-found freedom with him. During the past two years he had sensed that, while she seemed to have a good time when they were together, there was a reserve that he could not get through. But on this day she had an abandon about her that was totally beguiling. He spread out the picnic lunch which, he told her, had been prepared by the chef at the Marvin Hughitt, who had done so under duress because, he told Mr. Hoekstra, he could prepare a repast far better than what the gentleman was requesting. Please let him do a picnic basket lunch of which they could both be proud. Jonathan's excellent imitation of the very vain chef caused Holly to giggle.

"How you pamper me, Jonathan," she laughed.

"I love to pamper you and you certainly deserve it. You work so hard all week, even Saturdays, and you need a respite, so I hope you throw caution to the wind and enjoy it."

Yes, she thought, she could use a diversion, but she loved her work. Nursing suited her just fine and she and Randolph worked together as a smooth team, as one in caring for the sick and injured. They scarcely needed to speak as they labored side by side in a common effort. Despite his belonging to Sunny, Holly needed to be with him and to know that she would see him every day. She would never tire of that, but as the years passed she grew ever more lonely, and she had become fond of Jonathan Hoekstra. If she were completely honest with herself, she was probably thinking of possible marriage and the children she yearned for.

They were hungry and quickly devoured the lunch carefully packed in ice by the accommodating chef. Along with potato salad and pickles there were succulent wieners, pieces of coconut layer cake, and lemonade, which Jonathan had insisted upon because, as he patiently explained to the chef, his lady friend did not drink. The chef was incredulous that a picnic by the shore did not include a bottle of wine. However, he considered, wine with roasted wieners was unthinkable. Jonathan threw up his hands in a perfect imitation of the confused chef, sending Holly into giggles once more. He described all of this to Holly while he made a fire and deftly stripped thin branches from the many spindly bushes and trees which abounded, all the time speaking in the chef's imagined French accent. Holly was thoroughly entertained.

They roasted the wieners over the fire as the juices dripped into it, sending an aromatic smell upward that muddled their senses, an aroma sharpened by the fresh air.

When they had finished Holly sighed deeply in appreciation and smiled fondly at Jonathan.

"Delectable, doubly so since I didn't lift a finger."

"So glad you enjoyed it, Mademoiselle," he responded, placing a napkin over his bent arm in the manner of an uppity waiter. "I hope the entree was done to your liking."

He doused the fire and gathered up the remains of their meal. Then he took her hand and helped her up. "Let's walk a ways, to settle our lunch."

They walked on the beach around a wide curve of the lake. He took her hand and Holly was content. The feel of the sand beneath her feet enhanced the sense of liberation from the cares of the world. They paused for a moment to admire the birds as they wheeled in the sky against the cumulus clouds.

Suddenly Holly exclaimed "Oh!" and quickly drew her foot back as something skittered across it. She grabbed Jonathan in fright. They looked down and saw a startled garter snake hurriedly vanishing into the scrub.

"It's just a garter snake. It's harmless; it won't hurt you," said Jonathan, amused by her consternation, but noticing that she had not released him.

She shuddered. "I don't like snakes."

"It's all right. He's gone. You probably scared him, too. But please don't let go, Holly darling."

"Jonathan, really, I didn't mean ...."

He paid no attention to her protests. He gathered her into his strong arms and looked into her blue eyes intensely. As she looked up at him she was astonished to see love shining there, love for her. He held her and kissed her and she kissed him back as she felt herself yielding to his embrace gladly, gratefully. They clung together in their mutual loneliness and need. Holly's awakened senses were acutely aware of the cries of the birds, of the warm breeze caressing her, of the feel of the sand between her toes, and of the lingering, fragrant, burnt smell of the fire which had settled on their clothes.

"Holly, I love you. Will you marry me?" His brown eyes burned into hers.

She surprised herself by saying "Yes."

Chapter 11

Holly's wedding to Jonathan Hoekstra was set for the middle of October.

"It's the nicest time of the year," Holly said. "It's such a pretty season with all the fall colors and so comfortable."

"But this is so sudden," objected her aging mother. "There isn't enough time to do everything."

"Now Mama, don't worry. I'll take care of all the details. You won't have to do a thing."

"But Holly honey, does this mean you'll really be leaving us?" her mother asked plaintively.

She looked so befuddled that Holly felt guilty. It had been more difficult than she had thought to tell her of the engagement and upcoming wedding. This was the wedding she had longed for. It was her turn now, her life, her chance at happiness. She would be a participant in the stream of life, not just an onlooker.

"Yes Mama, I'll be moving out and into a nice home that Jonathan and I found on Idaho S.E. — you know, that really nice section of town. The Pyles live on that street, remember? It's not a brand new house, but it is very nice, and we'll be fixing it up. Jonathan is so handy that way. It's a two-story house with a bathroom upstairs and one downstairs. Imagine! How on earth did all of us manage with only one bathroom all the time we were growing up?"

"But Holly honey, what will we do without you? You've always been with us."

"You'll do just fine. You still have Madge and Opal and Hazel, plus Bernard, who'll be around to do any fixing on the place that needs to be done."

She began to cry and Holly put her arms around her.

"Please don't cry, Mama. I am so happy. You wouldn't begrudge me happiness would you? It's not as though I'll be moving out of town. We'll see you often. We'll be right here. You do like Jonathan, don't you?"

She hesitated. "Yes, of course, but he is a salesman, after all."

Her mother's remark would have made Holly angry if it were not so ludicrous. She was so serious and Holly had a hard time keeping a sober expression. She said patiently, "Yes, he is a salesman, but he has given up his sales route and all that traveling to settle down right here in Huron. He has accepted a job at the Sherman and Moe Drugstore as their pharmacist. He has an excellent reputation that is known in the trade, and they are glad to get him. They told him he will be a definite asset to their business. Now don't you worry your head about a thing. I have to go now. I must hurry and dress for the shower Gloria is giving for me. Isn't this exciting?"

She ran happily up the stairs to her room to don one of the new frocks she had purchased at Geyerman's to replace many of her outdated clothes which she now considered dowdy, if not frumpy. Wearing a nurse's uniform during the work week did not necessitate an elaborate wardrobe, but her life was very different now. She was engaged and had a diamond on her finger that she had thought pretentious, but which her friends had exclaimed over.

"Jeepers, Holly, flaunt it," demanded Rose.

Holly had never been one to flaunt anything and had been decorous to the point of appearing prim. It took some getting used to being in the limelight and the object of excitement and hubbub. She had become positively giddy shopping for her wedding dress, and the sales ladies at Geyerman's were happy to be selling one to such a good customer over the years. They were familiar with her size and taste after all the bridesmaid's dresses they had provided.

Holly took her mother with her on her shopping trip and she was treated royally by the sales ladies who carefully seated her on one of their plush chairs and presented her with a cup of tea. Holly tried on several gowns and noted that her mother was having a good time as she relaxed and watched as Holly showed them off. She chose a gown that she considered to be just right for her. Even so, Mama frowned at her selection. The white ankle length satin dress, although very nice, was not fancy enough to suit her. She should have a full skirt with petticoats and a flouncy veil. But Holly was firm in her selection. She was an old maid and such attire as her mother wished for would indeed be flaunting. The dress she chose had long sleeves and a lace bodice that fit her slim figure well. A lace collar was snug around her neck which she was comfortable in and which she felt was proper. The veil was not flowing, merely a beaded band around her head with lace that hung just below her waist. She chose low-heeled shoes that gave her a regal bearing without appearing to increase her height. The sales ladies were ecstatic over her splendid choice, ignoring her mother's slight frown, and meager remonstrances over the decision. The wedding had to be nice; it had to be just right. It was a mother's duty to make sure of that.

"But it will be nice, Mama. Really it will. I love this dress. It suits me. It looks good on me, don't you think?"

Mama finally came around to her way of thinking and had to admit that her baby had never looked lovelier. And to think that all of Holly's purchases would be delivered to her door took her by surprise. It had been so many years since she had bought anything new to wear that the afternoon of shopping with Holly was not only fun, it had been an eye-opener. They were so elated that Mama agreed when Holly suggested that they stop in at Sherman and Moe's for a soda and to say hello to Jonathan before they went home. Mama held back. What would Mr. Hoekstra think? He'd probably think she was checking him out, spying on him.

"Nonsense, Mama. He will think no such thing. Come on, I'm thirsty after spending all that money."

She was used to her mother's old-fashioned ways and her outlook on life, and it did her heart good to see how she had thoroughly enjoyed herself. She was right. Jonathan welcomed them warmly and she was delighted to see that her mother was considerably impressed with his appearance in his white jacket and in the respect the others in the drugstore accorded him. He even paid for their sodas, which helped to endear him to her. Holly chastised herself for not having spent more time with her hard working mother, who was often worn out. But she would soon change that. They would do things together and they would take her out often, she and Jonathan. He was very good with her reticent mother. He treated her respectfully, yet his sense of humor would bring a smile. It was going to be just fine.

Holly's upcoming nuptials were making her friends happy, too, and Holly submitted to their enthusiastic fussing.

"Golly Holly," said Daisy. "Everybody loves a wedding and yours is so special."

Yes, special. Finally Holly the spinster was getting married. She quickly thrust the unkind thought from her mind, relaxed and enjoyed the showers, the gifts and Jonathan's loving attention.

The feverish festivities brought a glow, making her look younger than her 31 years. She had expected to be an old maid like her sisters. She was aware of what some people thought about three old maids living in the family home along with a bachelor brother. It was perplexing to wonder about the lack of progeny in a formerly large family of ten children. She concluded that fertility had ended with her father.

She hummed as she put on her new lavender rayon dress with a collar embroidered with small yellow and white flowers edged with a darker piping, as were the short sleeves. She added a close fitting hat, white gloves with matching shoes and admired her new look in the old-fashioned oval mirror. She saw a tall, attractive woman in a smart outfit looking more youthful than she had remembered, and wondered what had happened to the person she was accustomed to seeing. She decided she liked her reflection and squelched her habitual command to appear modest and unassuming. She put aside for good her former opinion of herself and of the admonishment she recited to herself to maintain that appearance: after all, who am I going to impress? Now she knew. She was going to impress herself first of all, then the girls, and of course, Jonathan.

Suddenly she knew what it was to know the essence of one's self, with no apology, to know the core of what makes that person, to know her inner being and to rejoice in it, without any false modesty. She hugged herself and smiled broadly at her new image, then went downstairs swiftly before the feeling vanished.

The day of the wedding dawned bright and cool, a perfect day in October, but it turned cold and windy as the time for the ceremony drew near. Holly overlooked it; nothing could spoil her happiness. "At least the sun is still shining," she replied to her family's worried comments. By early afternoon the sun had disappeared and a chill drizzle began. Bernard assured her not to worry, that he would get her to the church on time and that she would not get wet.

For the past three months Holly and Jonathan had been getting their home ready to move into upon their return from their honeymoon. Jonathan had hired some of the work done, such as making sure the windows and their frames were tight and in good shape. He had the floors sanded and revarnished and put carpets in the living room, parlor and the upstairs master bedroom. The baths were outfitted with new modern fixtures and the walls were freshly painted. Holly had happily chosen new furniture and appliances, but not without first objecting to Jonathan's spending so much money. But he assured her that he had saved most of his money in his many years of sales and what better way to spend some of it than on their future.

Holly's head swam as she considered her good fortune. She had been so used to the old family home that was then showing signs of wear and tear that to be soon living in such an up-to-date home made it hard for her to comprehend. Jonathan took such good care of her. It was like her father used to take care of her. He was a decade older than Holly, but he was not an old man, and to be under his protective love was comforting.

Holly had moved all of her belongings to the new place, plus a small valise which held her things for the wedding trip. She left the wedding dress in her old room at home. She would get ready there with her mother and sisters to help. Bernard would transport all of them to the Methodist Church in his trusty old Ford that had seen a lot of miles.

Mama and Holly's sisters were bustling about in a state of excitement, considering their ages and her wedding being the first in which they had an active part. Her mother placed a string of pearls around the lace collar at her neck when she had dressed. Their luster was luminous, shining with an inner light.

"Papa gave them to me when we were married," she said lovingly. "It is fitting that you have them."

"Mama, thank you. They're beautiful!"

She hugged her mother, holding her closely. She looked into the eyes of her frail mother and saw tears of joy and pride. Her sisters' faces beamed. How precious they were and how she had taken them for granted for far too long. She hugged each of them and proclaimed her affection, causing them flustered pleasure. Madge, retaining her position as the one in charge, wiped her eyes quickly and said brusquely,

"You'd better hustle. Bernard is getting nervous. He's got that old car of his all cleaned out and all polished and shiny. Come on."

Holly took a last look around the familiar home. There was no pang of regret, only gratitude for the solid comfort it had provided for years. She was ready to begin her new life.

The wind whipped her wedding attire. She hung on to her veil and was grateful for the warmth of the fringed shawl Opal provided. Despite the wind and the cold drizzle they arrived at the church in no time and without incident. Bernard stopped at the side entrance to the church and escorted her inside. Impulsively she reached for him and hugged him fiercely. He lost his composure for a moment, but gave her a pleased smile and attempted to regain his staid expression. He patted her shoulder and promised not to be late to walk her down the aisle, then he returned to the house for the others.

Holly waited impatiently in the pastor's study and he went over the ceremony once more. In a short time Bernard reappeared and told her he had brought Mama and their sisters into the church where they were seated with Howard and his family from Brookings. Holly was eager to see them again and to visit with her nephews, the only issue which her family had produced. Well, perhaps she could make up for that was her happy thought.

Muted music emanated from the chancel. The pastor said, "Well, Holly, that's my cue. I have to leave you now. Are you ready?"

"Yes indeed," she replied and she hoped not too eagerly, but he smiled kindly and left to attend to his duties at the altar. Bernard solemnly offered his arm and they ascended the stairs to the back of the church.

Sunny was waiting, looking gorgeous in a pale pink satin dress. Marriage and children had made her even lovelier. They embraced and Sunny said, "Oh Holly, this is so wonderful! I think I'm more excited than I was at my own wedding." She handed Holly her bouquet of pink roses and exclaimed, "You look positively stunning. I've never seen you look so .... oh I'm so happy for you!"

The sounds of the wedding march sounded and Sunny said, "Here goes," gave Holly's hand a squeeze and started her slow walk down the aisle.

Holly took Bernard's arm. She was shaking and she took a deep breath. Her eyes sparkled and her smile was genuine, not the forced smile of years earlier at Sunny's wedding when she had walked down the same aisle toward the two men she was approaching.

There they stood, the two men she loved more than anyone else. Randolph was the best man and his tall presence made her heart skip. Why did he have to become more appealing with the years? But she directed her smile at Jonathan who was fairly bursting with anticipation and love. She vowed that she would love him with all her heart, that neither of her loves would ever know her conflicting true feelings for them.

The saying of the vows and the music evoked in her an intense feeling of commitment. Holly knew her life was forever changed and she was eager to take up the challenge of her future. The ceremony and reception passed quickly with a blur of happy faces, kisses and congratulations. Finally they left the church, got into Jonathan's Chrysler and, closely followed by some of the guests who merrily honked their horns and shouted words that were blown away on the brisk wind, they arrived at their home on Idaho Avenue to change clothes and begin their motor trip.

Mama and the sisters had momentarily forgotten that she would not be going home with them and were somewhat embarrassed to know that their baby sister would be changing her clothes in a house all alone with Jonathan. Maude laughed and reminded them that they were man and wife now and that they would all just have to get used to it. Having little to base what their imaginations brought to mind, all they could do was to blush slightly and stammer. Bernard drove them home where they had hot tea to warm themselves and to discuss every aspect and detail of the entire day, remembering it for the rest of their lives.

The wind was blowing red and yellow leaves along the street and gray clouds were scudding overhead. Jonathan parked in front of the house and sprang out, running to the other side to help Holly, ignoring the cars that had followed them with their horns blaring.

"Come here, my sweet, before the wind blows you away."

He took her hand, slammed the door and they ran up the walk. They turned and waved happily to their pursuers, and he opened the heavy front door with its frosted window decorated with etched designs. He lifted her and carried her inside.

"Jonathan! what will everyone think?"

"I hope the neighbors are all at their windows watching," he replied gaily. "I know our noisy friends are enjoying it."

81

He closed the door against the wind and the revelry and drew her into his arms and kissed her soundly, fervently. She thrilled to his ardor and when he released her they climbed the stairs arm in arm. The knowledge that she was in her own home, that her husband was at her side, quickened her pulse. At the door of the bedroom she paused. He took her hands and drew her in, embracing her again.

"I've a notion to make you mine this instant," he said huskily.

"Jonathan, please. Everyone saw us come in. What on earth will they think if we take too long to come out again?"

Reluctantly he released her and she just as reluctantly took off her small veil. In his gallant manner he said, "I'll change in the bathroom. We'd better get going before the weather gets any worse. Besides, you are far too tempting. But never fear, weather or not, I shall keep you snug and warm." He made a deep bow and closed the door, making her giggle.

She removed her wedding dress and hung it up carefully along with the veil, but she didn't put it into the closet with her other things. She wanted to look at it and savor it for awhile. She changed into her new traveling suit of light brown with a hat that fit closely over her dark waved hair. Jonathan soon joined her, filling the room with his towering presence.

His admiring look told her more than his words. "You are so beautiful."

She would have to adjust to being called beautiful, but she would love it while it lasted. Jonathan was only talking like an eager bridegroom, she told herself,

He picked up their suitcases and they descended the stairs. Holly glanced into the living room and sighed contentedly. "What a lovely home to come back to."

They locked the door and ran to the car, holding onto their hats against the prairie wind, as their friends honked their car horns and threw rice and shouted encouragement to the happy couple. They sent their friends another cheery wave, got into the car and drove off, escorted to the outskirts of town by the noisy entourage. When the cars turned back to town Jonathan's eyes turned from the rear view mirror with a relieved smile. Holly moved closer to him and he put his arm around her.

They had a reservation at the St. Charles Hotel in Pierre. Jonathan told her it wouldn't take more than two or three hours to drive straight through west on Route 14. He'd driven it many times. She would love it. All he had to do was to keep his eyes on the road, which was not easy with her beside him, he assured her. His strong, confident bearing and his loving smile made her feel like she was basking in the sun, although the rain had begun and thunder was rolling across the plains.

The scenery gradually changed. He told her about Pierre, the capital of the State of South Dakota, which she had never seen, and said they would tour the Capitol Building during their stay. It was a fine building, really something to see, and it was comparatively new. He said that it was still being used to house the current governor, Governor McMaster, until a suitable residence could be built. The St. Charles Hotel was said to be the best hotel between Chicago and Denver, and that all the furnishings had been brought from Chicago, he continued as they drove through the rain. It had been built in 1910 by Charles L. Hyde and the five-story structure of concrete and brick overlooked the City of Pierre, the Missouri River and beyond. He also said that their suite would have a magnificent view. He told her of the hotel's ballroom with a fancy ceiling and that he intended to twirl her around the dance floor until she collapsed in his arms.

Holly laughed at his merriment. He was obviously enjoying the trip with her, regardless of the thunderstorm. It was a familiar trip which he had made alone many times. The terrain was not as flat as they neared Pierre. It turned to low hills, with bluffs of various shades of green that extended along both sides of the wide Missouri River. He commented that they rather looked like Indian burial mounds, but were merely nature's handiwork.

They arrived at last and stopped before the St. Charles. Holly was properly impressed, thinking it to be an elegant place to spend a wedding night.

As they alighted, a young man in a uniform took their bags and they followed him to the registration desk in a large lobby with a high ceiling. Wide steps at one side led to floors above. An elevator was nearby.

"Mr. and Mrs. Jonathan Hoekstra," Jonathan said proudly. "I have a reservation."

"Ah yes, Mr. Hoekstra. The bridal suite is all ready. May I compliment you on such a lovely bride. The boy will take you up. I hope you enjoy your stay."

At that remark the bellboy had a smile that bordered on a smirk, but he was ignored as they rode the elevator in silence to the top floor. Jonathan gave the young man a dollar bill and he kept his silly smirk as he backed from the room. Jonathan locked the door, turned and they burst into laughter.

"Oh what he must be thinking," giggled Holly.

"No more talk about what other people think, my darling. All that matters is what we think at this moment. I love you and I want you — right now."

He took her in his arms. "Now," he murmured.

She spoke no objection. His passion soon swept her up in a passion of her own that she had not known existed. His lovemaking took her breath away. She knew she could easily really love this man.

Chapter 12

For the first time in her life Holly was truly happy. She loved the house she and Jonathan had chosen. It was big enough for themselves and for any company they might have. The upstairs master bedroom had a porch that extended the length of the porch below. Both of them were enclosed with lattice work which provided airy seclusion. Holly enjoyed the luxury of stepping outside the bedroom to greet the morning or just to sit there and read when she had the time, The independence of creating her own life with Jonathan, separate and apart from anyone else, was liberating. She blossomed in the warmth of Jonathan's love, and his happiness gave vitality to the life they made together.

The only cloud on the perfect setting was the absence of children. They had been married for three years and there were none, making Holly feel inadequate. Jonathan repeatedly assured her that it was all right, that although he understood her feelings the love they had for each other was enough.. Their lives were otherwise productive. They were secure financially, they got along famously, and he would never cease loving her. She must stop grieving over something that was perhaps never to be. But they would not stop trying, he said as he gave her a playful kiss. Holly knew she was blessed with more than others she knew and she gave thanks in her prayers, but she yearned for at least one child.

Then tragedy struck and the girls' thoughts were for Myrtle. A fire swept through her house one early evening in July, started by what could have been faulty wiring, according to the Northwestern Public Service. It was a very old house in need of repair. But speculation had it that Elmer, who had perished in the fire along with all of Myrtle's cats, fell asleep on the worn sofa with his lighted cigarette and started the blaze. Elmer had seldom been seen without a cigarette hanging from his mouth, except at Armour's where smoking was prohibited. Myrtle had been at a meeting of her church circle and returned to find everything she owned and loved had been destroyed, burned to the ground.

The news spread quickly among the girls and they gathered at the site to provide support. Myrtle stood staring at the charred remnants of what had been her home. Elmer's body had been taken away to Kinyon, the undertaker. Neighbors had come to offer her comfort. Their glum faces told the girls what they had hoped was not true. They rushed to Myrtle whose blank expression was in sharp contrast to the devastation smouldering before them. They surrounded her with loving arms and expressions of sympathy. The firemen had departed, leaving only a black, flattened plot of smoking embers. They were appalled to see the flimsy remains and wondered How Myrtle had survived for years in such squalor.

Holly spoke first. "Myrtle, you will come home with me. I have plenty of room. Myrtle, do you hear me?"

Myrtle continued to stare, trying to comprehend what had happened, with no idea of what she should do. Holly was shaking her shoulders and it brought her around.

"Oh hello, Holly. There's been a fire."

"Yes I know. Now come, Myrtle, come with me."

"They said Elmer died. He was burned."

She turned toward them, realizing at last that her friends were there. Her eyes, wide in her haggard face, shone with the understanding of the death before her. She couldn't move. Holly took her and walked her slowly to her car, the old Chrysler, as the others followed. Myrtle obediently did as she was directed. Holly sat her in the front seat and spoke to the others.

"Follow me to the house and we'll get some coffee into her. And Sunny, could Randolph come?"

They nodded in unison and drove off. Sunny drove home quickly. In only a few minutes everyone was assembled at Holly's house. Randolph arrived with his medical bag and talked gently to Myrtle, deftly examined her, looking into her eyes which were abnormally bright.

"She's had quite a shock," he said. "She mustn't be agitated. Does she realize what has happened?"

"Yes," answered Holly, already the proficient nurse at his side. "We brought her here until we can figure out what to do. She can stay as long as she needs to. There is plenty of room and there is an extra bathroom."

"Good. Give her something warm and then she should be in bed."

Daisy brought in the coffee and they sat in the living room with their miserable friend, uncertain as to what to say. The quiet was broken when Myrtle set her cup down and spoke.

"Thanks. You are all so good to me. I'm so mixed up, and so tired."

Randolph turned to Holly as he prepared to leave. "She'll be all right. She just needs rest and keep her warm. Despite the weather, shock could give her chills. It's good of you to take her in, Holly — typical of you." He smiled fondly at her.

"It's no trouble and I'm glad to help. I'll be back in the office tomorrow."

Myrtle was put to bed in the downstairs bedroom. Holly supplied the smallest nightgown she owned, but Myrtle seemed to be enveloped in it. As she left the room, Holly told her, "Tomorrow we'll see about getting you something to wear. Right now try not to think about what's happened. You need a good night's sleep."

The next morning they all reassembled at Holly's house, each bringing clean, durable clothing and other items to get Myrtle started again. This time they were determined to see that she was more properly provided for. Myrtle was overwhelmed with their generosity and, for the first time, they beheld tears in her eyes.

"I don't know how to thank you," she said. "I can never repay you."

They assured her that it was nothing and she should not fret about it. Next they would find her a place to stay.

Then there was the problem of Elmer's burial, what remained of him. Myrtle had very little money, and a sum from Armour's went directly to the mortuary. Holly assured Myrtle that she could stay with her and Jonathan as long as she wanted to, but it was clear that the arrangement bothered their house guest who hated to impose and who disliked being obliged to anyone.

After the least expensive of funerals and the committal service, the girls and their families returned to Holly's house for refreshment. Each family brought a dish of food and the repast was satisfying, if not somewhat stimulating with excitable children at "Aunt Holly's new house" and the variety of tasty foods. Myrtle appeared to be more relaxed, but didn't say much except to thank each one as her friends and their families left to return home. Then she helped Holly clear away the dishes and straighten up. She even dragged out the heavy carpet sweeper over Holly's strenuous objection.

"Myrtle, you certainly don't need to do that. I'll take care of it later."

"You know how kids are, Holly. Dropping crumbs everywhere. But aren't they cute? And they are growing up so fast, but so nicely. The girls are such good mothers, aren't they?"

Such a lengthy spoken opinion from Myrtle was a surprise. Holly was impressed and took it to mean that she had accepted what had happened to her and was preparing to continue somehow in her very different life.

But when she and Jonathan got up the next morning and Holly had her accustomed stretch by the door to the bedroom porch, she grew concerned when Myrtle could not be found. The bed in her room had been neatly made and all her second-hand things were gone.

She had left a note, which Holly read to the girls who had come at her telephone call. She read, as they listened in hushed silence.

"Holly and all,
I can't continue to impose and to accept your charity any longer. I'm going to visit my sister Enid in Nebraska where I can be of help to her

in case I stay there. Thank you for everything you've done for me. You are the kindest and best friends a body could have.

Love to all, Myrtle"

It was written in Myrtle's tiny script, but was clearly legible. They had no words for a moment. Then Daisy spoke.

"Well, I suppose it's for the best. It would be almost impossible for her to remain in Huron in her situation. Is this Enid the only relative she has?"

"She never spoke of her family very much, but Enid is really her only close relative. I believe she's a widow, too," replied Laurel .

Gloria said, "Isn't it odd — we think we know a person, a friend — and yet when something like this happens it's as though Myrtle is practically a stranger — but such a loyal friend."

Rose said, "But just how is she going to get to Nebraska with no money? And where in Nebraska?"

They gave that some thought.

"I remember. It's O'Neill. Maybe we should write to Enid to see if Myrtle is there and if she knows anything," said Sunny with a frown. "Her name is Enid Landburg. We know that Myrtle shouldn't go anywhere all by herself. You know how she is."

"Let's do that," said Holly. "I'll get my stationery and we'll compose a letter right now."

In no time they had a tactful letter of inquiry to Myrtle's sister composed and posted it at once by special delivery. Doing something positive made them feel better, assuaging the guilt they were needlessly experiencing. The closeness that existed among them had been compromised by Myrtle's misfortune, and they felt they had let her down. Holly promised that she would let them know what she found out when there was an answer to their letter.

However, the letter that arrived did not tell them what they hoped to learn. Enid appreciated their letting her know of her sister's predicament, but she had not heard from her nor seen her in years. She was welcome anytime she might appear, but she was completely ignorant of her sister's whereabouts. In the event she was found she would appreciate being informed.

"Now what?" demanded Rose. "We just can't do nothing."

It was Gloria who solved the mystery of their missing friend and a hurried meeting was called at her house. They met in the afternoon when the children were having their naps. Gloria's house was immaculate and she had coffee and home baked cookies prepared.

"How does she do all this?" asked Laurel. "Her house looks like something out of House Beautiful, her children are clean and well-mannered, and she manages company at any time with home baked cookies in the cookie jar. She really takes the cake and she makes me just a little bit annoyed with all her efficiency." She jabbed at her glasses which never stayed put.

They agreed as they smiled with amusement at Laurel, whose home was more or less clean, but cluttered with books and periodicals and encyclopedias in which she lost herself, sometimes at the expense of the family's supper.

Gloria entered from the kitchen with the coffee pot and they clamored to hear her news.

"I didn't get a letter nor have I heard from Enid. But a woman in the church who does charitable work came over one day and asked me if a Myrtle Black was a member of the Huron Fortnightly. I said yes she was, but we hadn't seen her for almost a month. Well, she said that she and others from the church had made their regular call at the County Sanitarium to take out some provisions to augment their larder, and she was sure it was Myrtle she saw."

"The County Sanitarium. You mean the Beadle County Poor Farm?" Rose's voice rose. "No! That can't be. That place is for paupers. Myrtle's not a pauper!" The connotation of the word made her flush in anger.

But they knew that Myrtle fit the description well. Expressions of shock and disbelief filled the room.

Holly was upset. "She didn't have to leave like that. She could have stayed with us indefinitely. I told her so many times."

Daisy offered, "We have to check this out. We have to go out there and see for ourselves."

"Yes, let's do that. We'll take some canned goods with us so it will look all right," said Laurel.

"We can't all go. Besides, we can't take our kids with us," declared Rose.

Holly spoke. "I'll do it. I feel responsible. I'll go out there next Saturday."

So it was arranged. Jonathan took a couple of hours off and they drove east on Cemetery Road to the poor farm. Holly's heart was heavy. It was a fact that such a facility was necessary, but it broke her heart to think that Myrtle had been driven to it. She would talk to her if, in fact, she was there and she would persuade Myrtle to return with them. They would think of something, find someplace for her. They had to. She was a lifelong friend. They couldn't just leave her there.

They stopped in front of a building which had formerly been a hotel located in Hitchcock, a few miles northwest of Huron. The two-story building stood stark in the sunshine on a section of farmland. The farm was intended to be self-supporting for the benefit of the residents, but donations were always welcome. Holly and Jonathan emerged from the car carrying boxes of canned fruit and were met by Mrs. Zella Grant, the superintendent.

"Good afternoon. Welcome, I'm Mrs. Grant."

"Good afternoon. We are Mr. and Mrs. Jonathan Hoekstra. We have some excess canned goods and thought you could use them."

"Of course we can. How thoughtful. Please come in."

They followed her into the house. A few old people were seated in a large room. Mrs. Grant said, "Sit down, won't you? I'll just take these jars into the kitchen. My, how nice to have some fruit." She took the box from Holly and Jonathan carried the other box into the kitchen after her.

Holly stood uncertainly, awkward in the presence of the pathetic people who stared at her with interest. She gave them a wan smile and walked to a wide window that looked out over a garden where vegetables were growing and maturing under the warm sun. Men and women, younger than the occupants of the room, were working the ground, hoeing and chopping out weeds. Suddenly, Holly drew in her breath.

"What is it dear?" asked Jonathan as he walked to her side.

"It's Myrtle," she whispered. "It is. Oh dear God, it's her."

Myrtle was working steadily in a garden row amidst the other workers and, Holly wondered amazed, why did she have such a look of contentment on her face? She watched, fascinated, as Myrtle straightened for a moment, holding her back, her hand over her eyes against the sun as she gazed at the expanse of green and gold stretching in all directions. Then she smiled and resumed her task.

Mrs. Grant returned from the kitchen. "Please sit down," she urged. "It's mighty nice of you folks to think of us. I see you were admiring our garden. We do try to be self-sustaining and it works most of the time, but there are times when we house some who aren't able to work and our resources get pretty scarce, so donations are welcome."

Holly's throat was dry and she swallowed with difficulty. "Mrs. Grant, I thought I recognized someone I know. Could you tell me .... that is, I need to ask ...."

"Of course, Mrs. Hoekstra. What can I tell you?"

She continued with a heavy heart. "Is there a Myrtle Black living here?"

"Why yes, there is. Is she a friend of yours?" she asked politely.

"A childhood friend, recently widowed. She was staying with me after a fire in which her husband died. Then she just vanished and my friends and I have been trying to find her. She left a note saying she was going to Nebraska to live with her sister, but her sister hasn't heard from her in a long time. Quite by chance we heard that she might be here."

"She came to us — oh about a month ago. She just showed up, said she was a pauper ..."

She stopped, seeing the distress on Holly's face. Jonathan put his hand on her arm.

"I'm sorry, but that is the qualification in order to live here. And she does qualify. We went through all the necessary paper work. She has no assets, nothing of her own. And she insisted she had no relatives, no one to look out for her. She has been here ever since. Now you mustn't feel so bad, Mrs. Hoekstra. Mrs. Black is perfectly content here. She is in good health, despite outward appearance; she's a hard worker and doesn't cause a problem. She really pulls her weight. I might say that, actually, she is very happy."

Tears sprang to Holly's eyes. "Could I speak to her?"

"Mrs. Hoekstra, I have no objection, but may I say something? Mrs. Black has given every indication that she doesn't wish to see anyone from her previous life. She made it clear that she prefers to be left alone to do her work, work she wants to do to justify her being here, she said. I honestly think that seeing someone such as yourself from her past — a life that ended so cruelly and abruptly — would be very hard on her. You can see for yourself that she doesn't appear to be troubled."

Holly rose and returned to the window. She watched, perplexed, as Myrtle continued to wield the hoe. Her face had lost its perpetual anxious expression and her movements were sure and certain. There was the unexplainable smile on Myrtle's face, the uncharacteristic serenity that Holly saw. Jonathan stood beside her looking at her in a manner that indicated he was in full agreement with Mrs. Grant. Tears flowed down Holly's cheeks. She felt Jonathan's arm around her shoulders and was grateful that he was there.

"Come, Holly. Leave it alone."

He thanked Mrs. Grant, who was considerate of their feelings. She thanked them again for their gifts and they left the house.

Holly cried all the way home. This was not supposed to happen, not to Myrtle, not to any of them. And, she thought angrily, why had she shut them out; how could Myrtle look so content? Jonathan said nothing, did not intrude on her grief. He dropped her off at home, holding her and reassuring her before he drove back to the drugstore that it was for the best.

After she had cried it all out, Holly called the girls, who came at once, and briefly explained Myrtle's fate. Sorrowfully they agreed to do nothing, to not even send a letter, lest it cause her embarrassment to know that her best and dearest friends knew where she was and that, furthermore, she wanted to be there.

In a few years Myrtle, barely into her forties, died and was buried in a pauper's grave, forgotten by everyone except those with whom she had shared her life.

Chapter 13

Holly and Laurel were seated at a table in the restaurant of the Tams Hotel.

"I suppose this is silly leaving one hotel and going to another, but I needed a change of scene," said Laurel as she fingered the coffee cup set before her.

They had come from the state convention of the General Federation of Women's Clubs which was held at the Marvin Hughitt. The Huron Fortnightly had been host to the 28th annual convention.

"It's hard to realize the club has been in existence for so long. What a triumph of our endeavors. Gosh, this coffee does taste good. I hardly had time to enjoy the banquet," Holly answered.

Membership had grown and the club was entitled to two delegates, the president and one other chosen by the group. Holly was president that year of 1927 and Laurel had been named the other delegate. Huron had been host only twice before and Holly had been extremely nervous about her responsibilities. Mrs. Sylvia Wallace provided her with much information plus programs from previous state conventions, all of which had proved to be invaluable. Mrs. Wallace was miffed at not having once again been chosen as a delegate. After all, she reminded them, she had the most experience, having attended several state conventions, and she had the freedom to travel anywhere at anytime, unencumbered by the restraints of home and children. They were aware of Mrs. Wallace's aversion to children and also knew of her considerable expertise, but felt it was time to chose someone else. She was mollified when Holly appointed her to a committee, along with Rose, to assist her in getting ready for the large group of women who were expected at the Marvin Hughitt. Rose could easily counteract any of Mrs. Wallace's high-toned ideas and Mrs. Wallace could counteract Rose's oft-times rash decisions. Rose could also coordinate arrangements with her husband, Clarence.

On one of their visits to the hotel to confer with Clarence, who had numerous helpful suggestions, he had thoroughly shocked Mrs. Wallace, as he gave his naughty wink at Holly. He said he had a dandy idea. He would place several signs in the shape of a hand with a finger pointing to restrooms, which ultimately led to the back door and outside to the trash barrels. He threw in this quaint idea at the end of a valid list of suggestions. It had made a hit when he recited it to other conventioneers, such as the members of the Elks Club, knowing it would get a riotous reaction. Rose knew what was coming and tried to suppress her loud laugh. Holly smiled, amused at Clarence's never-ceasing antics and, he was pleased to note, Mrs. Wallace's painted mouth dropped and she said huffily, "Well, really!"

But they knew Clarence and his capabilities and he settled down to business, expertly handling the large crowd of well dressed, nicely scented women who spoke impeccable English and had nice manners, while he valiantly salvaged what he could from his school days in an attempt to appear similarly inclined. The ladies were impressed, but it was mostly his charming wit and polite behavior that had done the impressing.

Under his direction things proceeded smoothly. He even found a decorative wood gavel when the one regularly used by the presidents somehow got lost. It was an even nicer gavel than the one the club possessed. Clarence graciously presented it to Holly as a gift from the management. He didn't wink and she accepted it, but she wondered what he was up to. When he said he wasn't up to anything, that he was just doing his job as manager of the hotel trying to please all the good ladies, she let it go at that. It was hard to know when Clarence was serious. He didn't tell her that it had been left behind by someone at one of the many conventions held there and he was glad for the opportunity to pass it on. But nothing was amiss when the outgoing State President, Lenore V. Polley, presented the gavel to the new president for 1927-1929, Mrs. 0. P. Shaw.

Holly and Laurel were relieved when it was all over. They had enjoyed the meetings and the reports and the banquet, but Holly had wanted it to be perfect. From the many compliments she received from those in attendance and from the officers of the State Federation she at last believed that all had gone well. But the nervous tension had worn her out.

So when Laurel suggested going outside for some fresh air and then continuing to the Tams for a needed cup of coffee, Holly accepted and began to relax and let down and enjoy the glow of satisfaction of a job well done.

"I'm so glad it's all over, Laurel. And I'm even more glad that you'll be the president next year."

She sipped her coffee, taking in the aroma and taste with its satisfying effect. "Mmm, that's good. Did you ever wonder how coffee could get you all perked up at times and at other times calm you down?"

She sighed contentedly and looked at Laurel, still fingering her cup, twirling it in the saucer, lost in thought.

"Laurel?"

Laurel looked up guiltily. "Oh I'm sorry. I heard you. I did. It's just that — I have to talk to you."

"Of course. Is something wrong?"

"Yes. No. I don't know."

Holly was baffled.

"I can tell you anything, can't I Holly? We are such good friends. You wouldn't hate me, no matter what I told you, would you? I couldn't bear it if you should hate me." She pushed her heavy glasses onto her nose and looked hopefully at Holly.

"Laurel, for heavens sake, what is it?"

"Oh golly, this will sound just terrible, but I figured if I talked to you, you could help me make some sense of it. I don't know what to do." She looked straight into Holly's eyes and said, "I'm in love with another man."

Holly was completely taken aback and she experienced a twinge of irritation as her happy glow went away and her coffee got cold. She didn't reply.

"Wendell works for the county, as you know, and he's gone a lot, especially in the summer when it's so busy. I know I can always find plenty to do and I love to read and to learn. Little Wendell is older now and plays outside a lot without as much constant care. His father is a good husband, really he is. No one could ask for a better provider. And he loves me dearly. Anything I want or need he gets for me, no questions asked. We get along...."

She paused and looked so forlorn that Holly's heart went out to her, but for the life of her could not understand what could be the problem.

"Heaven forgive me for saying it, Holly, but — well Wendell is not very smart."

Holly leaned back in her chair, resigned to hearing the worst.

"We entertain now and then and Wendell asked this man and his wife to come to supper last year. We hit it off right away. The four of us had such fun and their little boy and Little Wendell played together very well. Jim's wife, Paulette, and Wendell seemed to enjoy talking to each other as much as Jim and I did. We just clicked. It just happened."

Holly had heard those words before. Laurel had been involved with a married man for a length of time. It was disturbing news to know that one of their close group had been unfaithful, and to know it was Laurel, the smartest and the brightest, stirred emotions in Holly that she was in no mood to deal with just then.

"Laurel, I have no business getting involved in such a personal matter. This is something you must work out yourself."

"But Holly, I'm so torn between them. I love Wendell, really I do. But I long for — I need something more."

"Love is the most important, Laurel. Everything else comes from it."

"But I love Jim, too."

"Who is this Jim anyway?" Holly really didn't want to know but she could see there was no way out of the conversation until she had heard it all without alienating her.

"Jim Markham. He's the owner of the construction company that does all the county work and any other road construction around these parts. He's rich, but that isn't why I love him. It's because he is so smart, Holly. He has an education and he's so interesting to talk to. He has traveled and knows so much about so many different things. He learned about road construction in the Army in Europe during the war when they assigned him that duty. He excelled at it and when he returned to the states he decided to make his living at it, but not before his father made sure he got an education first. He graduated from Huron College with highest honors and his knowledge made him a wealthy man. "

Holly murmured, "I see."

"But it's not his money," she protested. "It's his brain and his sense of humor. There is such a wonderful feeling when we are together and talking about anything and everything under the sun. He invigorates me so, fills me with such enthusiasm. And we have fun. Sometimes I don't think Wendell knows how to have fun."

"Is this feeling mutual between you?"

"Oh yes. He told me he loves me."

Seeing the quizzical look on Holly's face, she went on.

"And, no, Wendell doesn't know, nor does Paulette. They don't have an inkling. We have met off and on for almost a year and, so far, no one knows a thing. Oh Holly, what shall I do? I know it's wrong. Wendell is so wonderful to me and I don't want to lose him, but I don't want to lose Jim either. I need what we have together. I'm at my wit's end."

"Well Laurel, I'm flattered that you think I could possibly help you, but I surely cannot make up your mind for you, nor set out your future course of conduct. Get some rest. We've both been very busy and you are overwrought. You're tired, too. I know I am. Think it all out very carefully and you might even say a prayer for guidance. You'll get your answer. I know it."

"But I had to ask you, Holly. You've gone through it. And you've handled it so perfectly. How do you do it working for Randy all day and then going home to Jonathan? I was sure you could help me."

Holly was flabbergasted at Laurel's logic. Had she, herself, set an example for her to emulate? It was true that she loved two men, just as Laurel did, but that love had been expressed to only one of them, her husband. Besides, all the girls knew of her love of many years for Randall. Their situations were not at all similar. Or were they?

"Holly, please forgive me. I shouldn't have said that. I apologize."

The former look of relaxation had turned to consternation on Holly's face and Laurel knew she had caused her much distress. Holly looked hurt and ashamed and she had no reason to be ashamed. It was she, Laurel, who was shameful. At the sight of Holly's sudden tears she was filled with remourse. Laurel rose and said, "Let's get out of here. Come on. I'll drive you home."

Holly quickly wiped the tears away and followed Laurel from the restaurant into the cool dark where no one would notice. They said nothing as they drove. When they stopped in front of Holly's house they sat silently for a moment.

"Holly, I'm sorry. I had no right to burden you with a problem I created. What I said was unforgivable, but I hope you can forgive."

Holly turned to her and smiled faintly.

"Let's forget about it. We are still friends. And you are right. I do know what it is like to love two men and just how impossible it can be. Go home to Wendell. Things will look better tomorrow."

"Thanks, Holly." Laurel was miserable. She had betrayed her husband and then made it worse by wounding Holly. Holly got out of the car and gave her a wave.

As she went up the walk to the porch its welcoming light and the soft light from the living room beckoned to her. She loved her home and she loved the good man who waited for her inside. She wiped her eyes carefully with her soft handkerchief, put a smile on her flushed face and opened the door.

Jonathan was asleep in his favorite easy chair with the paper on his lap. How peaceful he looked. He stirred when she closed the door.

"Holly. Madam President, how was your big meeting?"

She gave him a radiant smile. "It went wonderfully well. Just like clockwork. But I am so glad my job is finished. I am really done in. It takes a lot out of a person to have so much responsibility."

He rose, stretched, and went to her.

"You, my dear, are up to any task. I am very proud of you, and proud of myself to have had the good sense to marry you."

She twined her arms around his neck and held him closely to her. He was surprised at her sudden display of affection. He held her tightly and responded to her sound kiss.

"Well now, what brought this on?" he asked looking into her sparkling eyes.

"I'm just very glad to be here, at home with you. What a fortunate woman I am."

He turned off the light and led her upstairs to bed. She forced herself to not think of the unpleasant conversation she had with Laurel. She concentrated on her love for her husband and the privilege of being so lovingly cared for.

Chapter 14

As the 1920s neared the end of the decade and the frenzied Roaring Twenties came to a close, the stock market crashed in October, 1929, bringing financial ruin to the country. Huron did not escape and many people lost money and property. The Great Depression had begun.

To make matters worse, drought was pervasive in the Midwest. Rainfall was minimal and the little that fell soon evaporated in the hot, dry atmosphere. Snowfall was less than usual and did little to alleviate conditions. People were faced with the reality of poverty, a condition which put everyone in the same boat, eliminating class distinctions.

Population in Huron dropped from almost 12,000 to less than 11,000 when some residents moved to California, the Golden Land of Opportunity, in the hopes of making new lives for themselves.

Holly's mother died in 1930 and she had the worry about the welfare of her aging brother and sisters. They continued to live in the family home but were forced to take in boarders to maintain it. Teachers made up most of the boarders, along with aging widowers. Some teachers stayed on through the summer, finding it convenient and less expensive than returning to their small hometowns. Some preferred to work during the summer at part-time jobs. Their salary of $1,227 a year never quite met expenses and they were not paid during the summer months. They could have gone home by bus, as buses had routes into every small town not accessible by train but, as one irate teacher put it, it was annoying to say the least to be transported from place to place empty-handed by a young whippersnapper driving the bus on which she was riding who made more money than she did. Supper table conversations were lively and things seemed to go well with sufficient income, so Holly decided that her worry was unwarranted.

Despite worsening conditions which increased every year during the Dirty Thirties, the club members kept up with their active participation in the Huron Fortnightly. With the lives of each member becoming more desperate the comfort and understanding of their close association was even more vital to their lives. They added new members, one in particular, who expressed an interest before the state convention in 1927 held in Huron. She was invited to join and a Mrs. Maude Feinstein, the wife of a doctor who had moved to town, became a member. She quickly added a different dimension to the club. It was their first acquaintance with someone of "the Jewish persuasion" as one of the older women had put it, and they were intensely curious as to what she would bring to the membership. Her credentials were impressive: She was intelligent, cultured and well traveled, the kind of woman they always welcomed. Upon discussion as to extending her the invitation Mrs. Sylvia Wallace was the sole voice expressing some concern, but she was overruled.

Mrs. Feinstein was soon elected recording secretary and she proved to be a wise choice. She included every detail of the work of the organization in the minutes, and emphasized the fact that 75% of all public libraries in the land had been started by women's clubs, a feat of which they should be justly proud. Their own Carnegie Library stood as an excellent example of Andrew Carnegie's vision in the establishment of the many libraries that bore his name. She did more than merely set down the facts. She used very descriptive prose to document their activities, which on occasion, proved to be more enthralling than the actual event.

She wrote:

> "Members were in attendance at the Chautauqua meeting for a speech by renowned politician and orator, William Jennings Bryan, when the weather abruptly turned sinister, dark clouds formed rapidly, out of which a tornado (a common occurrence in the Midwest) plunged from demonic clouds and demolished the huge tent in which the meeting was held. The meeting was quickly adjourned and people scattered. There were few injuries, most of which occurred in the haste with which those in attendance made a hurried exit."

A subsequent reading of the minutes said:

> "Our president, Calvin Coolidge, and his good wife traveled by train through the State of South Dakota, including a stop in Huron on their route on June 15, 1927, enroute to the Black Hills for a summer vacation. He graciously stepped to the back of the train and spoke to the considerable throng assembled to wish him well. He does not appear to have a presidential demeanor and is by nature a quiet man, but the crowd was enthusiastic. It is the office of the president that calls forth the obligation of respect from the populace. A later photograph of President Coolidge while in the Black Hills is amusing, in that it depicts our mild-mannered, softspoken Chief Executive wearing an enormous cowboy hat. Local cowboys thought it especially amusing."

Mrs. Feinstein had the complete attention of the ladies of the club when she read the minutes of their meetings.

The unremitting progression of dreary, debilitating events that had become a way of life wore heavily on everyone during the decade of the thirties. No matter how hard they tried to remain hopeful, optimism was waning. But the members of the Fortnightly clung together; their friendship and purpose could not be broken.

Even the Cranes did not escape and faced more tragedy. Mr. Crane was forced to admit Mrs. Crane to the State Insane Asylum in Yankton. His wife was no longer the beautiful, capable woman he married. She had deteriorated to such a mental state that he could no longer cope with caring for her. Dr. Feinstein's diagnosis was manic depression and he told Mr. Crane that she could harm herself and others if not properly supervised. The commitment to the institution made him more lonely and reclusive. He stayed on in his rundown house with its overgrown, weed-infested yard and cracked sidewalk. His brooding increased. The obsession with the death of his daughter and then the hospitalization of his wife because of Butch's irresponsible actions never left him. He held at fault, also, the authorities over the lack of justice in the apprehension and prosecution of Violet's killer, even though they had long ago abandoned the case. His determination to do something about it kept him going, but he was a mere shadow of the former successful, strong, assured man he had been. He was thin to the point of emaciation. His eyes were sunken and his mouth was set in a permanent grim line. He had a mission and he couldn't die until it had been fulfilled.

It was Christmastime in 1931 and Holly decided to do something to raise the spirits of club members. She brought up the subject after supper one night in early December and found Jonathan in full agreement. She would have a party. It was her turn to have the meeting and she wanted to decorate the house, to find the tallest tree in town, buy lots of presents for the children and have the party on a Saturday afternoon, making it convenient for everyone and sparing the husbands from suffering through a party with a group of chattering women and noisy children. They could afford it and it really wouldn't cost much. She would pick out a gift for each child. Holly was nearing 40 and had given up ever having a baby but she still loved to be with the children of her friends.

"Do you realize how much work you are letting yourself in for?" asked Jonathan, smiling at her enthusiasm.

"Yes I do, but I can do it and it will be such fun. There will be a houseful, I know, and lots of noise and confusion, but I really want to do this," she said with her eyes shining.

"You know you can do whatever you want to do, my dear. And I'll help you where I can be of assistance. I just don't want you to take on too much and tire yourself out."

"Sunny will help me and I won't go to a lot of fuss. We'll have a great time shopping for the gifts and wrapping them. And we'll bake cookies and have cocoa with marshmallows, and — I'd better make a list."

Jonathan grinned to see her so happy. He could deny her nothing and gladly joined in the preparations. Soon a tall evergreen tree was erected in the living room in front of the big window resplendent with assorted fragile baubles from her mother's things. Jonathan first had the frustrating job of stringing the small grooved bulbs that kept going out, stretching his patience, because it was not easy to find out which one was defective. But at last it was done complete with a glittering pointed spire at its top. They stood back to admire their handiwork.

"Oh Jonathan, it looks just like a Christmas card."

He agreed and said he'd clean up the boxes and paper in the morning. It was very late and they were tired. The end results of any undertaking of his generous wife were gratifying, but her drive for perfection could wear him out.

There would be around 20 children with their mothers, plus the older club members, but Holly assured Jonathan that she wouldn't spend too much money. The joy of unwrapping a present, no matter the cost, would delight a child. Sunny was as enthusiastic as Holly and they went shopping. Montgomery Ward and J. C. Penney had everything for Christmas throughout their stores and toys were plentiful. During the Christmas season and especially on Saturday nights when shopping was heaviest, children would stand and stare at the multitude of wonderful toys: beautiful dolls, metal trucks, tea sets and red wagons, as they were warned not to touch. The lucky ones might find one of the longed-for toys under the tree on Christmas morning, but most of them had to be satisfied with less expensive things. It was harder on parents to not be able to buy their children their heart's desire.

Holly and Sunny went to all the stores and found suitable gifts at Newberry's as well. The car was filled with packages to be wrapped. Even that chore was fun and it wasn't long before they were wrapped in soft white tissue paper and tied with colored cord. Holly kept the coffee coming and they tasted each kind of cookie "to make sure they are all right" they told themselves. Jonathan came home to laughter in the dining room and found the table covered with boxes and wrapping paper and a mound of presents under the lighted tree.

"Well now, this is a welcome sight to come home to," he said.

"Doesn't it all look grand, honey?" Holly exclaimed.

Her face was flushed and she looked young and happy. Jonathan thanked his lucky stars for her. Sunny saw what time it was and hurried off to fix supper for her family. It was decided to leave the dining room table as it was and Jonathan helped Holly with supper in the kitchen. She and Sunny would finish the next day.

"The Tinkertoys are fun. Have you seen them, Jonathan? They're supposed to be educational, too. Imagine! They come in various sizes, but we got the small sets."

The day for the party neared and it turned icy cold, but dry.

99

"Why doesn't it snow?" Holly complained. "It won't be Christmas if it doesn't snow."

"It will snow, don't worry. We haven't yet had Christmas without snow. It will snow."

It did snow lightly, just enough to cover the gray landscape with a few inches to give it a Christmasy look.

"Just enough to have it tracked all through your clean house," Jonathan teased.

"It's much too pretty for me to object to a little tracked-in snow. It's just clean snow, not mud."

Nevertheless, she asked the guests to remove their overshoes on the porch to cut down on the clutter, she said, and she was glad she did as the boys had tromped through all the snow they could find, enjoying the change in the weather and getting their galoshes soaked.

The lights on the tree were lit at the early hour of 2:00 o'clock and all of them remained lighted and cheery. Compliments were showered on Holly and her beautifully decorated house. The children stood around the tree, excitedly exclaiming over all the gifts, seeking the ones with their names attached. Holly's face shone with pleasure as she welcomed all of them.

It was a happy gathering in the crowded living room. The regular meeting was dispensed with except for the recitation of the Collect. The children were hushed listening to the women's solemn voices in unison, not understanding, but knowing it was serious.

Then Holly said, "I'm so glad you could all come. We are going to have a party and to start it off we shall begin with refreshments. Do you all like cocoa?"

She knew everyone loved cookies, but was not that sure about cocoa and had coffee brewing for the club members just in case. The warm fragrance of cocoa simmering in a large pot emanated from the kitchen. Shouts of approval sent Holly and Sunny to fill the cups, adding a big soft marshmallow from cellophane bags. They carried trays of filled cups to the dining room table where crystal plates laden with Christmas cookies waited. Lighted red tapers shed a glow on the linen covered table. The smaller children ran to it as their mothers attempted to restrain them. The older ones hung back, not wanting to appear too eager.

They kept the plates and cups filled. Members sat on chairs in the crowded living room enjoying the festivities, watching the children close to the tree seated on the floor, as mothers repeated admonishments not to spill.

Holly was delighted. The house was awash with the warmth of the holiday that raised spirits that had been submerged for so long. She stood at the wide arched opening between the rooms and marveled at the passage of time. The oldest children were nearing their teens. They were all acquainted from the friendships of their mothers. Sunny's three were mingling with Rose's four redheads. Laurel's two, a boy and a little girl, were seated side by side. Daisy's four were happily poking the presents under the tree. The oldest had to wear glasses and it made him look intellectual like his father. Gloria was pregnant again, a seemingly perpetual condition. She was otherwise thin, surrounded by her five children looking like models from the Sears & Roebuck catalog.

Sunny appeared at her side.

"I'll pass more cookies. Saves the confusion of everyone traipsing to the dining room." She paused and added, "Did you notice Laurel's youngest? She's a living doll, but just who does she resemble? It's surely not either of her parents."

She didn't wait for Holly's response and Holly offered none. She had indeed noticed and often wondered if anyone had questioned the origin of the sweet little three-year-old with the black curls and dark eyes. Laurel doted on her. Nothing was ever said of their conversation at the Tams Hotel, but it was soon thereafter that Markham Construction Company joined the exodus to California to find better employment. Laurel had sunk into such despair that Wendell took her to Dr. Feinstein who determined that her moodiness was undoubtedly the result of her early pregnancy. Wendell was deliriously happy at fathering another child. Little Wendell was not so little anymore, so when Jennie was born he felt his life was complete. Laurel recovered from her personal trauma and was grateful for her beautiful little girl, the permanent reminder of her past secret indiscretion.

It was time to open the presents Holly was noisily told, and she was snapped from her thoughts. All the dishes had been returned to the table, the candles were snuffed and Jonathan came in to distribute the gifts to the excited thanks of each child. Children took to him readily and Holly considered it such a waste to have been denied the ability to give him his own. But she put those thoughts behind her and stood back to watch the opening of the packages that she and Sunny had such a good time selecting and wrapping. From the reactions it was clear that they had done an excellent job.

"Well, you've done it again, my dear," said Jonathan as he joined her.

"Aren't you glad we did this, Jonathan? Just listen to them. There's nothing like the sound of children laughing and having fun. This is what Christmas is all about."

He put his arm around her and a feeling of contentment flowed between them mingling with the smell of evergreen and candles which hung on the air.

Chapter 15

Holly's Christmas party was the last happy event the members of the club experienced for several years. Depression lay over the land like a heavy dark cloud that the sun could not penetrate, despite each summer passing with the sun blazing down unmercifully. Drought increased yearly with not enough moisture to coax seeds from the parched earth, yet farmers dared not to plant, being ever hopeful that each year would be a better one.

Money was scarce with little to spend on anything but food and shelter. Some people lost their jobs and their homes. Throughout the nation communities of Hoovervilles sprang up, so called after President Herbert Hoover, whom they blamed for their plight. Cardboard shacks covered with tar-paper became makeshift homes. People begged for a job or food. Some sold apples on street corners for pennies. Throughout the nation hard times came to 15 million unemployed people, amounting to 25% of the work force. Every community had soup lines with hundreds lining up every day for sustenance. In Huron there were 2,374 people on relief by 1934.

With the years of drought came dust storms which struck terror into hearts. Precious top soil throughout the Midwest was whipped into thick black clouds by strong, relentless prairie winds of up to 40 miles per hour. Blackness rolled out of the western sky turning day into night, blowing dirt into every crevice, pattering against closed windows like snow pellets and covering the land in desolation.

The Roaring Twenties had given way to the Dirty Thirties.

Crops were poor and prices for what could be harvested were even poorer. Farmers sold some of their livestock to get some cash, getting only five cents a pound for hogs. Dust piled up in ditches like black snow, covering fences, allowing cattle to escape, causing further losses. Farms were abandoned to a vindictive Mother Nature. Buildings crumbled from disuse and farmers became migrant workers earning $40 or $50 a month plus room and board. Hopelessness was pervasive.

The one crop that grew in abundance was the crop of grasshoppers. Grasshoppers of all sizes, from tiny green insects to large fearsome winged creatures two inches long, rose up from plants, weeds, brush — anything that managed to grow. They arrived in swarms, devouring crops and stripping bare every living thing. They clung to the sides of buildings and hung on screen doors, making going in and out a battle of wits to get through the door before the grasshoppers did. They stuck to clothing as people walked and were brushed off in disgust. Women were forced to hang laundry inside their houses, because to hang it outside was to find it covered with the voracious insects and stained with their droppings.

Winters were mild and the summer heat was unbearable. The hot nights gave little relief even though the darkness gave an illusion of cooling. Darkness brought an end to any breeze without a breath of air. Anything that came up green in the spring turned brown and brittle by June. Grass was nonexistent. Grime threatened to defeat even the most fastidious of housekeepers.

Holly did her best to keep Dr. Randall Thorne's office clean and sanitary, also keeping in mind the necessity to conserve water. It turned into a daily battle, dusting the waiting room and wiping down the examining room furniture, only to find it in the same condition when she arrived early the next morning. She had assistance from the office girl Randy hired when the press of his work grew too great for Holly alone to handle.

Dr. Thorne had numerous patients from area farms who came to him coughing and with aching lungs. The diagnosis was given as dust pneumonia caused by constant exposure to the violent elements. Some farmers had to be hospitalized. Sprague Hospital was soon filled to overflowing. The windows were kept open in all kinds of weather to clear their lungs, the doctors said. Patients required constant care, lest they expire in a paroxysm of coughing. They were given a serum to bring up the black sputum that afflicted their lungs. Mustard plasters were used to provide some relief. Yet in spite of all the efforts some died. Those who survived and had no money to pay for their care offered payment in sweet corn, chickens, eggs and garden produce, which doctors accepted. Holly was frightened at all the sickness. It was like a plague.

Rodents and gophers flourished, and enterprising men and boys with a vehicle drove around the countryside shooting them for their tails which fetched a nickel apiece. Others would drive out of town in an attempt to escape the heat, trying to bring in a breeze through rolled-down windows. Gas was only 18¢ a gallon, so it was an inexpensive diversion. They would report on the drifts of dirt, some as high as ten feet, against farm buildings. They searched the bright blue sky for a rain cloud, if only a wisp of one, to give them hope for rain.

An unexpected result of the numerous dust storms that ripped the topsoil from the earth was the uncovering of countless Indian arrowheads which were laid bare. The small, intricately carved stone specimens became a source of interest, and collecting and trading the artifacts became a popular pasttime.

Those who drove to Lake Byron hoping for respite from the heat returned with tales of the desolate condition of the once beautiful and popular spot. The lake had completely dried up. Dust was piled around the remaining cabins, filling screened porches. The shoreline was gone. One man reported seeing a combine in the middle of the dried up lake left there, rusted and unusable, by a farmer who had harvested what he could to feed his livestock. The prairie had become a wasteland.

President Franklin D. Roosevelt offered some hope during the thirties. The National Recovery Act regulated wages, hours and prices. The Civilian Conservation Corps engaged two and a half million men to work at $30 a month doing constructive work for the country, such as planting trees for wind breaks, building campgrounds and restoring historical places of interest. *The Huronite* reported one of the results of such efforts in the completion of Fisher Grove outside of Redfield, their neighbor 50 miles to the north, making the area a beautiful park suitable for picnicking along the James River. The Works Progress Administration hired many unemployed to build roads, bridges, schools and federal offices. The hard work was beneficial to previously unemployed men and to the country as the result of their labors.

The lack of cash renewed interest in entertaining neighborhood activities. People provided their own entertainment, often meeting in one another's homes on long evenings to play cards, work jigsaw puzzles, or just to listen to the radio to see how Fibber McGee and Molly were doing or what George Burns and Gracie Allen were up to. Bing Crosby made women sigh. Men preferred Eddie Cantor's energetic rendition of "Now's the Time to Fall in Love" since "Tomatoes are cheaper, Potatoes are cheaper—"

The 25¢ movie tickets were affordable to most at the State Theater. The Bijou was equipped with sound to better compete. Both theaters offered dish night and lucky women went home with a piece of a set of dishes each week, some of whom eventually assembled an entire set of dishes which served their families for years.

Movies gave the populace a brief, welcome relief from their woes. Shirley Temple captivated movie goers with her dimples and enormous talent, delighting mothers and making little girls envious, but everyone admired her singing and dancing. Fred Astaire and Ginger Rogers took people to another world with their sophisticated films.

Radios were a vital part of lives with upbeat music. Soap operas, so named because they were supported by advertisements of soap manufacturers, were a mainstay in the daily lives of women confined at home, but too often transmission was garbled with static, making steady listeners frustrated by not being able to hear what happened on Myrt and Marge, Our Gal Sunday and One Man's Family. Children came home from school promptly to listen to another episode of Little Orphan Annie, Jack Armstrong, the All-American Boy and Sky King. Holly and Sunny had a good laugh one day when an advertisement came over the airwaves on Sunny's Admiral radio claiming that "Rinso gets out storm dust: Only 22¢ for a large box at your local grocer." This declaration was followed by the Rinso white jingle. The women agreed that the writer of that line obviously didn't know what he was talking about and surely did not live in the Midwest. The game of Monopoly came out in 1934 and was the rage for years. Groups of players gathered regularly for the fun of trying their skills with play money and strategy. The fantasy of becoming wealthy — or bankrupt — also gave an education in economics.

In December, 1933, Prohibition, which proved to be a failed experiment, was repealed and the liquor industry resumed business as usual. Enterprising folks had made their own beer for years and, while some enjoyed the orange drink and root beer which the brewery produced during that time, most were ready for some oldtime lager with a bigger kick. It was not known for sure that Butch had a hand in the resumption of the manufacture of beer at the brewery. It was, however, common knowledge that he did exactly as he pleased. He was successful in eluding authorities, and he made plenty of money with his own underground operation, along with his illegal establishment of prostitution. None of these things could be proved and none of the allegations inspired the ambitions of lawmen to investigate. It took a lot of courage to cross Butch. And it was argued that the male of the species could not easily be changed in his pursuit of pleasure and liquor. Even the local Women's Temperance Union left Butch's name out of their examples of the result of intemperance.

In 1933 the state convention of the General Federation of Women's Clubs was held in Aberdeen at the Alonzo Ward Hotel. Mrs. Sylvia Wallace was again chosen as a delegate, in addition to the president, Maude Feinstein. They decided to take the train to Aberdeen after prolonged discussion about the merits of that mode of travel and that of a long bus ride. The inconvenience of changing trains at Wolsey to get to Redfield and on to Aberdeen, a total distance of about 100 miles, and the inconvenience of the bus which stopped at every small town along the way was examined. The bus would cost less, but it would take longer to arrive at their destination. Train travel was more in keeping with their stature and positions in the club, according to the ladies who were making the trip, and they were accustomed to train travel. A bus ride could be very bumpy over the graveled roads, quite uncomfortable, they pointed out. The women were highly fashionable and members could not imagine them seated in a noisy, jolting bus, crammed with assorted passengers who could be undesirable. They had nothing on which to base that assumption, but it made a convincing argument. So they took the Chicago, Northwestern and the ladies were satisfied.

Upon their return Mrs. Feinstein presented detailed minutes of the convention. Mrs. Wallace brought programs and brochures which set forth the good works of other clubs in the state, such as providing scholarships for worthy young women, beautification programs for their various communities, donations to charities, and more. Despite their different backgrounds, the two women had progressed from being polite adversaries to friends working in a common cause, which was the betterment of their own community through the efforts of the Huron Fortnightly. Their money and stations in life also bound them together, as the lack of those things bound those less fortunate together. They were enthusiastic about Aberdeen and very pleased with their accommodations, plus the fine shopping the town provided. They specifically praised the Olwin Angell Department Store, a large establishment of three floors filled with anything anyone could want and serviced by attentive, cultured sales ladies. Upon description of their eventful trip renewed interest in being a delegate was infused in members. The work of the club never waivered through the years.

During the early thirties modern day desperadoes roamed the country, making a living of sorts by robbing banks. Among those struck was the Northwest Security National Bank in Sioux Falls, the state's remote city in the far southeastern corner. Supposedly it was John Dillinger's gang, and a shoot-out and hostage situation made for considerable excitement. For years afterward an indentation in one of the columns by the front entrance to the bank was pointed out as having been made by one of the misspent bullets fired during the getaway. So in April, 1933, when the Security National Bank in Huron was robbed in similar fashion, rumors were rampant that it was Dillinger's gang. It was soon proved otherwise when the culprits were captured, being only bungling burglars.

The original members of the club were getting older. Hair was beginning to gray, making them feel even older because of the trying times in which they lived. Rose's bright red hair faded a little, and Holly's graying hair only reminded her that she was aging with no satisfaction of having something to account for it. Jonathan, ever the courtly gentleman, told her it just made her more appealing to him. She didn't believe it; after all, Sunny's beautiful hair had merely grown a pale gold, the color of wheat, but she was grateful for her husband's remark. Mrs. Feinstein, although about the age of Mrs. Wallace, made no apologies for her artfully coiffed steel gray hair. Mrs. Wallace, on the other hand, never seemed to gray, which they considered to be a family attribute, until Rose disclosed in a low voice that the reason for her still untouched tresses was that she dyed it. She had seen Mrs. Wallace making a purchase of hair dye at Perriton's

Drugstore. However, as the years passed, Mrs. Wallace's raven hair made her look much older as skin lost its firmness and wrinkles appeared. She needed glasses but she refused to wear them. Her vanity caused her to deny the necessity and she wore a small pair of spectacles which were attached to an ornamental brooch on her ample bosom, from which she pulled them to peer whenever it was necessary to read. Her subterfuge didn't fool them, but no one made mention of it, knowing that each of them had a foible to deal with. No one was perfect. Mrs. Wallace rationalized that her strange glasses were just an enhancement of the total image she projected. Rose made the astute comment that she was certainly successful in that endeavor.

The club donated books to the Carnegie Library on occasion and included 'Madame Bovary' by Flaubert, a French writer. Mrs. Wallace thought it was a scandalous selection, but she was reminded by Mrs. Feinstein that this was a modern age of enlightenment and they certainly didn't condone censorship. Gloria countered with being in agreement with Mrs. Wallace and gave her opinion about the new novel by Margaret Mitchell, 'Gone With the Wind,' asking if any had read it. Daisy replied that she had and liked it and that she thought Rhett Butler was very appealing, sort of wicked but nice, was the way she put it. Gloria continued to object and pointed out the insinuation of unseemly behavior written in the book, plus swearing. Rose snapped back that such was life. Gloria said it would have no place in her home and expressed gratitude that it had not been selected to donate. As it turned out, 'Gone With the Wind' was made into a movie and became one of the most popular ever made.

Gloria's sixth child had been born and she was more thin than usual and looked older than her years. She worked far too hard and was run down by constant child care and in having to do so much alone while her husband, Neville, was on the road selling insurance. She sorely wished she'd get his own office but he couldn't afford the overhead in such hard times. He was better off driving from town to town with only his car as an expense.

So it continued. The members of the club remained loyal in the bonds of friendship, despite the personal deprivations each of them suffered.

Chapter 16

On a Saturday morning in September, 1935, Holly was dusting her furniture and listening to the radio. A tenor was singing 'Pennies from Heaven', a popular song of the decade, which did little to bring people out of the doldrums.

Movies had become a thriving industry which provided a temporary escape. Actors rose to stardom romping merrily through fantasy tales that were immensely appealing. Errol Flynn, Cary Grant and Tyrone Power were just a few of the romantic leading men who remained popular for years. Glamorous stars such as Jean Harlow, Carole Lombard and Joan Crawford set the styles women tried to emulate. It was easy to be pencil thin as they were, due to the lack of hearty meals. Hair was worn longer and more sleek as the flapper look went out. But clothing was another matter. No one could afford satin dresses displayed on the silver screen. Many women were already remodeling their outdated clothing, most of which was made from fine fabrics to begin with, but for the majority a new frock was simply too expensive. Some children went to school in homemade dresses and shirts made of colorful cotton, cloth that came from larger-sized flour sacks designed to be easily ripped apart for just such purpose.

As the song on the radio ended Holly wished that "each cloud contained pennies from Heaven", preferably a rain cloud. Her tasks were interrupted by the ring of the telephone. It was Jonathan calling from the drugstore.

"Holly dear, would you do something for me?"

"Of course. What is it?"

"Gloria has a prescription that she needs right away. The baby is sick and our delivery boy is out somewhere. I don't want to wait until he gets back as Randy said she should have it soon."

"I'll be right down, hon."

She would have to hurry. The Fortnightly was meeting for a luncheon at 1:00 o'clock and she was looking forward to it. It was a catered affair at the Evergreens sponsored by the two ladies who had become unlikely staunch friends and allies, Mrs. Sylvia Wallace and Mrs. Maude Feinstein. She hoped Gloria could attend this time, but it was doubtful. She had missed several meetings that year due to the press of her social obligations within the church and the children, and she refused to slow down her hectic, but organized life. Holly took off the bandana that she wore to ward off any settling dust, removed her apron and washed her hands. No need to change her dress. Getting the prescription to Gloria was more important.

"Tell her I've put the cost on their bill," Jonathan said when she picked up the small package.

At her expression he added, "The Jones's run up a monthly bill. I shouldn't be telling you this, but as a close friend of Gloria's I think you ought to know. The store doesn't make demands, but there is a substantial balance on it. Check things out while you're there, will you? Randy also said that his office has an outstanding bill, as you may already know from his office girl. He bills according to need, but he has treated the entire family for various ailments and has more than once explained to Gloria that some of the reasons she comes to see him for are not necessary, that she could treat the sniffles and earaches at home. He thinks she's much too solicitous. They are healthy, active kids when she gives them a chance to be. Don't mention what I said. It's that 'a word to the wise' — you know."

Holly was surprised to hear Jonathan's pronouncements, but she nodded and left for Gloria's house. She found her waiting anxiously at the front door holding her squirming, fussy baby. He was almost a year and a half, but seemed small for his age.

As she opened the door Gloria said in surprise, "Holly, I surely didn't expect you to have to personally deliver this for me, but thanks."

"Jonathan called me because the delivery boy was busy and he said you needed this right away."

"Come in to the kitchen. Will you hold Jeffie, please, while I take care of this? I'm supposed to mix it with his milk. Something's bothering him. It began yesterday so I took him to see Randy, remember? He's done so much for the children and for all of us for that matter. What a good friend he's been all these years. He's such a nice man, so patient and kind, a wonderful doctor. You must absolutely love working for him." She was mixing a powder from the package into milk, then poured it into a bottle. "It's only an upset stomach, I think, but he's so irritable."

Holly listened as she looked into the wide-eyed gaze of the small boy in her arms. Yes she loved working for Randy. Gloria came with the bottle to retrieve her baby.

"How do you do it, Holly? That's the first time he's stopped his fussing. You really should have had babies."

Holly gave Jeffie back to his mother. Gloria thrust the nipple into his working mouth and his distress was eased as the warm liquid soothed his stomach.

"I should have had him weaned by this time, but he loves his bottle and he is so little. Besides, it's easier." She stated it almost as an apology. "Do you have time for coffee? I've got some on the stove."

They sat at the table in the large kitchen. Gloria's house was immense with five large bedrooms. It was a lot of house to keep up even with the help of her mother. They sipped coffee and admired Jeffie who dozed off at last, giving them a chance to visit.

"Please excuse the mess. I've been so busy I haven't had time to do much except take care of the baby."

Holly surveyed the kitchen and found no mess, but according to Gloria's standards she supposed dishes in the sink constituted a mess. She had seen worse at Rose's house and Laurel's. But Gloria aspired to being the perfect wife and mother and maintained an immaculate house, clean, well-mannered children, and continued church work and other social duties. The strain had become so obvious to the others. Gloria missed too many meetings, always sincerely wanting to be there and very apologetic for shirking her duties to the club, although when it was her turn she never declined. Her children became exemplary models that other mothers pointed out to their own children. But to those who knew her best Gloria was too strict, making her children timid to the point of being afraid to be children. They kept their counsel, but were worried as she became thinner and in a chronic state of exhaustion. They could see what she could not — that she had set an impossible goal for herself, for the glory of God, she told them. Her life and the lives of her family must exemplify what He expected of His flock. They held their tongues when she recited the reasons for her Spartan schedule, but it was hard not to say something. Rose had a particularly hard time keeping quiet. Daisy, whose insight saw clearly what the problem was and the simple solution for it, wondered aloud about the obtuseness of those who could not see it, to Rose's complete agreement.

Holly said, "I don't know how you manage all of this, Gloria, the children, this big house and tending to Neville. You're so fortunate that he is so successful in his insurance business."

Gloria was hesitant. "Yes," she finally replied, keeping her eyes on Jeffie, "but not many people are buying insurance these days. Everyone has been hit by the Depression. And we do have some bills — but I just won't worry about them. Neville says they will be paid. God will provide. Besides, I have far too much to do to concern myself with anything except for what I must do."

That remark would have to suffice for any questions that Jonathan and Randy might have. She could not pursue the subject.

"It looks like you won't be able to come to the luncheon today."

"I'm afraid I can't. I know I've missed some meetings and I'd really love to be there. The Evergreens is so nice, but with the baby not well I have to stay home. My mother is so good about helping out but I can't ask her again so soon, and I am rather tired."

"We do understand, Gloria. I'll extend your regrets. Now I must run. As you can see, I am the one who is in a mess. I have to clean up and get going."

She rose and prepared to leave. "Don't get up. Sit and relax while you can. Call me if you need anything. The coffee hit the spot. You always did make the best coffee around."

Gloria smiled and waved as Holly left by the back door. She sat motionless in the quiet for a few minutes, letting the weariness drain from her tired body, until the children burst in asking for their dinner and waking the baby who set up a startled wail. For a moment she envied Holly who had only an adoring husband to tend. She had a good job and was free as a breeze to come and go as she pleased. She quickly asked God for forgiveness for thinking such a wicked thought and tended to her hungry brood.

As she left, Holly tried to deny what was obvious. Gloria was pregnant again. She was very thin, but her condition was apparent. This would be her seventh child. How on earth would she manage?

She returned home, had a quick bath and brushed her short waves till her hair shone. She slipped into a blue crinkly crepe dress on which she had splurged at Montgomery Ward for the sum of $3.95. Wards and Penneys did not want for customers. Their prices were within the range of most people. Specialty stores had a harder time of it. Some women renewed old skills and sewed their own clothes, and some children never knew the thrill of having a brand new dress or shoes until the forties arrived. They had to be content with handmade clothes or hand-me-downs from their older siblings. Penney's also featured crepe material at 49¢ a yard but Holly was not on good terms with a sewing machine, much to her late mother's chagrin, so she considered herself lucky to be able to afford a "store bought" dress.

She looked at herself in the cheval mirror and, as usual, despaired of what was reflected, but decided with a sigh that it was the best she could do. She concluded that the two ladies in charge of the luncheon would more than make up for any lack of fashion sense that anyone else lacked.

She was right. The two former rivals stood side by side at the entrance of the Evergreens to greet their guests. It was the first meeting of the season and since they had the September and October meetings they decided to combine them and have it catered at the tea room, thereby offering a rare outing to the members and saving themselves the preparations involved in entertaining in their own homes.

Mrs. Feinstein was always elegantly dressed and they often wondered where she got her clothes but surmised that most of them had come from Kansas City where she and Dr. Feinstein originated. Her gray rayon dress was simple but nicely cut. It was set off with a plum-colored hat with matching gloves and shoes. Where on earth had she found plum-colored shoes? Mrs. Feinstein was a pleasant mystery. She and Mrs. Wallace could accomplish any task so adroitly that it appeared to be easy. But the two women had money, they were childless with nothing to tie them down from what they enjoyed doing. In belonging to the Huron Fortnightly there was so much they could do toward improving cultural awareness in the community and at the same time retain positions of authority in any capacity, performing their responsibilities capably.

Mrs. Wallace was also fashionably attired in a pale pink outfit with rose-colored accessories. Her small glasses were affixed to her bosom by her ornate pin. Members were relieved to see that Mrs. Wallace had the good sense to leave her fur coat at home, as it was her custom to retrieve her fur from its hibernation at Eiler's Furs at the turning of the first leaf in September. But even she knew it would be a grievous faux pas to wear a fur in those troubled times. Otherwise, the Depression had little meaning for her.

The Evergreens was a boarding house and tea room run by Mrs. Jennie Corley, who had converted her large home into a profitable enterprise to help make ends meet. She was a short, ordinary looking woman with glasses attached to a velvet ribbon around her neck. They were perched on her nose most of the time as she peered through them at her guests. She was strong despite her size and could carry the heaviest tray with plates of her delicious food. Tables and chairs with padded cushions were set throughout the downstairs rooms. White linen cloths and napkins adorned each table. Long lace curtains hung at the tall windows, filtering the light. Women who ordinarily could not afford to patronize the Evergreens and Mrs. Corley's teas were taken from their frugal present time and swept back to an era when times were better, when refined ladies conversed in cultivated tones as they enjoyed the tasteful service of the Evergreens.

Holly felt out of place. She hadn't had enough time to get ready, but she smiled and trusted that no one would take notice of her perceived inadequacies. She sat at a table with Daisy, Rose and Sunny. Laurel sat apart with other members. She had not felt completely at ease with Holly since her confession of infidelity some years previously, although she knew she had no reason to fear that anyone but Holly knew of it.

As they sipped tea after lunch Holly told of her visit with Gloria and of her pregnancy.

Sunny said, "I knew she was because Randy told me. I know he's not supposed to talk about his patients, but Gloria is our friend, his too, and he didn't think it was wrong to tell me something that would soon be obvious anyway. What will she do? She's far overworked now as it is and she won't let up."

"They have to be in a bind financially," said Daisy. "After all, how can anyone afford so many children and that huge house and all?"

"I wish we could do something for her, make it easier, but what?" Rose was getting her ire up. "I wish we could shake some sense in her."

"We can't interfere. I know they need money, but we can't just hand them any," said Holly. "Besides, there aren't many of us who could contribute enough to make a difference."

They pondered the dilemma as the tables were cleared and the meeting began.

When they stepped from the tea room onto the porch into the fall sunshine it was as though they had just departed from a step back in time, from a simpler, more secure life. The sterile landscape greeted them, bringing them back to the harsh present.

**Bearing gifts of food at
Mr. Crane's house**

Chapter 17

A foot of snow fell in the winter of 1936 after several mild winters. Farmers rejoiced at the much needed moisture and Huron residents hoped for the beginning of the return to normal weather to ease conditions in the Dust Bowl. Spring brought brighter prospects, but it would be two or three more years before anyone believed that the Depression had really ended.

Gloria's seventh child was born too soon in early February, 1936. She and her baby needed hospitalization for more than two weeks, an expense Neville could ill afford. Gloria's labor was difficult, leaving her spent and weak. Dr. Thorne urged her to consider some form of birth control which she rejected. She recovered slowly but got some much needed rest before going home with her small baby. Dr. Thorne prescribed iron capsules to help the depleted iron in her system. Gloria wasn't pregnant again until 1939.

As conditions improved throughout the land so did everyone's spirits. Radios were filled with the smooth music of big bands: Benny Goodman, Glenn Miller, Tommy and Jimmy Dorsey: and Harry James among them. The bands traveled all over the country, playing in ballrooms that were packed to the walls with couples dancing and swaying to their popular music.

Some of the dried out, old buildings in Huron were destroyed by fire, the worst being in April, 1938, when the Penney store burned, taking with it a half dozen adjacent buildings. Fire fighters battled the blaze for six hours to contain the fierce flames. The buildings were rebuilt, but folks in town commented that the only disaster that had not occurred during the Dirty Thirties was a flood.

The meeting of the Huron Fortnightly was held at Daisy's house near the Huron College campus in January, 1938. As usual, Daisy was not quite prepared, having been hostess that afternoon to a tea for the professors' wives. Such events were customary and Daisy's husband, Professor Melvin Moberly, was always proud of the turnout when Daisy was entertaining. She was wiping the last of the cups and saucers and dessert plates when the first members arrived for the evening meeting. All the lights in the house were blazing to welcome them in from the frigid weather. Daisy met them at the door with the dish towel in her hands.

She smiled in welcome and said, "Come on in. Make yourselves at home. I'll be with you in a jiffy."

Her guests straightened chairs in the living room and picked up books and magazines which were strewn over the wool rug. Daisy's afternoon soirees were animated and she thoroughly enjoyed the repartee and lively discussions. But time slipped away and if she had two meetings on the same day she often was not ready. They understood and always helped her pick up the clutter. Her opinions and viewpoints were interesting and sometimes at odds with the rest of them, but she made them think. Daisy was at her best in the company of people who had an intellectual sense, such as the wives of the college professors. And when the meeting consisted of couples from the faculty she was inspired by the inclusion of the male point of view. At those times a late evening was certain, sometimes including rousing arguments. There were some evenings when Melvin had to come for her to go to bed long after the last guest had departed. He would find her asleep in her chair surrounded by the latest publication or a new book.

Their children were well-read, which made them proud of their offspring, especially the oldest. He would take a book to bed with him and fall asleep, so one of them would always check to see if he had removed his glasses and turned out the light. Their children all did well in school and their eagerness to learn was admired by the members of the club who, in turn, emphasized to their own children the example they set.

"I'm sorry about all the stuff lying around. I just didn't get to it after the women left. Just stack it in a corner."

There were things stacked in most of the corners in Daisy's house but she knew just where everything was.

After the Collect had been said and the minutes of the previous meeting had been read by Mrs. Feinstein, she paused hesitantly. Then she spoke to them in an uncharacteristic, faltering manner as she brought up the uneasy situation in Europe. She evoked blank expressions and realized that they had no idea what she was talking about. She mentioned her apprehensions about the specter of war and the rise of a questionable leader in Germany by the name of Adolph Hitler.

"Why on earth would there be another war?" asked Rose. "We just finished one a few years ago."

"War has always been a scourge," replied Mrs. Feinstein. "This one could be even more widespread. It already has the look of genocide."

She could see that the members were clearly puzzled, so she dropped the subject. They could see that Mrs. Feinstein was troubled and it was only throughout the next decade that they understood .

The meeting continued. Daisy said, "I learned this afternoon that Mrs. Crane died at the asylum in Yankton."

There were murmurs of sympathy and surprise. She had almost been forgotten.

"I think it would be in order for the club to send a message of sympathy to Mr. Crane. Some of us remember the Cranes from our younger years," said Daisy.

Laurel asked, "Does he still live in that old rundown house?"

"Yes. What a pity to see it in such bad shape," she replied. "Years ago it was a showcase. It's tragic."

Rose offered, "I think we should do more than send a card or a letter. Some of us should go over there and see how Mr. Crane is doing, maybe take some food, something like that, to let him know he is thought of in his loss, not foreseaken."

"A good idea. I'll be glad to go with you," said Holly.

No one but the two of them were able to follow through with the idea. So on a Saturday morning after Mrs. Crane's funeral, Rose and Holly drove to Mr. Crane's house with a loaf of homemade bread and a casserole. There had been no funeral as such, only a commital service that was held before the club knew of it, which upset the remaining original members of the club who had known Violet's parents, as they would have all been there. It was very cold that January and they could see that the walk had not been shoveled in a very long time, but there were footsteps in the snow that made a path of sorts to the door of Mr. Crane's house. The old house appeared to be sagging. Snow covered the yard and straggly brush around the porch. The house was dark and looked unlived in.

"Holly, just look at that. It's positively pathetic. That poor man."

They got out of Holly's car and plodded through the snow to the uneven wood steps and up to the enclosed porch.

"We'd better go onto the porch or he'll never hear our knock," said Holly.

They pushed the creaky door open on its rusty hinges and stomped the snow off their overshoes. There was no rug on the sagging floor on which to wipe them. The dirty windows of the dark porch made it appear darker than the cold midday light indicated, and they began to wonder about their good intentions. It was not at all as they had remembered. But they knocked on the heavy door to the house. The oval window in the door was covered on the inside with a torn curtain. There was no answer. They knocked again and heard a stirring inside. A man's face appeared through the torn curtain, startling them with its intensity. It was a ravaged Mr. Crane who stared out at them.

He shouted, "What do you want?"

"Mr. Crane, it's Holly and Rose. Could we see you for a minute?"

He frowned, then opened the heavy door a few inches.

"Yeah, who is it?"

"It's Holly and Rose. You remember. We were good friends of Violet."

They were alarmed at the expression that crossed the old man's face and stepped back. He frowned again and peered at them intently.

"I don't know any Holly or Rose. Violet isn't here. She was murdered. What do you want?"

They were uncertain as to what to do, but Holly smiled at him bravely and said, "Mr. Crane, we've brought you something. It's from the club members. We want to express our sympathy for the loss of Mrs. Crane." She struggled to express herself without further upsetting him. "We remember her, too, with fond memories. We've brought you some food — in case you need extra for company you may have," she said lamely as his sunken eyes glared at them.

Then they filled with tears and a wave of remourse swept over Holly and Rose at having caused him pain. They shouldn't have come.

He gave no flicker of recognition. "Just leave it there on the floor," he said gruffly, but he added as he closed the door against them, "Obliged."

The door slammed shut but not before they got a glimpse of the dark, messy living room which was filled with unidentifiable rubbish. Holly and Rose stood rigid for a moment staring at one another. Then they turned and left the porch, carefully picking their way down the slippery steps. Safely in the warm car they let out sighs and sat with the memory of Violet's formerly gracious home and of the afternoon teas with Mrs. Crane's beautiful, fragile china, and of the good times that were such a part of their memory of Violet. It all seemed incomprehensible after what they had just experienced.

Finally Rose spoke, wrinkling her nose. "Did you see that living room? The junk heaped all over? And that awful smell."

"That poor, poor man," replied Holly. "We must do something. Tell someone. He should not be left alone in that filth. How can we convince him to accept our help?"

"Holly, give it up. You can't fix everything for everybody. Some folks don't want help and as much as tell other folks to mind their own business. We've done the best we could. I think he took the food because he needs it, not out of gratitude, and he certainly won't be having any company. He didn't even know who we are. He's really scary."

They duly reported their observations to the club at the February meeting. Nothing could be done except to report it to Mr. Crane's church whose members did the best they could, but their efforts were, on the whole, wasted. Holly continued to fret despite Jonathan's entreaties to let it rest, to devote her worthy efforts to those more likely to welcome them.

Gloria was a concern of her friends, also. She was not at all well in her eighth pregnancy. She had come to see Randy for her regular appointment in August, 1939.

Holly took her into the examining room. Gloria was thin and looked older than her years.

Randy grasped her hand and smiled, "Gloria, how are you feeling today? Has the morning sickness let up?"

She didn't reply as Holly helped her onto the table. She sat for a moment with her hand at her aching back.

"Won't this be your eighth child?" Randy asked in concern.

She nodded as she laid down for the examination and Holly placed her feet in the stirrups. She gave a low moan and said apologetically, "Sorry. It's really nothing. My back hurts a little, that's all."

Holly held her hand as he examined her. When he finished he said, "Everything appears to be all right, but you must gain some weight or you will have another tiny baby. You must get stronger for the baby's sake and your own."

"I do eat, but it doesn't seem to do much good. Even with mother's help I just wear it off taking care of the children and everything else I must do. The older ones do help, but it is really my job to take care of it all."

Holly helped her to sit up. Randy listened as he washed his hands, then he turned, picked up Gloria's medical file and looked at her solemnly. "Gloria, according to this you are forty-four now. Is that right?"

She nodded .

"That is not a good age to have a baby. It could be very dangerous for you and your child. Actually, it's mighty risky for a woman in her thirties."

She smiled at him weakly. "After all these years it's just a part of my life. Look at the pioneer women. They managed. I'm just fine."

He looked straight into her tired eyes and said, "Gloria, you are not just fine. You are undernourished, completely worn out, and your health and that of your baby is threatened. How will you take care of your family if you are sick and unable to function?"

Gloria responded with a smile and said, "I'll be perfectly all right. God will provide. He will take care of everything."

Holly could see that Gloria's attitude was upsetting Randy, but he controlled himself and said, "It is commendable that you think that way, Gloria, but you have a certain responsibility, too. I am going to make a suggestion for you to consider. After this child is born you must take serious steps to avoid another pregnancy. You must not have any more children." He brushed aside her protestations. "Because if you do, I cannot guarantee what your future will hold. I cannot guarantee that you will not deteriorate beyond recovery."

She began to cry and shook her head vehemently.

He continued, "There is an alternative — a simple procedure that can be performed after birth. I can make sure that you won't get pregnant again."

Gloria stopped crying and her face flushed with anger. "You mean tie my tubes! Never! It's sinful. It's not permitted. No, I will not let you do any such thing."

Holly patted her shoulder. "Now, calm down, Gloria. Randy wouldn't do anything without your permission."

Randy persisted. "Well, then at least let me talk to Neville."

Gloria became so furious that Holly put her arms around her to control her shaking. Gloria glared at Randy, unable to speak.

"Will you at least continue to take the prescription for iron? Your blood is dangerously low in iron. It's not a remedy to really do you the most good, but it will help."

As Gloria collapsed in Holly's arms Randy threw up his arms in exasperation and left the room.

By the end of 1939 the Depression had officially ended. The song of the hour was "Happy Days are Here Again." The rumblings of war got louder and Kate Smith sang "God Bless America" over the radio to appreciative listeners. Edgar Bergen and Charlie McCarthy renewed people's sense of humor.

Gloria went into early labor and gave birth to a premature sickly little girl. On New Year's Eve the priest gave Gloria last rites and she died in Neville's arms.

Chapter 18

Disbelief, sorrow and anger filled the hearts of the members of the Huron Fortnightly, especially in those who had known Gloria from childhood. They gathered in a back pew of the St. Martin Catholic Church for the funeral. Most of the church was filled with the large group of family mourners who had come to bid Gloria good-bye.

It was a lenghty ceremony, the first Catholic funeral many of her friends had attended. Their interest was held by the statues lining the walls and by what Rose called "the show" that was presented, and she had to be forcibly restrained when the priest intoned that he "was certain that Gloria Jones's sins had been forgiven and that she would soon be in Heaven."

Later at Holly's house where they had gathered Rose sputtered, "Sins! What possible sin was Gloria ever guilty of except for being too saintly for her own good. And just what did that priest mean saying that she would soon be in Heaven? For goodness sake! What would keep her out? Honestly..."

Daisy interjected, "Rose, calm down. Don't get yourself all excited. That's the way they believe."

Laurel changed the subject. "What on earth will Neville do with eight kids to take care of? The baby is not well and the younger ones need constant looking after. Sure, the older ones can help, but someone has to take charge. Her mother is too old to take on something that strenuous."

Sunny said, "Randy is so dejected about her death. He tried so hard more than once to help her and to save her life at the end. She just wouldn't listen to him; then it was too late. It is so sad."

Holly nodded. "Randy did everything he could. He's lost patients before, but this has really gotten him down. Losing a friend is devastating. Do you realize that out of the original nine of us there are only five left. What is happening to us?"

Rose angrily spat the words, "Maybe we're getting old."

By 1940 Holly's family was further diminished and only the aging Madge and Opal remained in the family home. They continued to take in boarders but hired the help necessary to maintain it and to keep it running smoothly. Holly felt guilty about the situation but was reassured by Opal.

She said that she and Madge enjoyed their boarders and that it was very nice to be waited on and to have someone else do all the work.

In that same year the Campbell Park band shell was built not far from where Holly grew up. It pleased her to see that the area remained beautiful and pleasant with band concerts and other events which were held there. Huron's educational system was of the highest quality and it led the way in the Midwest in initiating Parent Teacher conferences, a staple in education and information.

On Armistice Day winter returned to normal with bitter cold and snow as a blizzard blew out of Montana, plunging temperatures to twenty-one degrees below zero and causing thousands of dollars in damage to telephone lines which buckled from the weight of the sleet which covered them.

And in 1940 a brothel sprang up north of town across the tracks. It was whispered that it was Butch's doing and, worse, that Miss Janet Moselle was the madame in charge of both of Butch's illegal operations: His big house which he built at the end of World War I, around which rumors abounded concerning bootlegging and prostitution and gambling, and the brothel.

The friends were aghast at the news. Holly said emphatically, "Oh I can't believe that. Miss Moselle would never be a part of anything so disgusting."

"No one ever sees her," said Rose. "In fact, no one seems to know what happened to her. Maybe it is true."

"Well," said Daisy. "We know she had practice in that sort of thing." They looked at her, shocked. "You remember, when she bought some kind of birth control years ago."

"But isn't she too old for that? I mean, what man would —" Laurel's face turned red.

Daisy countered with, "You all know that a madame doesn't participate in the goings-on. She just sort of — runs things, keeps records, takes care of those fallen women."

"How does someone come to such an end?" asked Holly. "I just don't understand it at all."

Rose snapped, "Holly, sometimes you have your sensible head in the sand. Life is not always as we would like it to be. You worry too much."

Nonetheless, they pondered the life of Miss Moselle, their mentor for music and culture. She had imparted her knowledge to the young people of an earlier time and was now living in the depths of degradation. They also thanked their lucky stars for their fortunate circumstances.

In his 1940 Christmas card was a letter from Howard in Brookings written on the college's letterhead. Holly opened it eagerly, but her happy anticipation soon turned to dread as she read at the end of his letter:

"I don't know how to put this, so I shall just plunge ahead. Dwight and Albert have joined the Navy 'to do their part' is the way they put it, to get their service out of the way before the war scare gets more pronounced. They have put aside the rest of their college until the end of their enlistment. Gabrielle and I are heartbroken, as you can imagine, as we do not think the United States will get into any war. But they insist that they will be back in no time at all, that their service will fly by and they will return to resume their education. They have such brilliant minds. We hate to see it wasted in the military. I pray that what they believe will be so.

Wishing you and Jonathan a Merry Christmas,

Your brother, Howard"

On December 7, 1941, after vainly trying to ignore the possibility of getting involved in war for most of the year, the catastrophe of Pearl Harbor brought it painfully real to the United States, and the world erupted. Families experienced the grief of abruptly losing a loved one on a sunny Sunday morning in the most beautiful of spots, Hawaii.

Holly received a telegram from Howard and went numb reading his words, words which matter-of-factly told of the deaths of his only children, his two sons who had been together throughout their service and who had been on the battleship Arizona which sank to the bottom of the harbor.

She collapsed in Jonathan's arms and cried, "How much more are we to endure? This is so unfair!"

They picked up Madge and Opal and drove to Brookings for the memorial service. Howard and Gabrielle welcomed them but they could not be comforted at the loss of Dwight and Albert.

"We don't even have their bodies," sobbed Gabrielle. "We never will. What are we to do?"

Holly stayed as placid as she could for Howard's sake, but as they prepared to return to Huron, Holly said in a low voice as she threw their few things in their suitcase, "My family is disappearing. Soon there will be no one left to show that we existed at all. Why? How could this happen to one family?"

Jonathan could not console her. Mingled with the sorrow was an anger he had never seen in his usually composed wife. She turned to him and said, her eyes blazing, "I'm glad we had no children. Glad! It would be inevitable that any child of mine would be torn from me. Dealing with death has become a way of life and I'm sick of it!"

They didn't speak on the way home. Madge and Opal were quiet in the back seat. Holly was rigid with rage beside Jonathan. He knew it would be futile just then to try to ease her distress, but it tore his heart to see Holly's handsome face so contorted.

123

Christmas that year was not a merry one for the people of the United States.

The hopes and optimism that followed the end of the Great Depression were crushed as the inevitability of a lengthy war became a fact. Fierce determination to avenge Pearl Harbor and to drive out the demonic forces of Hitler, Mussolini and Tojo swept the country. A strong patriotism rose from the ashes of despair of the Dirty Thirties and became the prevailing spirit of the people.

The Fortnightly was no exception. As the war in Europe and the Pacific continued, members pledged to buy Defense Bonds. Once again they brought the Red Cross alive with familiar efforts to aid the boys "over there". They became nurse's aides and participated in air raid warden duties. Rose thoroughly enjoyed donning a helmet and draping binoculars around her neck when it was her turn to be on duty to scan the skies for possible enemy attack. Her children were excited and proud of their mother's contribution to the war effort. The General Federation of Women's Clubs around the country were urged to "not bicker", that in unity there was strength, and to set an example in every community.

Everyone in Huron did their part. The athletic field on Huron College campus was converted to victory gardens. Almost every household had a victory garden, growing and preserving much of their own food, thereby releasing processed foods for the armed forces. Tin cans were collected to be added to other items of scrap metal to be used in building planes, tanks and weapons. Rationing was a necessity to conserve scarce products and to make sure that everyone got a fair share of the goods available. Ration books were issued entitling the bearer to purchase certain amounts of food, gas and other commodities.

For every pound of used fat brought to a butcher a housewife received two points in exchange to be used for meat. An "A" sticker on an automobile entitled a motorist to purchase three gallons of gas per week for necessary uses only, no joy riding. Tires were impossible to obtain, so recapped tires of synthetic rubber were used. The Firestone Store sold recapped tires for $7.00 each. Shoes were rationed and people were forced to have their old shoes resoled, often with a substance less than satisfactory, since rubber had gone to war. The Service Shoe Shop resoled patrons' shoes for $1.00 and they had plenty of customers. The Red Owl sold round steak at 26¢ a pound plus thirteen points. Lampes sold beef liver at 20¢ a pound plus four points. Jack's Market sold pork cutlets at 12¢ a pound plus three points. Sugar was at a premium and also rationed. Women who canned fruit in the fall cut back on the sugar used to make the syrup to sweeten it. Coffee was never wasted and used sparingly. And so it went.

Excitement occurred during that time, along with a tragedy, when a B-17 Flying Fortress crashed and burned southwest of Huron. It was to have

124

been a routine training flight from the Rapid City Air Force Base, but twelve young men died for their country without ever having gone off to war.

At the meeting of the Fortnightly in October, 1944, Maude Feinstein was absent, an unusual occurrence. She was one of the most faithful members, and had held the position of secretary many times. It fell to another member to read the minutes of the previous meeting and without Mrs. Feinstein's verve and flair for reading them they lost much of their impact. Holly decided to stop to see her on her way home from the meeting.

Dr. and Mrs. Feinstein lived in one of the old Victorian houses near the downtown area. The house and yard were kept in immaculate condition. She had been there a few times when the club meetings were held at the Feinstein home. It was furnished in a rather old-fashioned way, but it was tidy and pleasant. Holly was not sure just what she would say, but it was so unlike Mrs. Feinstein to not be at a meeting or to call to say she wouldn't be there.

She climbed the cement steps and knocked on the door. There was no answer and she decided against knocking again and turned to leave when the door opened and Mrs. Feinstein said, "Holly, hello. Come in."

Holly smiled at the older woman and entered the house.

"Mrs. Feinstein, I hope you will excuse me for coming over, but we missed you at the meeting. I thought I'd stop on my way home to see if you are all right."

Mrs. Feinstein led her into the living room and motioned for Holly to sit down. She had not yet looked directly into Holly's eyes. When they were seated Holly could see that she had been crying. Her face was wet with tears and her eyes were swollen.

"Oh dear. I am so sorry if I have come at the wrong time."

Mrs. Feinstein looked gratefully at Holly and said, "You have come at exactly the right time, Holly. I think you will understand." She wiped her eyes and said, "Dr. Feinstein and I have just learned the news from Poland, the homeland of our people. We are Jewish, as you know, and the news from Europe is terrifying, Hitler has been decimating Jews wherever he goes, set on conquering the whole of Europe, probably the entire world in his mad pursuit. Just recently, on October 2nd, he caused to be slaughtered 250,000 Poles in an uprising against him."

"How awful! Are any of your relatives among them?"

"That's what is so torturous. We don't know. We have no way of knowing. It happened in Warsaw where we both have family. It's terrible not knowing."

Tears flowed again and Holly was distressed to see what the war had done to a fine woman and her husband. Thousands of Polish people killed and for what? As if in answer to Holly's unspoken question Mrs. Feinstein said, "It's genocide. Hitler wants to purify — as he calls it — all people not acceptable in his eyes. They just happen to be Jews. We feel so helpless to do anything."

Holly felt helpless, too. When she left Mrs. Feinstein she appeared to have felt some better. She had fixed tea and they had visited for an hour while Mrs. Feinstein talked it all out. Holly didn't understand the antipathy toward Jews, but she could feel Mrs. Feinstein's pain. Surely such injustice would be halted. Certainly, sanity would prevail to stop such cruelty. Neither of the women knew just how long it would be before any justice was meted out and just how despicable the acts of Hitler would prove to be when the world finally learned the extent to which his madness reached. The world never forgot the Holocaust.

The war was traumatic for everyone. But eventually it ended. The war in Europe (VE Day) ended May 8, 1945. The war in the Pacific (VJ Day) ended September 12, 1945.

In Huron there was no State Fair in 1945.

As if to make a resounding end to all the travail, there was an earthquake in Huron in 1946, dropping temperatures for a time and creating an unusually brisk breeze. There were no casualties.

Shortly after the war Madge died at the age of 72 and Holly found that she had left her the family home. Opal insisted on remaining there, but was persuaded that it would be impossible to continue the operation of the house as she and Madge had done. So Opal reluctantly went to live with her little sister, Holly, and her husband Jonathan at their insistence. She didn't want to be a burden and puttered around the house while both of them were at their respective jobs.

Holly found that the family home which she now owned was in bad shape, too old to make any repairs feasible, plus being far too expensive if she did undertake them. One day Holly sadly sold the house to a developer who argued that the area would be an excellent place for new, smaller, compact homes, and the house was demolished. Johnathan insisted that Holly put the money in an account in her name alone, despite her protests that what was hers was also his.

Veterans came home at last. Their women came home as well; many of them had spent the war years working in defense plants, particularly in California.

They resumed their lives, but no one was ever the same.

Chapter 19

At war's end Holly was 52 years old. She had come to an acceptance of what life had done to her and to those she loved and no longer despaired. She counted her lucky stars, giving thanks in her prayers for the riches she possessed. The greatest of those riches was the love she shared with Jonathan and her friends. She had good health, security and a job she loved with a man she also loved, but she had made peace with that conundrum.

Dr. Randolph Thorne's practice had grown, as had his reputation as a dedicated, compassionate doctor. He still needed Holly; they worked as one, a team that knew what needed to be done for their patients. Their life together gave them immense satisfaction in their compatibility and in being able to heal people or, at least to make them feel better. When a patient died it still affected Randy, and Holly would remind him, "You can't save them all. Everybody dies." Yet she knew that a true physician wanted to heal, to see a recovery.

The country also healed after World War II, the war that had devastated the world and forever changed it. There was an eagerness to return to normal.

In Huron a badly needed new facility, St. John's Hospital, was begun by an order of the Franciscan Sisters from Chicago. It opened in 1947 just in time to admit the many patients who were stricken with poliomyelitis, commonly called infantile paralysis because children were most affected, even infants only months old. It struck mainly in the summer and during that year there were few areas in the United States that escaped the epidemic. Huron had its share of victims and swiftly 68 patients were admitted to the new hospital. The worst ones afflicted with the dreaded virus, a total of three at that time, were encased in iron lungs, tube-like machines in which the paralyzed patients lay with only their heads outside them. A bellows contraption beneath the iron lung forced air in and out of their lungs. Sometimes speaking and swallowing were affected in those patients. Arms and legs were exercised manually by nurses every day in a vain attempt to restore lost muscle function. Not many iron lung patients survived.

Holly said to Randy in consternation, "Those poor people. Will they regain the use of their limbs? Will they walk again? Will their withered arms function?"

Randy could only reply in frustration, "We just don't know, but we have the latest technology at our disposal. About all we can do is what we have done — bring down the fever, reduce the pain, and do our very best for them."

"Visitors complain that they catch themselves breathing along with those noisy, confounded machines. What a frightening illness this is — and so widespread."

Randy only shook his head.

Eventually, some of the worst affected were transferred to the Elizabeth Kenny Institute in Minneapolis, before the paralysis set in, for the new, controversial treatment of Sister Kenny from Australia. Chief nurses in Australia were called Sisters, which made for some confusion in the United States. Her use of hot, smelly, medicated packs on the affected limbs did not gain her the respect of American doctors at first, but the good results she obtained proved her method of treatment. The treatment reduced the spasms and shrinking and subsequent crippling of the affected muscles dramatically.

In 1947 there were more than 400 polio cases at Sioux Valley Hospital in Sioux Falls, one of the two largest cities in South Dakota. The epidemic peaked in 1948, but the decline in cases did not arrive soon enough for Laurel and Wendell Swanson.

They rushed into Dr. Thorne's office early one morning practically carrying Jennie, who was limp as a rag and crying softly.

"It hurts," she sobbed.

Holly quickly took them into the examining room and immediately ran for Randy.

"Randy, you must come right away. It's Jennie Swanson. Looks like polio to me."

He uttered an epithet and went with Holly at once. His fears were realized when he looked at her. She was writhing in pain, even though it was painful to move. Laurel and Wendell were trying to soothe her and looked up in relief as Randy and Holly rushed in.

"Something is terribly wrong. She is in so much pain. Her head aches and her joints are so stiff and each time we touch her it hurts. She woke up this way. Please tell us it's not ...."

"Let's have a look," Randy said kindly. "Please sit down and I'll examine her."

They reluctantly left her and sat down on chairs against the wall. Randy smiled at Jennie, his newest patient with the dread virus. She had grown into a beautiful young woman in the bloom of youth, not yet nineteen. Her dark eyes were full of pain; her black curls clung to her damp forehead. He helped her to lie down on the examining table but it was clear that every movement sent a stab of pain through her slight body. His touch was gentle, but Jennie cringed.

"It hurts all over," she cried.

He patted her hand and turned to her parents. To have to tell them that their daughter was another victim would be one of the hardest tasks he ever was forced to do. Putting off the inevitable and trying to appear calm he instructed Holly to administer aspirin, to wrap Jennie warmly and to fetch a wheelchair, even though he knew that she was fully aware of precisely what to do, and knowing that Holly understood.

Laurel and Wendell looked at him in fear. He could not muster a smile. He took a deep breath and said, "I'm sorry ...."

"No! No!" cried Laurel. "It can't be. Jennie is fully grown. It's children who get it. No, it must not be. Not my Jennie."

She clung to Wendell and sobbed.

"Don't cry, Mama," said Jennie in a small voice. "I'll be all right. Dr. Thorne will make me well. I know it." She looked beseechingly at Randy.

The weight of that hope and responsibility and the reality of the hopelessness of it lay heavy on his heart. But he managed a smile that didn't match his mood and said, "She will recover. It's just a matter of time before the fever and pain subside. Then we can determine how much crippling — if any ...." he added hurriedly as he saw the look of alarm on their faces. "It is entirely possible that Jennie will not have many adverse effects. Some patients come out of this with very little paralysis."

But he knew that she would be affected. He knew that the reality of their daughter's future would have to be doled out in doses. It was too cruel to have to absorb all the bad news at once .

Jennie was admitted to St. John's Hospital in the polio ward, the isolation area, and laid flat on her back, with not even a pillow at first. Later a small pillow would be allowed to relieve the strain on her neck. Dr. Thorne and Holly, along with her parents, appeared at her bedside shortly thereafter. Jennie was far from comfortable, but she brightened somewhat at seeing all of them.

In an attempt to be as optimistic as possible and to leave them with as much hope as he could, Randy said, "Some who come down with polio recover from the illness with little or no outward signs that they were stricken. Most have some paralysis which often diminishes, but which may require the use of crutches or braces. We can be thankful for one thing; at least it is not necessary to put Jennie in an iron lung."

He did not tell them that mortality was high in those patients. Holly looked at him in gratitude for the way he was handling the situation. It was very hard to see the suffering Laurel and her family were experiencing.

One day shortly afterward, on her way home from work, Holly stopped by the hospital for a brief visit with Jennie. She hoped she could cheer her up and tell her when they would eventually be moving her and that she could then have some company. She would be glad to be out of isolation. The risk of infection at the onset of infantile paralysis ran high during those years of the epidemic, and patients were isolated for the good of everyone.

As Holly passed the waiting room she saw Wendell seated alone with his head in his hands, his shoulders shaking in his grief. She went to him and sat beside him.

"Wendell, I am so sorry this had to happen to Jennie and to your family. She is such a sweet young woman. And she is stronger than you think. She will survive — it will work out somehow."

He looked at her. His face was twisted in anguish and wet with tears. She wanted to hold him, to comfort him.

He said, "Jennie is our life. She has brought so much joy to our family and now she is sick and will be crippled for the rest of her life. That beautiful child crippled! It's just not right. What did she do to have this terrible thing happen to her?"

"Wendell....."

He brushed away his tears with the sleeve of his work shirt. "I'll tell you something, Holly. If she doesn't get over this awful thing I don't know what I'll do. I love that child so."

"She is strong and she will manage."

He wasn't listening to her. He stared ahead out the window of the waiting room, not really seeing.

"I know Jennie isn't mine. I've always known. A man would have to be deaf, dumb and blind not to know. But I love her as if she was mine; I always have. How could anyone not love her? And I still love Laurel, in case you're wondering, and I've forgiven — him. I have a family that any man would be proud to have, a smart, loving wife, two great kids, the ideal family. Now this has to happen. Why?"

The following Saturday afternoon Laurel came to see Holly. They sat on the front porch in the warmth of the late sun. The bright landscape belied the sadness that oppressed the town and, in fact, the entire nation. Laurel was beyond comfort, more sad than when the two of them had their talk over coffee at The Tams so many years ago. The incident had not been mentioned to any one since that time. They sat on the wicker chairs and Laurel tried to speak, but tears soon filled her eyes and her voice broke .

"Holly, it's all my fault. I did this to Jennie. It's because of my foolishness and my selfishness. My silly vanity!"

"Laurel, you're talking nonsense."

"No, it's true. I brought on this tragedy. God is punishing me at last. God will not be mocked, Holly. I deserve whatever he does to me, but not through Jennie. It's too much."

Her sorrowful eyes looked straight into Holly's and Holly felt her pain. Tears streamed down Laurel's face, blurring her vision. She grabbed the heavy glasses off and dabbed at her cheeks. Anguished sobs emanated from her mouth as she stared guiltily at Holly, her confessor.

Holly got up and kneeled beside her, putting her arms around Laurel's shoulder. Laurel cried until she was spent.

"There, there. It's going to work out. You are much too distraught to think clearly. What happened to Jennie is in no way anybody's fault. Illness strikes people indiscriminately. We don't know much about polio and this is a real epidemic and all parts of the country have been hit. Some day it will be prevented and eliminated. In the meantime, innocent children are hurt, and that hurts us all."

Laurel lifted her head. Her eyes were swollen.

"I betrayed Wendell and this is my punishment. I just know it. I deserve it, but it is too much to have to take."

"Laurel dear, listen to me; you are not being punished. And you can bear it. You and Wendell will be given strength. He is miserable, too, and he needs you now more than ever. You mustn't foresake him. A lot is being required of you right now, I know, but remember your husband and daughter need you now, to say nothing of young Wendell."

"He's been so wonderful, such a source of strength. It's hard to realize he's a grown man now. He's so fond of Jennie and wants to be in the room with her, but they'll only let him stand in the doorway and look at her."

"You are very lucky to have him."

"Do you really think I can do this, Holly? I've never told Wendell about Jennie, you know."

"I know."

"He's a good man."

"Yes, Laurel, he's a good man."

They watched the sun go down like a red ball. Laurel gave a shuddering sigh and said, "Holly, you've been such a comfort. Thanks. What a good friend you've been to all of us over the years." She straightened, patted her hair, cleaned her tear streaked glasses and shoved them on her face. "All right. I'll take my punishment. I shall do the best I can. I owe it to my family; we'll stick together and beat this thing. Besides, Jennie mustn't see her mother in a perpetual state of quivering jello." She smiled. "Remember Myrtle's jello molds?"

Holly laughed softly. "How could we forget Myrtle's jello molds? Poor Myrtle. We were quite a group, weren't we? We still are."

Laurel stood up. "Yes, and thank God for you, Holly. You have held us all together. I do feel much better. It will be hard, very hard, but I'll do whatever it takes to make Jennie well again and to keep our family whole and together always."

They hugged and the friends parted. Laurel walked purposefully down the walk to the street to her car, giving Holly a smile and a wave.

When she had driven off Holly sighed and went into the house. She would have to see about getting a wheelchair and, with any luck in the near future, a pair of crutches. Jennie was going to need them.

It wasn't until 1951 that a vaccine made of three killed polio viruses was discovered. Dr. Jonas E. Salk came up with a safe and effective vaccine that he first tested on himself, his wife and his three sons. In 1954 a total of 1,830,000 school children were inoculated in a mass test throughout the nation. The test was entirely successful and, despite parents' reservations about purposely injecting their children with the "killed virus," it was only a matter of years before poliomyelitis was eradicated. Eventually the fear of the injections disappeared.

Thirty years later doctors would be perplexed when hundreds of thousands of polio survivors came to them with recurrent symptoms of the illness. They were not contagious, but pain and fatigue had returned along with difficulty of movement. They were forced to return to the use of wheelchairs, crutches and canes. These very real symptoms were devastating to patients who had formerly recovered and conquered polio, and were far more severe than the mere aging of the victims. Doctors who had never seen a polio patient finally diagnosed the ailment as "Post Polio Syndrome", which provided small comfort to those suffering from it, except to know that what they were experiencing was real and not "all in their heads" as they had first been told. The real blessing of the vaccine was that another crippling disease was eradicated.

In the late 1940s people hoped for a brighter future. In Huron a Sears & Roebuck store was welcomed, giving competition to Penneys with a new line of moderately priced merchandise. The Starlite Drive-In Theater opened and Rose complained that since her youngest was now driving, he and his girl friend were spending far too much time there.

"You know what those kids do out there," she said to Holly, her eyes flashing.

"Now, Rose, you were young once yourself and I can remember when you were pretty fresh at the Bijou."

"Well, that was different," she retorted.

The daughters of Holly's friends shopped at Sherman & Moe's drugstore and it was a popular gathering place for the young people with its soda fountain, still the same after years in business. It had a gumball machine and a nice glassed-in counter of toiletries and cosmetics.

Particularly popular was Evening in Paris, a potent perfume in dark blue bottles that was the rage for years. Cutex nail polish, especially in bright red, and Coty face powder completed the dressers of many of Huron's young women.

Women had grown used to working hard during the war and in earning their own money in factories and munitions plants. It was their money and they didn't have to account for it to anyone. When the war ended they were determined to keep on earning it. They saw nothing wrong with women working outside the home, but they ran into stiff opposition and resentment, with dire prophesies of their children being neglected and the weakening of the father's role in the family. In some cases the prophesies came true, but on the whole, families survived and thrived.

When veterans returned from the war there were postponed weddings finally being performed; they married the ones they left behind. The weddings were austere, because no one could yet afford the customary traditional wedding with a large guest list, the bride's white gown and veil and the many bridesmaids. Men and women took up the lives they had hoped for before the war changed everything. Most marriages lasted, but some fell by the wayside. Divorce became more accepted, not the disgrace it once had been.

Throughout the turmoil of the war years and adjusting to new lives most people hung on to the values they grew up with, although there was a feeling that they were a minority, with the majority living lives that reflected a more broadminded view of life and love.

Holly had no trouble keeping her values intact, but she was getting tired.

PART III
FALLING PETALS

Chapter 20

It was July 31, 1953, Holly's 60th birthday. She awoke early and considered the busy day that lay ahead of her. As much as she shied away from her birthday celebrations, family and friends insisted on making more of them than she wished. But this day was certainly a milestone and she would make the best of it.

It was Friday and Randy had given her the day off.

She had objected, "That's not necessary. It's just another day and I really don't mind coming to work."

"Take the time; enjoy yourself. Consider it a birthday gift if you like. Stephanie agrees with me. She can handle the office without you," he replied, not knowing what his words did to her.

If Holly thought seriously about it she knew very well that Stephanie could handle it. She was a very capable young woman, not a nurse but indispensable in running the busy office and in keeping records up to date, tasks Holly had long ago relinquished. Stephanie was attractive, in addition to her clerical attributes, and Holly had to be very stern with herself when she admitted that she just might be a trifle jealous, because she and Randy had a good rapport. Get over it, she told herself. You are behaving like a silly old woman. She was forced to admit that the young woman was a distinct asset and that Randy displayed no interest in her other than the excellent manner in which she did her job. All three of them got along admirably. Besides, she rationalized, she wasn't that old, not yet anyway.

Holly got out of bed and walked to the pleasant bathroom next to the bedroom. How lucky she was. She loved her comfortable home. Jonathan was so good to her. Actually, he spoiled her and she loved it. She washed the sleep from her eyes and before she left the room she surveyed herself in the large mirror. Yes, the image seemed to say, she really was 60 that day, but her bearing was still gracefully erect. She had gained very little weight over the years. Her thick hair was generously streaked with gray. She avoided looking at the lines around her eyes and mouth. With a sigh she returned to the bedroom and put on her light nylon robe and walked onto

The poor mailman & Opal

the open porch shaded by the trellis. Twining Boston Ivy covered it and she stepped confidently outside. No one would know she was there. The vine quickly took over anywhere it found easy access to climb, but she loved the cover it gave and the shade, plus the mass of red leaves in the fall, which provided a brilliant display of color.

July had been hot and humid, as usual in South Dakota. The night had not cooled down much, but the early morning was fresh. She looked out at the familiar scene before her and smiled in contentment. How peaceful it was, so quiet. The neighborhood consisted of moderately priced homes in an older part of town filled with families and happy children. The return to normalcy once again felt good, since the Korean War had ended only days before. Everyone fervently prayed it would be the last war they would have to endure. The sons of her friends had escaped being drawn into the war, for which they were all grateful. She shared Sunny's feelings about her oldest, Scott, who could continue his education.

Sunny had said with feeling, "Who on earth ever heard of Korea anyway? And there are two of them, north and south, just like our own Civil War. Good night! When will the nonsense of making war end?"

Scott looked so much like his father that Holly's heart gave a leap whenever she looked at him. A sweet nostalgia swept over her, a painful reminder of her ever-present feelings for Randy.

She stretched leisurely in the morning air. She might as well enjoy the day. She was 60 no matter if she celebrated or not. It would be another scorcher and too hot to move very fast. Randy's office was air-conditioned and she really wouldn't have minded going in to work. Jonathan was thinking about adding air conditioning to their house, but the idea of those ugly machines in the windows did not appeal to Holly. The ceilings were high and a good fan kept the rooms comfortable if the house was shut up in time in the morning and the hot prairie wind was kept out.

Her long stretch was interrupted by Jonathan's loving arms as he appeared behind her.

"Happy birthday, my dear," he said.

He turned her around and kissed her soundly.

"Jonathan, what if someone sees us?" she asked, slightly flustered.

"Holly dear, are you still worried about what other people might be thinking? At this stage in our lives why should it matter one whit?"

"You are absolutely right," she said with a happy smile and hugged him closely and kissed him just as soundly.

He grinned at her. "Well, I certainly don't feel like I had just kissed an old woman, considering my own advanced age."

He didn't appear to be ten years her senior and she counted herself to be one of the lucky women in having such an attentive, passionate husband after almost thirty years of marriage.

"Come on, I'll fix breakfast," he said.

"Jonathan, I can do it. Just let me get dressed."

"Nothing doing. It's your birthday and I'll fix breakfast. Come the way you are."

Her day was starting out nicely. Breakfast from her adoring husband. Lunch with Sunny, Rose, Laurel and Daisy. Supper prepared by Opal, then an evening of cards with Sunny and Randy. She would surely have to fast for a few days after all of the festivities.

After breakfast Holly enjoyed a long tepid bath with plenty of scented bubbles to prepare for the rest of the day. She declined Jonathan's optimistic offer to wash her back, because she knew what that would lead to and, besides, she wanted to soak and think. She was going to step over another dividing line in her life and she needed to ponder a few things.

She dressed carefully in one of her soft chiffon dresses. She enclosed her waist with a beaded belt which combined nicely with the necklace of glittering stones that Jonathan had fastened around her neck. She added a touch of makeup and, having become thoroughly relaxed and assured by Jonathan that she would be the most beautiful woman at the lunch, she decided that she looked not bad.

When she left the house the heat was heavy in the air. The girls were meeting at the airport cafe, arriving separately in their individual cars. The airport was a few miles north on the flat, treeless prairie. The drive was short but uncomfortably hot and she was glad when she reached the cool oasis of the air conditioned cafe. Their decision to have lunch at Charlotte's Cafe came about because of its good food and also because the five of them had had ample quantities of birthday cake in their lifetimes, so they would enjoy the apple dumplings which were a popular feature.

Laurel made the reservation and requested a corner table so they would have privacy while the five of them celebrated "the onset of our old age" as she laughingly put it. Holly was the last of them to turn 60. When she arrived the others waved merrily to her. She joined them in the corner away from the wide windows where waves of heat emanated from the outside, even though the blinds were drawn.

"Happy Birthday!" came from the girls as the other diners turned to see who the celebrants were. Orders for lunch had been given and they sat back and sipped iced tea in a cold glass graced with a slice of lemon. They gradually cooled off.

"This is for you, Holly," said Daisy as she placed a gaily wrapped package before her.

"You know we don't exchange gifts," Holly said.

"It's not much. We just wanted to give you a little something, one that you can ...."

"Daisy, don't tell her what it is."

Holly unwrapped what looked like a small book, only it was filled with blank pages.

"You can put down your remembrances, as I was about to say before I was interrupted," said Daisy.

"Thank you, all of you. I'm not much of a writer, but I do want others to know the things of importance to me. I'll fill it with my thoughts, starting today."

They had become closer over the years, realizing their own mortality as people they loved died. They were important to each other, having shared love and friendship since they were children. Joy, heartache and disaster had touched them all and they knew they could count on the others when they were needed.

They continued as members of the Huron Fortnightly, but had fewer duties, declining election to the club's offices, deferring to younger members who brought new life to the club's continuing good works. Membership had remained stable, with two delegates to the annual state convention. Interest had been high when the 50th anniversary of the General Federation of Women's Clubs was celebrated in 1949. It was held in Mitchell and was a high point in the years of its existence. The delegates returned with gold colored booklets of the history of the activities and accomplishments over the previous 50 years and filled with messages from former presidents.

Holly was at ease with her cool drink and gazed with affection at her friends. Daisy was slender and spritely. She had been compelled to wear glasses and complained bitterly about it, but if she was to continue with her reading and study she had to be able to see. Laurel laughed at her, telling her that she had worn those awful thick glasses ever since she could remember and thank goodness for modern technology because nowadays they didn't have to be as thick as they used to be.

Laurel was matronly, but still very pretty. She still made use of her brilliant mind. They were glad to see that she had lost the tense, nervous look she once had. Only Holly knew that she and Wendell had their talk, declared their love for one another and, along with young Wendell, had come to terms with Jennie's crippled condition. The composure on Laurel's face softened the lines that her previous guilt and worry had put there.

Sunny was tall and slender, as was Holly, and the two of them still caused heads to turn with the stately bearings they were born with. Sunny's golden hair was streaked with silver, enhancing her elegance.

Rose was heavier than she ever had been and, with her short stature, looked like a cuddly doll. Her fading red hair shone beneath a sheen of white. Her bright eyes betrayed her prickly nature. Rose was the only one of them who had taken a job, except for Holly's nursing career.

Rose said she needed something to keep her occupied, now that the children were grown and Clarence was thinking of retirement. She wasn't sure she would like his being at home all the time. She smugly informed them that *The Huronite* had taken her on part-time to write human interest stories.

"It's pretty tame stuff and they are not to be opinion pieces, but I can usually sneak in something. I never run out of something to say," she declared. She received a small remuneration on whatever they accepted. "Small is right," she said indignantly.

They laughed at their roly-poly friend who exuded enthusiasm and the courage to say what she thought, although her tongue got her into hot water more than once. For all of her energy Rose put on pounds, but as Sunny expressed it, "She's so darn cute."

They devoured a large salad and relished the delicious apple dumplings and another glass of iced tea and reluctantly concluded their time together. Each of them had duties that demanded their attention. Laurel had to pick up Jennie from her job at the library, a job where she could remain seated for much of the time. She moved around quite well and her improvement had been steady since her bout with polio five years before. She had discarded the crutches and had a limp, which bothered her family more than it did Jennie. Laurel had become so proud of her and of how she managed her life. She was 25 and had become independent and, although she still lived at home under the protective care of her parents, she talked of moving to her own apartment. This was causing some consternation, but she assured them that she could manage just fine. In addition, she had met a nice young man, which only increased her parents' worry. They had taken care of her for so long that they feared no one else could do so properly. Her friends tried to make Laurel see that it was time to let go. Jennie was a grown woman and needed to try her wings.

Daisy commented that she understood Laurel's feelings because many of the female students no longer lived at home even when they attended college right there in Huron. Huron College had dormitory rooms for 99 girls, which caused some distress in parents. But, she added, it was a modern time and such was progress. Daisy had to go to a tea of the professors' wives and it was at the president's home so she had to be there, but she said she had imbibed more than her share of tea that day. She would just sit still and listen. Her friends could not imagine that she would really just sit still and listen, knowing Daisy's affinity for good conversation. It was taken for granted that Melvin would be fending for himself at supper time.

Rose said she had to do some writing. She clearly enjoyed her avocation. It was with relish that she confided that it would, of course, be in accordance with the limited boundaries of *The Huronite* but she had a project she was working on, a news story that would set the town of Huron on its heels. It would be a front page story, not a small column that would be put wherever it could fit in. Her energy was enviable, but the others were eager to return to their homes and change clothes.

Holly and Sunny were the last of them to exit the cafe, waving to the others as they hurried through the shimmering heat and got into their cars and vainly tried to wave the heated air through the windows.

"We'll see you tonight; please don't fix anything to eat," implored Sunny with a groan."

"Opal is taking care of everything. I so wish she wouldn't fuss, but she is so eager to please. She seems to want to justify her living with Jonathan and me. I just don't have the heart to dissuade her. But I'll try to hold her down on the refreshments. Wear something comfortable. No need to dress up to play cards."

As Holly drove up to her house she was startled to see Opal brandishing the garden hose at a confused mailman who was being soaked in the process. She jumped from the car and ran to the side of the house.

Opal was not a large woman. She was in her mid-seventies and had long ago given up trying to keep up with fashion because she considered most of it to be immodest. She still wore her dresses long, well below the calf. Her footwear was the old-fashioned kind with a medium heel and laces well over the top. Her white hair was piled on top of her head in a neat twist. But Opal was feisty. It was clear that something had upset her.

As Holly approached she could see that Opal was wielding the garden hose wildly about and that the water was turned on full blast. The mailman looked about to drown. No matter which way he turned he was assailed with a stream of water. Water dripped from his cap and he was frantically trying to shield his mailbag from being filled and ruining the mail of the United States Post Office.

Holly quickly turned off the water. It was the only way she could get Opal's attention.

"What on earth is going on?" she asked, endeavoring to look stern but not succeeding very well. Opal's determined face filled with annoyance stared into the flustered expression of the mailman's.

He said, totally unnerved, "I really apologize, Mrs. Hoekstra, but I was only trying to get a drink of water. Didn't want to bother anybody. This heat gives a body a thirst."

"Well, why didn't you just ask?" said Opal, completely out of sorts. She added to Holly, "I had gotten the house all ready and the yard all picked up and had just chased some of the kids away because they were playing with our garden hose. You know how they like to tease me, don't you Holly? I just got inside when I heard the water running again and I took myself outside to put matters to right and shoo away those rascals. I turned on the hose as high as it would go to teach them a lesson and poor Mr. Murphy got all wet."

"Why didn't you just shut off the water, Opal dear?"

"It gushed out so hard I couldn't and then Mr. Murphy tried to get the hose away from me and I was trying to steady it and, mercy me, the poor man got soaked."

"I'm afraid some of the mail got wet, too," said Mr. Murphy. '

"I am very sorry about this, Mr. Murphy. And I know Opal is sorry, too, aren't you dear?"

Opal made an inaudible sound as she stared at the wet grass.

"Please come in and dry off, Mr. Murphy. And let me get you a cool drink of water."

"If it's all the same to you, Mam, I think I'd best be going. I'm late on my route as it is. I've got considerable mail left to deliver. Thanks anyway."

Mr. Murphy tipped his sodden cap as water trickled down his neck. He walked across the grass and continued down the sidewalk, shaking a leg as he went.

"Really, Opal, such a fuss. Poor Mr. Murphy is soaked to the skin."

"Did you see that, Holly? He cut right across the lawn — didn't use the sidewalk at all."

Holly laughed and led Opal back into the house. Despite her urging to not prepare a large meal there was pot roast with potatoes, onions and carrots baked with it, sliced tomatoes from the garden and baking powder biscuits. She had also baked Holly's favorite cake, white with a fluffy white frosting laden with coconut.

Supper was scheduled for 6:30 and Sunny and Randy arrived on time, along with Jonathan, who had driven up at the same time. Happy greetings were exchanged and Jonathan went upstairs to change from his white clothes, his pharmacy clothes he called them. The men were comfortable in short-sleeved shirts. Holly and Sunny had removed their confining hose and slipped into canvas sandals and sundresses. The house had become heated with Opal's cooking and baking, but a large revolving fan gave off a steady hum and a soothing breeze.

Opal soon called them to supper and flushed with pleasure at the exclamations of approval at her laden table set with the good china on the Irish linen. The men were ready for the robust fare which she had prepared, having worked hard all day. Sunny and Holly took small portions, enough to not hurt Opal's feelings, but not too much after their ample lunch. Opal joined them at the table but leaped to her sturdily shod feet regularly to serve them. But Sunny overrode her refusals for any help and helped her clear the table and serve the cake. Opal's energy seemed to be unflagging from the compliments heaped upon her. They could hear the clatter of dishes being washed from the closed kitchen door.

"Now that's what I call celebrating a birthday," said Jonathan, squeezing Holly's hand and smiling at her with affection. "All day without having to lift a finger."

"It's really been grand, but Opal works far too hard and I can't make her slow down," said Holly. She chuckled and related Opal's misadventure of the afternoon with the hose. They joined in her laughter. Despite her age, Holly's older sister had spirit.

They reminisced, as older folks are likely to do. Daum's Auditorium had been demolished in 1950 marking the end of an era.

Sunny commented, "Daum's held so many good times. Remember when Lawrence Welk played there? He was very young, but just think, he's famous now."

"Huron needs a larger place. The town must be 12,000 now, and we have the new arena which is more suitable, plus we get the state basketball tournaments with all the revenue it generates. Sioux Falls doesn't even have an arena for all its size," said Randy.

Jonathan gave Holly a look. "Well, one thing that hasn't changed over the years is our wives. They have only become more dear. "

"Jonathan, you must stop; you're embarrassing me."

"But isn't it nice to hear?" replied Sunny. "Randy says nice things like that all the time."

Holly quickly squelched an unseemly reaction to Sunny's words and said briskly, "Well then, are we ready for some cards? I think Sunny and I can easily take on the two of you flatterers. Since I am the birthday girl — and I use the term lightly — I get to choose, and I choose gin rummy."

They retired to the living room where the card table and chairs were set up and were soon engrossed in a battle of wits. Opal emerged from the warm kitchen, set the dining room to rights and joined them, plopping herself down in one of the easy chairs. She was soon fast asleep, oblivious to the amiable chatter around her.

It was almost 11:00 o'clock when Sunny and Randy departed after hugs all around and promises to get together again soon. Holly submerged her pleasure of being in Randy's arms briefly, but it remained with her long after the door had shut, the lights were turned out and Opal was roused from her nap and led into her bedroom.

Only then did she tuck the memory safely away into her mind to recall. She gave her full attention to her husband as he took her into his arms and she was hearing him whisper, "I do cherish you."

In their bed she relaxed as a cool breeze wafted through the window and let the tiredness drain her body. She had had quite a day. Sixty years of her life had gone. Somehow it didn't seem that long. She counted herself a fortunate woman and she looked forward to the future, which held so much promise. She wondered how many more years there might be.

Chapter 21

Jonathan was twirling Holly around the living room as the phonograph played 'Dancing in the Dark.' Holding her closely and murmuring endearing words of love in her ear. Holly's dancing skills were still intact and she was enthusiastically responding to her madcap husband. It was their 30th wedding anniversary. They were thankful for a quiet evening at home and that they had not mentioned the date to their friends and that it had not occurred to any of them to observe it.

"I want you all to myself," he had said. "We have both been far too occupied; we need some togetherness."

She had happily agreed. Opal, true to form, had prepared a romantic dinner, complete with candles set precisely on the Irish linen, used only on special occasions. She disappeared into the kitchen behind the door and left them alone. They urged her to join them but, as she quaintly put it, she knew when to "make herself scarce".

They enjoyed having Opal with them, but occasionally she got a little confused and they found it necessary to keep track of her, something they had not had to do. She would be forgetful and it became necessary for Holly to remind her sometimes to bathe.

"You have your own bathroom, Opal dear. Please feel free to use it as often as you like."

"I don't want to run up your water bill."

"Nonsense. Use all the water you want. And please, remember to put your soiled clothes in the hamper."

Opal thought nothing of wearing her clothes for days at a time; then Holly would lead her into her room and insist that she bathe and put on fresh clothing. On the day of their 30th anniversary Opal was alert and receptive, her usual competent self.

Jonathan was in high spirits. He was in good health and loved his job at Sherman and Moe's pharmacy. He had an able young assistant who eagerly awaited Jonathan's retirement. He often stressed the advantages of Social Security, a dandy program for old people. Jonathan did not look his age, which he credited to Holly's good care, but he wanted to work until he was 72, at which time he would draw his hard-earned social security and also be allowed to earn as much money as he pleased without his benefits being reduced. At that time he didn't know what else he would do, but he had fun leading the lad on. He would get his job soon enough.

Holly was also considering retiring. Jonathan looked forward to the time they would be together most of the time. They had married late in life and he had plans for activities to enjoy while they could. They had never taken a lengthy vacation. They had heavy work loads, plus being involved with the activities of their close friends. They had visited the Black Hills in the western part of the state, of course, and planned to make it a yearly event. And when Jonathan's sister in Michigan died they flew there for the funeral and spent a few days while Jonathan took care of her affairs. They took time to drive around briefly and the sight of Lake Michigan took their breath away.

"Just look at all the water, Jonathan, and those waves! It's more like an ocean," exclaimed Holly.

Jonathan had many plans for their future and his enthusiasm was shared by Holly. She could still work part-time and fill in when needed. Some of the younger patients at the office thought she was too old to be a nurse. They didn't feel that way toward Dr. Randolph Thorne. He was a mature, wise physician in their eyes and doctors were supposed to be of an age. It all made Holly smile. To her, Randy was still the handsome man she had loved for years. His glasses were stronger with bifocal lenses and his posture was not as straight, but to her there was no change.

She loved her husband, too, and as the years went by she loved him even more. She loved him very much. She was perplexed by this unnatural state of affairs. The girls seemed to have forgotten all about it or dismissed it from their minds; they seemed unaware of Holly's continuing dilemma, but for Holly there was no solution. Was it sinful for her not to feel a vestige of guilt? Am I deceiving Jonathan, the finest husband a woman could have? Will God punish me? Laurel was sure God was punishing her for her infidelity. But that was different. Wasn't it? Or is my behavior as deviant?

Holly's notion of deviant behavior certainly did not fit the definition of the word and, despite her age, she was comparatively naive. She was a decent, caring woman who lived by her values, the values instilled in her by her parents. Eventually, she gave up trying to solve the puzzle and considered herself enriched by the love she felt for both of them.

Their dance did not seem to be tiring Jonathan but it was wearing out Holly. After several whirls to 'Dancing in the Dark' and 'You'd be so Easy to Love' Holly flung herself onto the sofa.

"Enough! Jonathan, where do you get all that energy?"

"I think it's the company I keep," he smiled.

His adoring good nature melted her rapidly beating heart. She stretched out her arms to him. He sat beside her and drew her into his arms and they breathed deeply from their exertion, content and at peace with the world as the phonograph ran down.

On a Saturday afternoon a few days later in late October Holly answered the ring of the telephone. It was Rose.

"Holly, I need to talk to you and I don't want to do it over the telephone."

Her voice held an urgent conspiratorial tone which intrigued Holly. She told Rose to come over and she put on the coffee pot to await her arrival.

Rose soon appeared in the driveway and left her car in such an obvious attempt to look nonchalant that Holly had to laugh. Despite Rose's rotundity she bounded up the steps to greet Holly.

She marched inside and said, "Good. Coffee. I have a lot to tell you." Without urging she walked to the kitchen and closed the door.

"Where's Opal?" she asked.

"Opal is taking her nap. You can speak freely. Rose, what on earth is so important that you couldn't tell me on the telephone?"

She set a cup of coffee in front of her and Rose helped herself to one of Opal's oatmeal cookies.

"Well," she said leaning forward in her chair. "Remember when I said I was working on a news story?"

Holly nodded and sipped her coffee.

"It's an expose of sorts. About Butch."

She paused and looked at Holly for her reaction. She wasn't disappointed. Holly's mouth dropped and she put down her cup.

"Rose! You're not!"

"Yes. I've been working on this for almost a year . It has to be accurate. No one has ever been able to get the goods on that awful man. He's gotten away with every offense in the book and no one, not even the law — or should I say, especially the law — has been able to do anything about it. Well, I've kept my eyes and ears open in driving around Huron getting my stories for the paper, human interest mostly, just mundane stuff, and I've also done research at *The Huronite* in their old newspaper files. Older folks, business people who have been around for years know more than they've been willing to tell about Butch and his operations, which, by the way, includes gambling."

"But Rose ...."

"Oh I've been careful and no one has any idea of what I'm on to. You know how men think. What does a woman know? Or what would she do with it if she understood it? The usual mindset of the, male animal. I declare, Holly, one of these days I'm going to prove to all of them — I swear I'm going to write ...."

"Get on with it, Rose."

"Right. Well, Butch doesn't have any interest in the brewery anymore, but I learned from reliable sources — I love to say that," she giggled. "I've learned that he's still in that ugly house that he built decades ago and he still owns the brothel, but this is 1954 after all, and he is still guilty of plenty of offenses, beginning with Violet's death, as far as I know, and I believe I have enough on him to bring him to the attention of the state, maybe even the federal authorities. He'd get his comeuppance at last and I'd get a top notch story which would be an asset for further writing, to say nothing of being rid of that man."

"It sounds mighty dangerous to me Rose. Have you thought this out? I mean really thought about it? And what in Heaven's name do you expect to do to accomplish all this? Surely what you've found out must be a matter of record."

"It is a matter of record and the people I've talked to in regard to Butch swore me to secrecy about where I got my information. They wouldn't talk to me unless I promised to not use their names — they're still that afraid of him."

"Why don't you enlist the help of the police? You say you have all the evidence."

"Holly, I need more proof. I need photographs, real proof. I've caught a glimpse of Butch — he's really disgusting looking — a perfect shot if I had my camera with me. A recent photograph of him would add a lot to my article. But it was in broad daylight and he would have spied me taking his picture. Even I wouldn't be that foolhardy."

"Rose, what on earth could I do that would help you, and I'm not so sure I'd be willing to."

"I need to get some photos and I need to get them very soon. I need you to come with me. I have a great new camera with an attachment to take pictures in dim light. I spent all my money on it, even my grocery money. I don't want to get caught, of course, so I'm going to do it at night. And I need you along to drive my car and be my lookout while I snap them. They will be the clincher to my story. Please say you'll do it. It would be of enormous help."

"Oh, Rose, I don't know."

"Come on Holly. Where's your spirit of adventure?"

If Holly ever had a spirit of adventure it had vanished long ago. She was about to turn Rose down in no uncertain terms, but Rose kept up the pressure, giving all of her reasons for needing Holly's assistance to complete her project. She said there would be absolutely no risk. She just wanted to get some photographs and return to town; that was all. The weather would be turning soon and she couldn't wait until spring. It demanded immediate attention. All that was missing were the incriminating pictures she would get. She didn't even have to tell Jonathan. After all, she reasoned, how could he worry if he didn't know what she was up to?

In the end, Holly grudgingly agreed to drive Rose's car. When she asked when Rose wanted to do it she replied that very night after supper.

Holly gasped, "Tonight? So soon?"

"Yes. I found out that once a week dumb old Butch — remember when we called him that, dumb old Butch?" Rose chuckled. "Once a week on Saturday night Butch goes to the brothel and checks on — things. If I could get pictures of his coming and going and maybe even of some of the customers — Holly did you ever wonder just who the customers are? Haven't you been the least bit curious?"

Holly was getting exasperated. She certainly could not let Rose go on this fool's errand alone.

She said, "All right. I don't like this one bit, but you can't go out there by yourself. When are you going to pick me up?"

"Nine o'clock."

"But at that hour what on earth shall I tell Jonathan?"

"Just tell him we're going to the second show at the State."

"I can't lie to him."

"OK. Then we'll buy tickets, go into the theater and leave again. That way you won't be lying."

Holly sighed and wondered what she was getting herself into. She also wondered if Rose had told her everything, because she knew Rose and her persuasive ways. She would withhold anything that would lead to Holly's refusal.

Shortly before nine o'clock Rose drove up and Holly kissed Jonathan goodnight. Saturdays were busy at the drugstore and when he came home he was tired. He liked to read the paper, listen to the radio and go to bed. He was regularly lulled to sleep in his chair while listening to a symphony broadcast from Minneapolis or St. Louis. "Have a good time," was all he said. Holly was filled with guilt for deceiving him as she and Rose left the house. He didn't even ask where they were going, so trusting was he, so they didn't follow through on the charade of buying movie tickets.

It had cooled off considerably and the wind was brisk. They got into Rose's car and headed east. Rose said they would go by way of the brewery. Holly was filled with apprehension.

The brewery was located on the east side of the James River. It was a towering structure on a hill. Two big ice houses and a wash house sat adjacent to it. On the other side of the road was an irregular pile of large rocks settled against the hill as they made their approach. Blume's Brewery had closed after the war. There had been a series of owners and Butch had not been an employee "a man of property", as he used to call himself, for many years. Why Rose thought he might be in the area was beyond Holly; she

147

could easily have gotten a photograph in the daylight. But she was going to keep her head and see to it that Rose did not get too capricious and put both of them in danger or, at the very least, in an awkward situation. Someone had to be in control and Holly figured she was it.

The October night was getting colder and was black as pitch. Holly grew uneasy. Making matters worse, the wind which had picked up all day had blown up a storm, the first of the season. They could see the trees near the brewery begin to bend and sway from the force. They heard thunder and the blackness was punctuated with streaks of lightning which illuminated the road ahead as if it were daylight.

"Rose, don't you think we should do this another time? How can you get any decent pictures in this weather?" Holly said nervously.

"We're here, aren't we? Might as well do what we came to do."

Lightning lit up the road ahead of them. The car's headlights shone on the steep hill. They could see the brewery at the top, stark and forbidding against the black sky. A swirl of dry leaves swept across the road. Rose pulled over and turned off the headlights and the ignition. Except for the roar of the storm it was eerily quiet.

Holly said in alarm, "What are you doing?"

"We can't be seen. The lights will give us away."

"Rose, I just don't like this."

"Holly, you are such a worry wart."

"And you, Rose Koning, are getting more reckless with age," Holly retorted.

Rose switched on the overhead light and was adjusting her state-of-the-art camera.

"Butch's ugly house is just over the hill. As soon as I'm all set we'll trade places; you'll drive slowly to the house and I'll get out and quietly take my pictures. If he or any — that is, if he's not there, we'll drive to the brothel."

"Oh Rose, you can't be serious."

She switched off the overhead light and said, "OK, I'm ready. Let's trade places."

Holly sighed in resignation, they got out, taking care to not slam the doors, and got in on the opposite sides. Holly wished with all her heart that she was home with Jonathan.

Rose whispered, "Now, start the car quietly — don't turn on the lights — and we'll creep up the hill and sort of glide over and — Oh God!"

They stifled a scream. A wide flash of lightning lit up the blackness with an accompanying loud bang of thunder. Silhouetted against the blackness on top of the hill, clearly outlined, was a huge man staggering under the weight of what looked like a body. Another lightning stab revealed the man to be Butch, weaving and raging unheard obscenities as he stood

148

against the wind whipping at him. All at once he stopped and raised the body above his head. It looked like the lifeless form of a woman. They gasped as the violent storm seemed to direct its fury toward Butch when he looked straight at them. His red eyes bored into them and he dropped the body. He swayed and continued to mouth his maledictions and started to take a step down the hill toward them. Suddenly a loud crack was heard in a brief lull in the night's turmoil and he stopped, then crumpled to the road and lay still.

Holly and Rose were rigid with the horror of what they had witnessed. It was as if the lightning had etched the image on their brains. They couldn't speak and let out their breath in a rush. They looked swiftly to their left from where the sound had emanated.

"Holly, that wasn't thunder. That was a gunshot," whispered Rose.

"I know. Rose, this is too much. Let's get out of here."

Rose made no objection. They said nothing as Holly backed silently down the hill until she could turn around. She turned on the car lights and drove as fast as she safely could back to town as rain and dead leaves hammered at the car.

Chapter 22

The next day the Sunday edition of *The Huronite* displayed a glaring headline in large capital letters.

LOCAL WOMEN WITNESS MURDER

Huron man Werner Bruno shot and killed

Two More Bodies Discovered

by Rose Koning

Late Saturday night during the violent thunderstorm which swept through Huron, a Huron man, Werner Bruno, known in this area as "Butch", was shot and killed in the vicinity of the old deserted Blume's Brewery, where he had formerly been employed.

The body of Janet Moselle was also found beside the body of Werner Bruno. Both appeared to be in their seventies. Both were long-time residents of Huron. Janet Moselle's body showed no sign of a gunshot wound.

The third body was discovered across the road from the brewery. It proved to be that of Eugene Crane, an elderly retired banker who had been a recluse for a number of years. Alongside the body of Eugene Crane lay an antiquated shotgun which appears to have been the murder weapon in the death of Werner Bruno.

Mrs. Jonathan Hoekstra and Mrs. Clarence Koning gave police eye witness accounts of the incident. Police did not say why the women were in the area.

Police are continuing their investigation.

"Incident! Is that what you call it, an incident! And did you have to bring our names into it?"

Holly was totally out of sorts with Rose. She raised her voice and accused her of a less than accurate account of what had happened. Rose quickly defended herself, pointing out that *The Huronite* was thrilled to have an eye witness account by one of their employees and had hired her on the spot to continue with a series of articles. She couldn't just leave Holly's name out.

They were exhausted and distraught, but Rose had recovered sufficiently to type her story for the Sunday edition of the paper. They had been up most of Saturday night being questioned by the police and undergoing further interrogation by their husbands who had been roused from sleep and confronted by policemen at their doors who requested their presence at the station where they would find their wives.

Holly had never been so embarrassed or humiliated, but Rose began to enjoy the situation. She had the upperhand in having witnessed what had happened and the sudden change in her plans had given her her big chance. Clarence found no comic relief in his wife's escapade and was as grave as she had ever seen him which made her more subdued. Jonathan was bewildered and disappointed in his wife, who was in tears and asking forgiveness for her actions, actions which were completely unlike her.

They gave their statements to the police as Jonathan and Clarence listened dumbfounded. Rose did most of the talking. Holly looked morose and sat staring at her clasped hands. The editor of *The Huronite* soon appeared, rumpled from dressing in haste, having been called by a young rookie reporter who had been assigned night duty at the police station. His excitement in his exclusive evaporated when the editor gave the entire story complete with a byline to Rose. He didn't hide his anger at the snub, but Rose didn't notice. She perked up at once. Holly just wanted to go home.

The Sunday issue caused the biggest stir Huron had seen in years. Daily issues sold out quickly. The lurid details came out over successive days and rumors abounded from people who remembered Butch from his younger days and the trouble he had caused. Old-timers nodded their heads and made somber pronouncements about how "the truth will come out" and "sooner or later misdeeds are punished". Everyone agreed they were glad that their old nemesis had received his just reward and was finally gone.

Rose's carefully worded articles held the front page for most of the week. She was proud of how she was handling the story, but she held back some of her notes which she had taken so long to gather. She planned to write a book soon and use the story, including additional information that only she had. Clarence came around to her thinking and took pride in her detective work and in how she had rebounded from the traumatic event which she had seen. Her zest for life was contagious.

But it did not rub off on Holly, who asked Rose in some irritation, "Really, Rose, is it necessary to dig this all up and to prolong it so with your piecemeal information?"

"Sure it is and I have the backing of the paper. It's really working, isn't it? I was the one who got to the bottom of what could have been a real mystery — the only one who was willing to do it, I might add. And it made me a full-fledged newspaper reporter, soon to be famous writer." She laughed.

Holly did understand, but she was as miserable as Rose was excited. Furthermore, whatever Rose wrote, everyone knew that Mrs. Jonathan Hoekstra had been accompanying her. She had embarrassed herself and her husband and she had betrayed his trust. She never imagined that she could do such a thing. She told him again that she was sorrier than he could ever know. His heart melted as she cried and he held her, comforted her, but she couldn't bring herself to forgive herself. She had been a part of a ghastly adventure. The town was abuzz with talk about her and Rose. Rose reveled in it, but Holly surely did not. She wanted to stay in the house and pull down the shades until the awful episode was forgotten, but Jonathan would have none of it.

"You can't hide, Holly dear. This will all blow over. You and Rose are not responsible for what happened. It was pure coincidence that you were there. And if you think about it, your being there has been of tremendous help to the police. Now please, just forget it."

She tried to forget but it was difficult on some days at the office. Everyone knew that Dr. Thorne's nurse had been out in a questionable part of town at night in a storm and looked at her in a different light. Randy knew she was distressed; he touched her shoulder and said, "You must ignore the curious who ask impertinent questions and stare. You know how people are — the gorier the news, the better. Some people have decidedly salacious natures."

"But it was so awful. We were terrified. He looked straight at us and he looked like he was about to start down the hill toward us. And poor Mr. Crane. I should have talked Rose out of her outrageous plan."

"You know that no one can talk Rose out of anything once she makes up her mind. Besides, if you hadn't seen what happened the police would not have wrapped up this mess so quickly."

She knew he was right, but her sensibilities had been shattered and she didn't like the feeling.

Monday's article contained additional information.

CORONER RELEASES FINDINGS IN MULTIPLE DEATHS
Police say deaths are related
by Rose Koning

The scene of the multiple deaths of Werner Bruno, Janet Moselle and Eugene Crane which occurred last Saturday night was gone over thoroughly by the Huron police. They issued a statement to the press giving their preliminary conclusions based on their findings and the coroner's report.

Police findings indicate that Werner Bruno was carrying the body of Janet Moselle at the time he was shot. A direct hit to the chest from a few yards away was the cause of death. The coroner states he died instantly.

The coroner's report states that Janet Moselle's death was due to strangulation. Further information is forthcoming concerning the reasons for her being in the company of Werner Bruno.

The report further states that the body of Eugene Crane showed no unusual marks except for a bad bruise on his right shoulder, probably caused by the kick of the shotgun when it was fired. The shotgun was found beside his body in a grouping of large rocks on the opposite side of the brewery where the shooting took place. His death was due to a massive heart attack. Eugene Crane had been in poor health for a number of years.

There is no information regarding the two eye witnesses, Mrs. Jonathan Hoekstra and Mrs. Clarence Koning, for being at the scene of the incident.

Further information is expected.

Photographs from the files of *The Huronite* accompanied the article. They had been on file for many years and were taken in the daylight when the buildings were newer. Rose complained that if only she could have gotten current pictures with her camera that night it would add a flavor to the article. Holly told her that in her case the images engraved on her brain would never leave her.

The Huronite's Tuesday article continued the unfolding of the grisly happening.

AUTHORITIES GIVE REASONS FOR RECENT DEATHS
Police plan further interrogation
by Rose Koning

Police believe they have uncovered the reasons for the deaths of Werner Bruno, Janet Moselle and Eugene Crane, all victims in last Saturday night's tragedy in the area of the abandoned Blume's Brewery.

From interviews with people who knew all three victims it was learned that Mr. Crane held Mr. Bruno responsible for the death of his daughter, Violet Crane, in a boating accident back in 1919. Violet Crane was the only child of Mr. Crane and the late Mrs. Crane. Authorities familiar with the incident maintain that there had been little to go on in order to prosecute Mr. Bruno at that time, although that decision has always been in dispute.

Ostensibly, Mr. Crane planned his course of action over a period of time. According to those who knew him, he had repeatedly urged authorities to bring Mr. Bruno to justice, often to the point of harassment. Reportedly, Mr. Crane had been obsessed with retribution for many years. Police found that the area around the rocks where his body was found contained evidence that he had concealed himself there more than once. Cigarette butts and trampled growth littered the rock-strewn area. The heavy rain on the night in question pounded this evidence firmly into the ground and in crevices between the rocks. The shotgun found next to Mr. Crane's body was clean and oiled despite its age. It had been fired once.

Police will be interrogating the women in Werner Bruno's employ.

"Too bad they can't interrogate the patrons of Butch's place," said Rose in contempt.

"Honestly Rose, you are really enjoying all of this notoriety, aren't you?" declared Holly in a fit of pique. "And why are you allowed to print all of that information. Aren't police investigations confidential?"

"Yes, except the parties are all dead and there is nothing further to investigate — no trial, nothing like that. And yes, I am enjoying this. Furthermore, I'm not finished yet."

Holly frowned at her. What had happened to her friend? She was turning into someone she didn't know.

The Wednesday edition's article gave readers more.

WOMAN INFORMANT COMES FORWARD
Gambling added to illegal activities
by Rose Koning

Police have gained more information concerning the three deaths last Saturday night. Known only as Tess, the woman came forward with pertinent details as to why Werner Bruno, Janet Moselle and Eugene Crane died. The woman had been employed at Mr. Bruno's brothel north of Huron.

Tess told a story of intimidation, illicit gambling and murder in connection with decades of prostitution.

Janet Moselle, former music teacher in the town of Huron, did not seem to fit into the tragic episode which has been unfolding. She was thought to have left town. Tess stated that Janet Moselle was Werner Bruno's confidant; she kept his books for each of his activities and knew all there was to know about his business. Tess did not know how or why she became associated with Mr. Bruno, but said that Janet Moselle was terrified of the man.

Tess told police that she saw Mr. Bruno kill Miss Moselle after a violent argument. He discovered that his trusted employee had amassed evidence and all the facts concerning his illegal activities, which included Werner Bruno's connections with eastern gambling syndicates. Tess witnessed Miss Moselle's murder when Mr. Bruno flew into a rage. He also accused Miss Moselle of stealing from him, despite her denying it, whereupon he threw her to the floor and strangled her.

Tess did not know Eugene Crane, but felt an obligation to come forward with what she knew, since all parties are deceased.

Police searched the two houses owned by Werner Bruno, but found little. They were deserted, with signs of hasty departures. They expect to search the area around the deserted brewery.

More details are expected.

The girls gathered at Holly's house. Rose had brought them to try to cheer her up.

Rose urged them and said, "I can't stand to see her so blue. She cannot see that this whole thing was just a big coincidence. Please come with me."

It was Holly's afternoon off and she welcomed them when she opened the door and saw their cheery faces. She couldn't help smiling back at them.

"I'm so glad to see you," she said.

Opal looked in from the kitchen and saw that she should make a pot of coffee. When they were seated Rose spoke.

"Holly, we've come on a mission of mercy. We can't stand to see you in such a state. We've got to make you see that you are entirely blameless in this whole crazy affair and all because of that dumb old Butch. It was my idea and all my fault for making you like this. I'm sorry. But it's over and you must get over it, too."

Daisy added, "I agree. I really don't see why you are so uptight about it. You actually did a service by being able to help the police."

"It's just that I don't usually behave so rashly," she answered them, looking apologetically at Rose. "And I deceived Jonathan."

Laurel said with fervor, "We all know what a fine man your husband is and know that he has forgiven you, if in fact he even blamed you at all. Come on, snap out of it."

Sunny added, "They're right, you know. No one is placing any blame or disrespect on you except yourself. You are far too hard on yourself, Holly."

Sunny rose to help Opal who was struggling through the kitchen door with a tray of coffee cups and a plate of her ginger cookies. She smiled in appreciation and couldn't figure out why the tray seemed so much heavier than it used to.

Rose lifted her cup and said, "To our good and faithful friend, Holly, who is much too sensitive for her own good."

They laughed and lifted their cups. Holly had to laugh in spite of herself.

Daisy said, "Werner Bruno — I didn't know that was Butch's real name. What a wasted life with nothing of value to show for it. I wonder why he was always so mean, so cruel?"

Laurel asked Rose, "How much longer are you going to drag out your articles? It's been almost a week now."

"It should make you all feel better to know that my last article on the subject appears in tonight's paper. They have found more bodies, you know."

"Rose, you scamp! How could we know?" scolded Sunny. "It seems to me that you have had far too much fun with this entire business. You are showing us a side of yourself that none of us has seen."

Rose gave a delighted whoop and her round body jiggled with mirth. "I know. And I'm loving it. The exclusive story is all mine and the police treat me like a very important person. I am enormously satisfied. *The Huronite* gave me, a woman 60 plus, my start in serious writing away from the society page and justice has been done, at last. But I must admit, not at all the way I envisioned it. What a strange twist life sometimes gives us."

They were gratified to see Holly's gloom lift. She gave a deep sigh and thanked them for their efforts. She wasn't perfect. Her recent behavior was proof of that. She would now concentrate on resuming a normal life and on trying to forget the black night that had destroyed her sense of morality for awhile. She lamented the fact that life had such a sordid side, but she would stress the positive and the good that life held.

The Thursday *Huronite* was delivered late that afternoon with the headline:

MORE BODIES FOUND IN CONNECTION
WITH RECENT MURDERS
Police close multiple murder case

by Rose Koning

Huron police found four more bodies in following up on information provided by their informant known only as Tess, a former employee of one of the deceased, Werner Bruno.

In excavating the ground around the two houses owned by Werner Bruno, nothing was found. Excavation of the ground around the abandoned Blume's Brewery disclosed the bodies of four females. It is suspected they are the bodies of women who were part of the prostitution ring of Werner Bruno. Tess told police that four young women had disappeared over the past few years. The coroner stated that all four had been strangled. With Tess's help police hope to identify the bodies and to notify next of kin, if at all possible.

On Wednesday Werner Bruno's house and the brothel were boarded up and condemned.

The bodies of the three people found last Saturday night were released by the coroner for interment. It was learned by *The Huronite* that Eugene Crane has been buried beside his late wife per instructions of a cousin. Janet Moselle has been buried in a corner of Riverside Cemetery, according to a county official. Werner Bruno's remains are buried at an undisclosed location. Obituaries are found on page 4.

The police have declared the strange case solved in a satisfactory and speedy manner. They expressed their thanks to Mrs. Jonathan Hoekstra and Mrs. Clarence Koning for the help they provided to the police in the conclusion of this matter.

The folks in Huron were glad to have it end. It had been lurid and exciting, but the events were nothing of which to be proud. They did take a perverse pride in knowing that the news had been reprinted in newspapers around the State of South Dakota.

Rose was ecstatic and made immediate plans to write her Great American Novel. Holly's emotion was one of immense relief.

A few weeks later Holly was puzzled by the arrival at her door of a strange man who inquired about a Mr. Werner Bruno. She didn't like his looks and didn't let him in, but referred him to the local police and to *The Huronite*. The man tipped his hat and left.

Chapter 23

The November meeting of The Fortnightly was held at Sunny's house and Holly wasn't going at first. She had called Rose to tell her about the stranger at her door after her series of articles on the recent infamous events, and Rose had surprised her with the news that she had been greeted by the same man. He was dressed in a three-piece pin stripe suit and fedora, which were definitely eastern clothes and certainly not of the area.

"He didn't impress me as being the least bit interested in what I had to say, and I didn't tell him much you can be sure, and I didn't mention your name, Holly. He gave me the impression that he was from a publication somewhere on the east coast. He was vague, but he led me to believe that they might be interested in the story behind my articles. He indicated that he would be in touch with me after the first of the year. That was quite an outfit he had on, wasn't it?"

"Rose, you don't suppose he represented a more sinister organization, do you? After all, with everything you uncovered, it's likely that certain people could be somewhat nervous."

"Oh Holly, of course not. I've said it before and I'll say it again: You are such a worry wart. Now you have to change your mind and be at the meeting. It will look funny if you don't. You know you have to attend a meeting eventually. Might as well get it over with. No one will act differently toward either one of us."

But they did. Members were discussing the unpleasant events that two of their members had been involved in and stopped abruptly when Holly and Rose came in. But they presented broad smiles and pretended there was nothing out of the ordinary.

Holly usually loved going to Sunny's house. She and Randy had purchased one of the newer homes in the south of Huron. It was a rambler with most of the rooms on one floor. It looked so spacious with large windows which let in the light. The homes had been built over a reclaimed swamp and most of the residents had a sump pump to keep basements dry. There were not the tall, old trees which shaded the older parts of town, but trees had been planted, as well as lots of shrubbery on the wide yards. The houses that sat esthetically on the prairie still had the look of openness of the plains. Holly loved her home, but started to realize that she really wasn't as modern as her friends. Nevertheless, she and Jonathan were happy right where they were and would probably live out their lives in their home.

Sunny's bright living room easily held the members of the club. She was president that year and began the meeting with no mention of the late scandal. Proceedings went smoothly and at the close of the meeting Sunny said, "I have some sad news. We are losing one of our members, a woman who has done so much for The Fortnightly. Mrs. Maude Feinstein is leaving us soon at the end of the year."

Mrs. Feinstein stood and smiled her dignified smile as murmurs went around the room. With sadness in her voice she spoke to them.

"Yes, it's true. Doctor and I will be leaving in a few weeks. He is closing his practice, leaving it in the capable hands of a fine young physician, Dr. Abner Rosenthal. We have been planning retirement for some time now and will be moving to Florida. I think we shall enjoy the nice warm temperatures. We have friends who have retired to Ft. Lauderdale and, after visiting there, we are looking forward to it. However, I shall sorely miss this fine group of women. Never have I enjoyed such friendships. You all accepted me unequivocally and I have thoroughly enjoyed my association with each and every one. Thank you."

Her last words were said with difficulty. Mrs. Feinstein was overcome with emotion and wiped her eyes with her linen handkerchief.

"Your kind words give us much to live up to, Maude," said Sunny. "The club will just not be the same without you."

Daisy added, "And none of us filled the capacity of secretary as well. It was such a pleasure to listen to the Minutes of the Meeting. "

They smiled in appreciation. Mrs. Feinstein's way with words certainly kept their attention.

"I suppose you will be flying to Florida," said Laurel.

"No, we've decided to go by train and see the country. The good old Chicago and Northwestern to Omaha will start us on our way."

Mrs. Wallace seemed to be deeply affected by her friend's departure and she struggled to keep her composure. Tolerance of Mrs. Wallace was often sorely tested over the years because of her oftentimes expressed statements of passing judgment "for the good of the club." Her early antagonism of Mrs. Feinstein which had changed to deep affection for a close friend was good to see, and together they had accomplished much working through The Fortnightly. Mrs. Wallace had grown old and, while she was not senile, she had become more pronounced in her attitudes and criticisms.

"People must get that way when they grow old," Laurel had said with an impish smile, since her friends were all in their sixties.

However, Mrs. Wallace had to be in her late seventies. She had changed little in appearance except for the set expression on her wrinkled, made-up face. Her jet black hair only intensified her aging, a fact she could not see. She was heavily corseted in the belief that she retained her girlish figure, a figure that had long ceased to exist. The Spencer foundation lady who made house calls to women with a "challenging figure" was a competent sales lady who declared to her eager customer that Spencer undergarments would enable her to retain her figure and that her clothes would enhance her handsome visage. Her tummy would be held in and her breasts would be lifted to their former outline. But when Mrs. Wallace was seated her bosom lifter appeared to rest on her full abdomen, their twin cups looking ludicrously akin to the tips of rockets. Members endeavored not to stare at her, lest they fail to contain their amusement. They could not embarrass her and they all felt sorry for the old woman who could not acknowledge the passage of time.

Holly reminded them, "We'll all be old someday."

After Mrs. Feinstein's announcement, Rose stood and said,

"I know my articles in *The Huronite* have been a source of controversy for members of the club, but I am a writer after all." She said this with some bravado and continued. "But as a direct result of those articles and the exposure it gave to me I have an opportunity to really get down to business and do some writing with some depth, articles for national magazines, maybe even a book about this whole unsavory affair."

Exclamations of surprise came from some of the women; there were also a number of words of disbelief. Rose went on.

"So Clarence and I are going to travel and I'll write articles about the United States as we travel and submit them regularly to the magazine that has made the offer to me. There's no reason we can't just close up the house and be gone for a few months. The kids are grown and on their own. I am so excited about this great opportunity and I hope you are excited for me."

Holly had been taken by surprise. "What magazine has contacted you, Rose?"

"One I never heard of, a new one, not your regular run of the mill *Saturday Evening Post* or *Colliers*. It's called *Traveling Across America.*

"But won't traveling be expensive with food and lodging and all?" asked Sunny.

"It would be, but we will be self-sufficient. Clarence bought one of those trailers — one of those shiny silver things. It's called an Air Stream. He said our car will be able to pull it easily. They're very light weight, you know. We'll eat and sleep in the trailer and just pull into one of those campgrounds each day. We'll be all set."

Seeing their doubtful expressions she continued, "Come on now; it'll be wonderful. We'll meet all kinds of people and see the country while I type out my articles on my reliable Royal typewriter. I'll even type you regular letters as we go."

"We're just concerned about you, Rose," said Daisy. "This is quite an undertaking. You and Clarence aren't so young anymore. When do you plan to leave?"

"Next spring as soon as we can. The timing is perfect, and what else would I be doing now that most of us are retired? I'll miss all of you here in the club, of course, but I want to do this. Don't worry. We'll be fine."

But her friends did worry. They knew Rose's impulsive ways and how they always seemed to get her into trouble. One day she had said to her close friends in confidence, "Do you know what I think? I think J. Edgar Hoover's FBI men are checking into this whole mess that's been uncovered."

"Oh Rose, what an imagination!" declared Sunny.

After the November meeting as Holly was helping Sunny clean up, the subject of the long ago Gypsy fortune teller's predictions came up. They laughed in remembering their eagerness to believe the strange woman.

"Do you remember what she told Rose?" asked Sunny.

"No, I can't say that I do," Holly replied.

Sunny put down her dishtowel, positioned her hands as though she cradled a crystal ball and solemnly intoned, "'Your sharp tongue gets you into trouble. Your future may not be so bright because of it and you will have surprises in your life' — something like that."

They laughed at the recollection. Holly said, "Ah yes, but do you remember what she told me? She said that I'd have many children. She told Myrtle the same thing."

"You're right. It was so silly. But she did hit it on the head with Rose."

Holly chuckled, "How could she miss, for goodness sake? Rose has always been too aggressive for her own good."

They dropped the subject and Holly drove home to Jonathan and told him all the news.

In the spring of 1955 shortly before Rose and Clarence left Huron for their long road trip Laurel had a dinner party for them with her friends and their husbands present, ten in all. Conversation was lively at the table. Rose was exuberant and Clarence was in rare form, cracking jokes and reciting various tawdry verse throughout the meal, causing them to hold their sides with laughter. Clarence expressed his pride in his wife as she was positive about her very bright future, making a place for herself in the male dominated profession of writing at her "advanced age" as she put it, and paving the way for other qualified women. Nothing was going to stop her from attaining her goal.

"But we shall all miss you terribly," complained Daisy. "All of us have been nearby all our lives and now you are trekking off into the country and who knows the dangers you may encounter."

"Nothing bad will happen to us. Why on earth would it? Clarence and I are harmless."

She was greeted with hoots and smart remarks at that utterance.

They all met at Rose and Clarence's house on the day of their departure. Their children were there and Teddy was explaining the workings of the gleaming Air Stream trailer to one and all. The girls had each brought food to tide them over in case there was a long stretch of road between towns. The men shook Clarence's hand and clapped him on the back wishing him well and urging him to stay off the center line on the highways. Clarence retorted that he always thought that the center line meant a driver was to follow the dotted line. Finally, everything was ready for departure, hugs and goodbyes were said, and the couple got into their dependable Buick. They moved slowly from the curb and into the street and waved until they turned a corner and were out of sight.

"That's some rig, that's certain," admired Teddy. Then he and his brother and sisters waved merrily and were gone. The group was quiet for a moment.

Holly sighed and said, "Well. Rose always was full of surprises."

Laurel added, "She'd better write often, even if it's only a postcard."

Shortly after the Koning's departure the girls were occupied with Laurel's news that Jennie was to be married in June. They were so happy for their handicapped daughter who had overcome many obstacles that had been placed in her path since the onset of polio in 1948. Jennie had been true to her word, had moved from the protective love and security of her parents, and lived alone in a compact apartment close to the library. Her family was excited and making elaborate preparations for the wedding. Jennie's 32 year old brother was planning all sorts of mischief at the wedding of his beloved sister and paid no attention to his young wife proclaiming to Jennie that he would do no such thing. Laurel eagerly informed the girls that Jennie's young man's name was Bob Schmidt, a common enough name, that he was hard working and adored their Jennie. He was employed as manager of the Coast to Coast store and made a good salary. They were all invited to the wedding, of course, and plans were made for a bridal shower.

"We may be getting old," said Sunny, "but we still have plenty of energy when it comes to important events."

"It keeps us young," agreed Holly, "but do you ever feel that you and I have spent an inordinate amount of time in the kitchen?"

"Some people would say that that is where we belong."

161

They laughed at that. Then Holly said, "Rose is going to miss the whole thing, shower and all. But her letters sound happy."

The two old friends worked as one in preparing an afternoon bridal shower for the daughter of a dear friend. They were a little slower in their movements, but their capabilities had not diminished. The shower would be at Holly's house at her insistence. It was to be on a Saturday afternoon in May and invitations had been sent.

Holly was upstairs relaxing on the porch outside her bedroom. The landscape was green and the Boston Ivy had begun its long climb. She watched as a car drove up in front of the house. She was pleased to see Teddy, Rose's oldest, and rose to wave to him. She stopped when, from the hurried walk and look of distress, she realized that something was wrong.

She spoke to him over the balcony. "Teddy what is it?"

"Aunt Holly, please, I have to talk to you."

She hurried from the bedroom and down the stairs wondering what could have upset him so. He was normally a happy go lucky young man filled with gaiety and enthusiasm.

In his haste to speak to her Teddy had opened the front door and come in and was pacing the living room. He looked at Holly with dark beseeching eyes and went to her, tears streaming down his face.

"Aunt Holly —they're gone. Mom and Dad are dead."

She gathered him to her and he sobbed on her shoulder. She was rigid with shock and devastated for Teddy and his brother and sisters. She stared across the room, seeing nothing, as she held him, patting his shoulder and holding his head as he cried.

"Come," she said. "Let's sit down, then tell me what happened."

They sat on the sofa and Teddy pulled out his handkerchief and wiped his face, trying to compose himself. He took a telegram from his shirt pocket and handed it to her. Silently she opened it and read:

> To Theodore Koning
> Huron, South Dakota
> Regret to inform you of deaths of Clarence Koning and Rose Koning result of traffic accident. Crash of vehicle and trailer cause of death. Call number below for details.
> (signed) Sgt. Frank Desmond
> Highway Patrol
> Battle Mountain, Nevada

"I called the number, Aunt Holly, and this Sgt. Desmond seemed like a nice guy. He offered condolences and answered all my questions. He is even making arrangements to ship the bodies back."

He collapsed into sobs once more. Holly couldn't utter a word, just let him cry it out. It was unbelievable, unthinkable.

Teddy gave a shuddering breath and said, "This Sgt. Desmond said it happened on a lonely stretch of road, that it must have been a one car accident, but he didn't understand it at all, because the weather was clear, the road was in good shape and it happened in the morning. So it couldn't have happened because of their being tired or sleepy. I just don't get it, Aunt Holly. How could this happen?"

"I don't know, dear. I just don't know."

Teddy added, "Sgt. Desmond did say the driver's door was all bashed in, but it could have happened when the car and trailer somehow jack-knifed and rolled. Mom and Dad were underneath —" He choked back a sob. "Aunt Holly, what should I do? I don't know what to do."

She looked at his ravaged face and her heart went out to him in his grief. She would do anything she could to help, as would the rest of the girls.

She said, "First of all, the bodies — they should be delivered to the funeral home and arrangements made." She could see how those words hurt him. "I'll go with you."

His red-rimmed eyes were filled with gratitude. "Aunt Holly, thanks. Sgt. Desmond said Mom and Dad will be on the Chicago and Northwestern from Rapid City day after tomorrow. They have to do autopsies and then they'd know more ...." He couldn't go on.

"All right. Now, you must go home and be with your family. We'll take care of everything as soon as they — arrive. Would you like Welter Funeral Home to take care of things?"

He nodded sorrowfully and got up. He looked years older than he was. She hugged him to her again and told him that everything would be all right, although she really didn't know how. They said goodbye sadly and she went to the telephone to give the news to the others as tears welled up and spilled over and she cried.

Once again the girls and their husbands attended a funeral at the Methodist Church where much of their lives had been spent. It was more than they could bear to see Rose and Clarence lying in adjacent coffins. They were still in shock. The autopsies showed no abnormalities in their broken bodies. Rose and Clarence were active, healthy individuals who had been in an automobile accident. The cause of death in each of them was the accident. The car was in good running order before the crash. Grief was mingled with bewilderment in those who knew the Konings. None of their friends remembered a word of the sermon or what music was played. Sorrow lay upon them, smothering any other feeling. Rose and Clarence were buried in the Restlawn Memory Garden south of Huron, a beautiful new cemetery laid out on the South Dakota prairie.

It was extremely difficult, almost impossible to take up their lives after the tragedy. It was incomprehensible to their friends that people so vital and who seemed indestructible should be taken so abruptly and so violently. It made no sense.

But life did go on and in a few weeks Jennie Swanson and Bob Schmidt were married, giving them all something positive to look forward to. They were married in June in an outdoor ceremony at the beautiful Riverside Park near the James River east of Huron. In the middle of the park a stone archway graced an area which was surrounded by hardy prairie flowers. Paths wound through a mass of petunias, daisies, zinnias, phlox, blue iris and sweet William. The couple presented a sharp contrast with Jennie's dark beauty and Bob Schmidt's blond good looks. Jennie's walk was only slightly unsteady as she approached the arch on Wendell's arm. As the bride and groom stood beneath the arch their families and friends watched with happiness. The vows were spoken clearly and with love shining on their faces. Warm sunshine cast dancing lights through the trees as though a myriad of butterflies had come to the wedding. The devastation of the recent deaths was dissipated somewhat in the glow of the golden afternoon. Hope was renewed in the beginning of the young people's lives.

Time brought additional changes.

There was excitement and worry when the Huron Theater caught on fire as 650 children watched The Three Stooges. All were safely evacuated.

A large motel was built north of Huron called The Plains. An added attraction was a 24-foot high pheasant which stood at the entrance and a sign which proclaimed Huron to be the "Pheasant Capital of the World".

A Lewis Drug Store, one of several throughout the state to be built, soon appeared on the south edge of Huron, as well as a Dairy Queen with its delectable treats.

The Huron Symphony boasted 60 players and presented a choral concert featuring Handl's 'Messiah', Haydn's 'Creation', Mendelssohn's 'Elijah' and Mozart's 'Requiem' to an appreciative audience.

Holly remained troubled about Rose and Clarence's deaths. Something about the entire incident was just not right.

Rounding out the decade was the destruction of Blume's Brewery on May 26, 1959, when it burned to the ground, leaving only charred stone walls.

Chapter 24

It was early summer, 1962. Holly was seated in the corner of the porch on the balcony outside her bedroom where she was hidden behind the ivy which was climbing inexorably to the roof. The thick greenery gave her the seclusion she needed from time to time, when she fled to the comfort of the porch behind the ivy where a curtain of shade surrounded her in a cocoon of protection.

It had rained most of the day and the dusty air was washed away, leaving the pure fresh smell of a thorough cleansing. It should have buoyed her spirits but it only made her sad. She and Jonathan had just returned from Opal's funeral and burial. The sense of a burden having been lifted and the relief of knowing that her sister's suffering was ended was overcome with Holly's ever-present guilt. The feeling that she had not done all she could for Opal remained with her. Of course she had no reason to feel guilty. Jonathan reminded her that Holly had done far more than anyone else could in caring for her remaining sister. She had even gone the extra mile in providing loving care and shelter. The girls had been at the small funeral, along with a few old people who remembered Holly's family, and they pointed out that Opal had lived a long, useful life of 85 years. But Holly's nurturing nature was left with a void, an empty feeling.

Holly thought of how poor Opal had become senile, requiring constant surveillance due to her forgetfulness. She had deteriorated from her sturdy, sprightly self into an aging child. So Holly retired in 1960 to devote her time to caring for her. She was still a good nurse and there was no one better who could take on the task. Besides, it was time to retire.

But Holly became exhausted in her unending vigil in tending to her. Opal was so confused most of the time, often walking away from the house. If she managed to get the heavy front door open she would fail to close it and the next morning they would begin the search for absent-minded Opal. In winter the risk was enormous. She would take outdoor excursions without being properly clothed, sometimes being barefoot, when they would find her on the sidewalk, crying and holding her icy feet. She was close to frostbite late one night when they found her and rushed her to the hospital. It was sheer luck that they found her in time. Eventually the warmth and color returned to her frigid feet, but not before all concerned were so alarmed that they knew that Opal had to be confined. Randy urged Holly to place her under some kind of supervision for everyone's sake, Holly's included.

Holly's devoted care over the previous two years had been difficult. It had been necessary to lock Opal in her room at night. It hurt Holly to do it. After all Opal had taken care of their family for so many years and this was no way for anyone to be treated. But it had to be done so she and Jonathan could get some rest and be prepared for the next day's continuing watchful protection. Opal's condition had worsened and she liked to wander through the house at night and turn on the water or the electric stove and then forgetting to turn them off.

Holly became completely worn out and Jonathan was worried about her. When the Tschetter Nursing Home opened in 1962 Opal was one of the first residents to be admitted. Holly resisted at first, but Jonathan insisted. Opal had gone willingly with them when they drove her to the home. She loved to go for a ride. But upon arrival and being shown to an unfamiliar room she became frightened.

"Is this my new room, Holly?" she had asked plaintively. "I like my old room better. Please let's go home."

Her distress at being told she couldn't go home just then, that she would be staying in her new room, and that she would like it a lot in no time tore at Holly's heart. The nurse said she would soon get accustomed to her new surroundings, but Opal began to cry as Jonathan led Holly from the room, causing Holly to cry.

"She'll only get more upset if we stay, Holly. She doesn't understand right now, but she'll get used to it and even grow to like it."

Holly's ears rang with Opal's pathetic cries. A few weeks later Opal died peacefully in her sleep.

"It's all my fault. I did this to her. If only I hadn't put her there she'd still be alive. I could have continued to take care of her," Holly wept.

"Now dear, be sensible. She was 85. Do you honestly believe she would have lived longer in her confused state, wandering around the house endangering herself and possibly us as well?"

Holly knew he was right but she needed to be alone for while. So she had retreated to her haven of refuge behind the ivy to think things out. She pondered the thought that she was nearing the age of 69 and wondered if she, herself, would end as Opal had, dependent on others. If she became a burden to Jonathan she couldn't face it. Dear sweet Jonathan who loved her so very much and who was such a support to her in every circumstance should never have that burden. At 79 he was still a vital, passionate man, a bit slower in his movements perhaps, but everyone she knew, their friends and acquaintances were slowing down. Actually, as she thought about it, Huron was turning into a town of elderly folks. Her thoughts were taking a morbid turn and she shook them from her head and thought of other things. True to his word, Jonathan had retired at 72, much to his young assistant's delight. He had patiently waited for the job of chief pharmacist at Sherman and Moe's Drugstore. He gloried in his new position, a position he had earned, but he had to admit that he had a storehouse of knowledge learned from the old retired man.

Holly and Jonathan had a good life, enjoying retirement and each other. They were content. Jonathan liked to travel and, although Holly was not as enthusiastic about it, they managed to take several trips. They drove a new car on their vacations, a new car every other year, which was the only sure way to know you owned a reliable vehicle according to Jonathan. But he was beginning to complain that they surely didn't make cars the way they used to.

"Golly, you slam the door and it sounds tinny," he said as the years passed.

In her spare time Holly volunteered at St. John's Hospital finding it most satisfying. The nursing instinct that was hers responded with empathy to the patients and they responded to her, She especially loved being with the children who returned her love, calling her Grandma Holly. Holly decided she liked being called Grandma Holly. After all, the girls were all grandmothers. It made her feel like one of them.

Holly breathed in the fresh clean air and her thoughts turned to others in her life. She was grateful to Jonathan for leaving her to her reveries during her periodic seclusion behind the ivy, but sometimes she wondered if she really was getting old when she would sit alone and think and slip into her old lady mode as she called it. She had seen so many she knew and loved leave her. She was still around and at her age that was not unusual but, with that line of reasoning, those who had died before her had gone on ahead too soon. Her own small, intimate circle was diminishing. She had been deeply saddened when Howard died, with Gabrielle following soon after. At the time, she consoled herself that she still had Opal. Now she, too, was gone. When she seemed to brood over such things, Jonathan would remind Holly that she was, after all, the youngest in her family and, while she had so many brothers and sisters for a long time, she would be the one who had to see them go, one after the other.

She sighed. Laurel and Daisy were now widows, but they had their children and grandchildren. Holly had none. She shook her head to rid herself of such thoughts. She would not feel sorry for herself.

Many of the original members of The Fortnightly were gone. Even steadfast Mrs. Sylvia Wallace had succumbed to old age. She had been found on the living room floor of her home one afternoon when the paper boy became concerned by the accumulation of *The Daily Plainsman* on the front porch. He called it to the attention of his superiors and police

167

were notified. They arrived at the house immediately, discovering the poor woman on the floor. She had been dead for several days. The members of the club were extremely upset because none of them had inquired when Mrs. Wallace missed the last meeting, which was most unusual for her. She had lived alone for many years and had no immediate family. Her life was The Fortnightly to which she had contributed much, despite her idiosyncrasies. Holly felt she was becoming a regular at funerals, most depressing.

She stirred as a warm breeze wafted through the leaves of the thick vine. She knew the pleasant summer day would soon turn into a hot, humid one. The 1960s had begun with lots of snow, causing the James River to rise, cresting at over sixteen feet and flooding Riverside Park. The recent heavy rains had caused some concern, yet few people objected to an over-abundance of rain in South Dakota where water was a premium commodity. Oftentimes, after a rainfall during day or night, dust could be seen blowing down the streets. The older generation, remembering the Dirty Thirties, never wasted water, which was something the generation of the sixties seemed to not comprehend. One simply turned on a faucet and water issued forth. What was the big deal, as their frequently used comment went.

Huron's population was over 14,000 when the 1960s began. It was the beginning of a new decade, a new era with much promise, but the promise was never realized. During that time when Lyndon B. Johnson became president, he proclaimed his administration would bring about vast changes in the Soaring Sixties. Holly didn't like what the decade was turning into, as well as others in her generation, and stated with indignation one day that the times were more akin to the Sorry Sixties. It was the beginning of an assault on the lives and mores of the older generation by the younger generation, which got progressively worse, spilling over into the seventies. The ridicule and blame was at first hurtful and puzzling, feelings which turned into consternation and anger, emotions which proved to be futile. There were valid complaints about the laxity in the proper upbringing of children. Parents were not as strict. There was growing disrespect for authority.

Even education was affected with different teaching methods which decried memorization and the facts of history. Modern math problems took up an entire piece of paper, complicating a simple multiplication or division exercise, turning out students who could not do basic arithmetic. The young began to dress in frayed, sloppy clothing, as though they had stepped out of the Great Depression. The lack of good personal grooming was apparent. Holly found it embarrassing to even think about the relaxed sexual behavior that began to be prevalent. Daisy had filled her in on that to Holly's shock. Daisy said she thought it was abhorent, too, but that it was nothing new; there was just more of it. It used to be called "free love." But

Holly's sensibilities and been jarred from her naive complacency and she didn't like it.

She considered the prices of everything which cost more and more as she got older. Habichts charged 99¢ for a pair of nylon hose. An automatic clothes washer at Sears sold for the sum of $168, outrageous. Red Owl's bread was 23¢, not so bad. One could hardly bake bread oneself anymore for that price. Ed & Eb's hamburger was now 3 pounds for 99¢. Tires at Montgomery Ward sold for $12.88 each plus trade-ins. How could one operate a car at such prices? Jonathan was not the least bit disturbed by it and continued to drive a new car no matter what the price was. The cost of almost $2,500 for a new Biscayne at Verschoor Chevrolet caused Holly to offer an objection.

"Jonathan, do we really need a new car so often? That's a lot of money, money we could use for more important things."

"Like what? Our old age?" he retorted with a twinkle in his eyes .

She dropped the subject and concluded that men love their automobiles somewhat like the men of old who valued their horses as their sole means of transportation so much, and why so many horse thieves were summarily hanged.

However, Holly considered it an entirely different matter to pay 49¢ for an angel food cake at Ruby Ann's Bakery and to buy Butternut coffee at 59¢ a pound as refreshment when she entertained The Fortnightly. It was surely easier and cheaper than beating all those eggs to make the cake from scratch. Besides, with the Gold Bond stamps that many merchants gave with purchases, she could add a new item to the house, such as those horse bookends she had chosen and the table lamp by Jonathan's favorite chair. She sometimes wondered if she was becoming miserly in her old age, but decided that thrift was a virtue and let it go at that .

She sighed again, patted her gray hair and decided she had done enough moping for one day. Opal was at peace and she would remember her as she was, not the sad creature she was when she died. She owed the rest of her life and her energies to Jonathan, who was always so understanding.

She got up and walked to the porch railing and looked down on her familiar neighborhood, clean and bright after the rain. She smiled, perked up and decided to fix Jonathan his favorite supper, meatloaf and mashed potatoes. Then they would make plans to attend the State Fair in September. Eddy Arnold was one of the featured entertainers that year. She just loved his earthy singing.

Chapter 25

Holly and Jonathan were going to a party. They were hosts at a large gathering in the ballroom of the Marvin Hughitt Hotel on the occasion of their 40th wedding anniversary in the fall of 1964.

During the sixties and seventies it was not unusual for large parties to be held at the hotel or other rooms capable of holding 300 to 400 people. They were extremely popular, providing those who were invited with a special evening and giving the host and hostess a chance to reciprocate invitations. Everyone dressed to the nines on such occasions, a band played the popular tunes of the day and also of days gone by and decorations and refreshments made the room festive.

They had not mentioned their anniversary in the invitations. They did not want gifts, just the company of friends and acquaintances. Holly had included members of The Fortnightly, along with their spouses. They chose their anniversary because it was a good way to celebrate and, as Holly had said so many years before when they were married, "October is such a comfortable time of year." As if on cue, the specified day arrived with leaves turning color in the warm sunshine and a light breeze carrying the scents of autumn.

"It's going to be a beautiful day, Jonathan," she said from the bathroom as she swallowed two aspirins. Her 71 years were catching up with her, and despite the pleasant weather, her bones ached in the morning.

Jonathan appeared behind her and hugged her to him as he kissed her cheek. "A beautiful day for my beautiful wife," he smiled.

She had never gotten used to his calling her beautiful, especially those days. Good gracious, she was an old woman now, no doubt about it. But his constant love, which was expressed so beautifully made her look younger than her years as she responded. She touched her gray hair and looked at him in the mirror, smiling back at him. He was still a handsome man. Why was it that men got better looking as they aged, while women had to fight the ravages of time every day? His tall rugged frame was getting a bit stooped; he was a good deal older than she, but the love in his eyes gave them a brightness many old men didn't have. He took the aspirin bottle from her and joined in the battle against the aches and pains of old age.

**Holly and Jonathan
on their 40th wedding anniversary**

They were basically strong, healthy people, lucky to not be plagued with an illness or ailment which required prescription medicine.

Later in the day as Jonathan took a brief nap in preparation for a night of dinner and dancing, Holly went over the arrangements for the party one more time. She wanted everything to be perfect. Each of the large parties had a theme. Since it was October Holly chose the colorful theme of a successful harvest with fall flowers and pumpkins, along with a touch of Halloween. Guests could come in costume if they wished, but she knew that the older people would dress formally in their finest, more sedately than her younger guests. Satisfied that everything was in order, she looked forward to an enjoyable evening.

As they were dressing for the party Holly hummed happily. Jonathan gazed at her in contentment and pride. She had basked in that look for 40 years and knew she was one fortunate woman. She took a small package from her dresser drawer as he walked to her, then turned to look at her reflection one last time in the long oval mirror. She was still tall and slim and, she decided, adequate. Her new green silk dress with long sleeves and a close collar at her regal neck suited her modesty and the gown was a length that she liked with just enough flare to be flattering. She held out her hands with the gift.

He appeared surprised, but opened it to find a set of Black Hills gold cuff links. His look of pleasure made Holly smile. He immediately replaced the cuff links he had just attached with the new ones and admired the result. Then he took a long velvet box from his pocket and presented it to her. "For you, my dear."

Happily she opened it and gasped. "Jonathan, those are diamonds, real diamonds!"

He took the necklace from the box and fastened it around her neck where it sparkled against the soft material of her dress. She touched the gems in awe. "It's something I've wanted to give you for a long time — better than the glass beads I gave you on your birthday once."

"I love those beads and I still wear that necklace."

"You deserve only the best," he said as he kissed her.

"It's absolutely gorgeous. Thank you, I love it. Oh, Jonathan!" She threw her arms around his neck and they held one another close.

Dusk was falling as they left the house. A soft wind rustled in the trees and a harvest moon shone brightly. They got into their new Pontiac and drove off in a flurry of leaves.

Their entry into the Marvin Hughitt Hotel was met with cheery greetings from early arrivals. Holly suppressed a pang, remembering Clarence's droll greetings of years gone by. When they stepped from the elevator on the third floor she was satisfied with how the ballroom looked. The glorious fall colors were festive, the buffet table was set with a sumptuous feast. A large cornucopia was set in the middle of the table filled with the produce of the season. Tables were situated around the perimeter of the room, with pumpkins, corn stalks, colored corn, and greenery interspersed among them. She must compliment Sunny, Laurel and Daisy who had been such marvelous help in the decorating the day before.

Sunny was still a striking looking woman, still lovely, but she looked tired and, as they had worked she acknowledged that she had been quite tired but that she was taking iron for it and it would take a few weeks before she felt any better.

Daisy was late, as usual, and arrived ready to go to work with her hair mussed and her glasses crooked on her nose because they had broken and were held in place with adhesive tape. She told them she had just been too busy to have them fixed and hated to take the time. The prescription probably needed to be changed, too, but she'd get to it eventually. They gently suggested that perhaps she could see better if she would turn the house lights on sooner. Daisy was becoming somewhat eccentric. Without Melvin to check on her she would get so engrossed in her reading and writing that she easily lost track of time. The darkened interior of the house made it appear empty. She was chronically late.

Laurel, too, spent her time differently since Wendell died. She spent much of it with Jennie and her children. The others feared she was making a nuisance of herself as she chattered on and on about them. They inquired tactfully about how Jennie and Bob enjoyed her frequent visits and telephone calls, but it didn't seem to register. Laurel was totally engrossed in her Jennie, who had borne two children, a boy and a girl, making Laurel even more attentive. She loved her role as a doting grandmother .

As she looked around the ballroom Holly was satisfied with what she saw. The band was setting up at one end and early guests were milling about. Harry Eisele and his 7-piece band had been engaged to play for the evening. His band was popular in Redfield a small town 50 miles north of Huron, as well as being in demand in the towns for miles around. He had played the Marvin Hughitt ballroom on many New Year's Eve celebrations.

The music began with a spritely rendition of 'One O'Clock Jump' which brought dancers to the floor. It was a favorite with the older generation with enough spirit to appeal to the younger generation. Holly was right; the older guests were dressed stylishly and in formal attire. The dresses of the younger generation were very short, which was the style, and their long hair and the odd trousers of the young men made a definite contrast. But everyone was enjoying the music. She had requested a variety, music that the older generation loved, along with some current pop tunes. When 'Feelin' Groovy' was played Laurel said, "Holly, why on earth did you include such crass music at this great party?"

Daisy replied with her usual candor, "It's what the young people like and, besides, it does have a nice beat. We have to keep up with the times."

Laurel countered, "I can keep up, but I don't have to like it and, speaking of beat, did you see those Beatles on the Ed Sullivan Show? Where did they get such a name? And it's spelled incorrectly. Beetle is spelled with two 'e's not 'ea.'"

Daisy laughed. "Laurel, you really are behind the times. 'Beat' signifies the 'beat generation'. According to them they are beat because of the older generation's mistakes."

"Oh really," Laurel replied with a wry look.

Holly added, "We can't be stuck in the thirties and forties, Although I have asked that the band play lots of the beautiful melodies from that time."

'Moonlight Serenade' filled the room and the dance floor was packed with dancers of all ages.

But Laurel persisted. "Can't you just hear Rose if she were here: 'Just where is 'Winchester Cathedral' anyway? And what the dickens is 'A Hard Day's Night?' Furthermore," Laurel added, "those Beatles persons need haircuts."

Holly and Jonathan gave a hearty laugh as they joined the dancers. "We must really be getting old," Holly said. "Actually, I agree with much that Laurel said." She relaxed in Jonathan's arms to the smooth music and said, "They just don't write songs like they used to."

He swept her around the floor as 'Sentimental Journey' flowed from the mellow instruments. The band seemed not to tire of playing any kind of music, but excelled at the old standards. Jennie and Bob had come to the party and the girls wondered who was staying with the children because Grandma Laurel was at the dance. They smiled as they witnessed the couple's love. Bob carefully guided Jennie around to the slower melodies. The residue of muscle weakness which polio had left had not yet prevented Jennie's being able to do almost anything, but with care. How in love they were.

The party was in full swing and Holly noted with satisfaction that everything was proceeding as she had hoped. After a rendition of the 'Jersey Bounce' the band took an intermission. People lined up at the buffet table and soon the tables around the perimeter of the room were filled with happy, enthusiastic guests who expressed their appreciation to Holly as she and Jonathan walked around the room in welcome.

Jonathan said, "Well, my dear, I've said it in the past and I have to say it again. You've done it again, really outdone yourself."

"It is going well, isn't it? But I had a lot of help. What a grand way to spend our anniversary."

Word soon spread that the occasion was the 40th wedding anniversary of their host and hostess and the band swung into 'The Anniversary Waltz' to the applause of everyone. Holly and Jonathan were the center of attention as they danced slowly around in the center of the room.

Laurel and Daisy watched with tears in their eyes. "They're still so much in love," said Daisy. "Sometimes I really miss my Melvin, but if I keep busy I don't think about it so much."

Laurel agreed. A few tables away Sunny said to Randy , "Isn't that sweet, Randy? It's such a joy to see those two so happy."

Randy put his hand over hers in agreement as he kept his eyes on the couple. As they danced by Sunny waved gaily to them and for an instant Holly's eyes met Randy's and a thrill of connection passed between them. It vanished abruptly as laughter filled the room. Jonathan swung Holly back into a dip and kissed her as he lifted her up. The moment was gone. Only Holly and Randy were aware of the something that had passed between them. The feeling remained with her and she chided herself that it was only the nice romantic feeling of the occasion and of Jonathan's abiding love, nothing else. Besides, she scolded, I am far too old to have such feelings. Save them for your husband. It did not occur to her that her reasoning was quite illogical.

They moved off the dance floor as applause followed them. Her face was flushed. "Jonathan, what will everyone think!"

"My dear, at this late stage, I hope they all paid close attention."

The gala eventually came to an end. 'Good Night Ladies' came from the band as the last remaining couples danced dreamily and they reluctantly took their departure. It had been a success. Holly and Jonathan remembered it with pleasure. Their guests remembered it with thank you notes and telephone calls. Holly was content and satisfied with a job well done.

One day the thought occurred to Holly that she seemed to have the knack of having a party or a gathering of some kind just before catastrophe struck, just as her first Christmas party had been held before the Depression took hold of the country. Her party was the last one for awhile when the beginning of 1965 saw the beginning of another war, making merrymaking unthinkable. The Viet Nam War, which was to prove to be the most futile conflict the country had ever involved itself in brought despair to those who had suffered through too many wars in their lifetimes. There was little support for the war and patriotism was at an all time low. Daisy's youngest grandson was called up and it was with disbelief that she watched him depart on the train and be speedily transported to an unknown Pacific country.

The girls were aghast. "How many more senseless wars are we to endure?" Holly said to Jonathan angrily. "It is all so useless. Haven't we learned anything after all these years? Tell me why we are over there.

Where is Viet Nam and of what value is it to risk the lives of our young men? I just don't understand it."

"I know, dear. But what can we do? Now please don't get so agitated. We must support Daisy and her family."

The Soaring Sixties fell with an audible thud with an escalation of the drug culture, scandal and the assassinations of John F. Kennedy, Robert Kennedy and Martin Luther King, Jr.

There were some positive occurrences. An honor was bestowed on one of South Dakota's own. Vice President Hubert H. Humphrey was honored by Huron College at its graduation exercises in 1966. He and his wife, Muriel, were given honorary degrees. His beginnings were humble, working in Humphrey Drug in Huron, a store begun by his father in 1931 . His interest in politics led him to Minnesota where he became Mayor of Minneapolis, then United States Senator from Minnesota, and eventually becoming Vice President of the United States. While his run for President on the Democratic ticket was unsuccessful, he was held in high esteem by the people of South Dakota. Muriel Humphrey served out the remaining ten months of his third term as Senator when he died in 1979.

In 1968 the Huron Nursing Home opened with an adjacent Sunquest Village building for assisted living. The Super City Shopping Center north of the Chicago Northwestern Railroad was destroyed by fire, but was eventually rebuilt southwest of town during the 1970s. The Little Zee gift shop opened downtown and remained a popular shop for many years.

But the 1960s saw tragedy strike many families in the state as servicemen and women in Viet Nam were returned home for burial or hospitalization. Daisy's worst nightmare came true. Her grandson was one of the many who were killed. He was returned to his family and laid to rest next to his grandfather, Melvin Moberly, in the family plot, a space which Daisy had assumed she would some day occupy long before her children or grandchildren. She sank into a deep depression. Her children and their families could not console her, could not reach her. It wasn't natural for young folks to die before their elders she said to them. They watched over her the best they could, but Daisy kept to her home and her books and writings. She finally asked them to leave her alone for awhile, that she would be all right. They acceded to her wishes, but checked on her regularly.

Daisy continued her life, paying scant attention to her surroundings or her everyday tasks. One day her daughter found her at her desk with her head down amid scattered books and papers. She was dead of carbon monoxide poisoning. A bird's nest was found in the chimney and she had neglected to have her furnace checked for too many years. In the basement they found boxes and litter close to the old furnace. The filter was thick with soot.

Holly, Sunny and Laurel stood at Daisy's casket and wept together. It didn't have to happen was uppermost in their minds. Laurel spoke what was in their hearts.

"Now we are only three."

Chapter 26

The three women became even closer after Daisy's death. They spent much time together, clinging to their friendship and often recounting the early years and the nine little girls who had grown to womanhood together. The three of them lived for the present, could not forget the past, and tried not to think too far into the future lest the thread that bound them together should break.

They visited often on the telephone or in person. They had lunch at the Plains or shopped downtown or at the Super Shopping Center until a fire destroyed it in 1968. Their shopping trips were more of a social outing or window shopping and browsing, perhaps making a purchase of some inconsequential item. Being amidst other people and the activity made them realize that life, indeed, does go on. They also felt a sense of loss, that that same stream of life was passing them by. They viewed it as a plus if they happened to run into someone they knew, a familiar face who fortified their existence.

Jonathan and Randy didn't object to the closeness of the tightly knit group, knowing the intense loyalty they held for one another. The men considered their occupation with each other was a good diversion for their wives while they, themselves, had the opportunity to pursue interests of their own. Randy had been retired for some time and had renewed his interest in playing the piano. He had found some old piano pieces in a box in the basement and entertained Sunny on many an evening with his expertise. As Sunny had said, he was no Van Cliburn but he did have a nice touch. He also spent time researching and writing a paper to be submitted to a medical journal on his experiences in the treatment of polio patients and of the disease's effects on them years after the initial infection. His opinions were controversial but he hoped that the controversy would lead to a better knowledge of the disease.

Jonathan puttered around the house, upgrading the old structure and making needed improvements. He and Holly did not want to move, so they decided to renovate. He hired a contractor and they worked on every room. At the start on any given room Holly took her leave and the girls made plans to be somewhere else. Holly hated the mess, but it made Jonathan happy and each room showed tasteful improvement.

Now, as Holly sat at the dining room table with a box of sympathy cards and a neat stack of small envelopes ready for mailing, she looked around at the refurbished house and cried. Tears fell on the pages of the book which had been given to her by the girls on her 60th birthday. Over the years she had jotted down important events, dates of births and deaths, along with a few thoughts of her own. The entries were not lengthy. She felt that her thoughts were of no consequence; it was only a record she kept for herself. She had no one to leave it to who could possibly be interested. For that matter she had no one to leave any of her things in the house that she had shared for so many years with her beloved Jonathan. She supposed that now she would have to think about that.

Her tears fell on the latest entry which gave the date of death of Jonathan Hoekstra at the age of 87. He was an elderly man, but healthy and strong with twinkling eyes, eyes that shone with love for her. He had refused to admit that he could not and should not continue to do the tasks he had always done. His bravado and stubbornness resulted in his death when he suffered a heart attack while shoveling snow. She had urged him to hire one of the neighbor boys, but he said there wasn't much snow and that he could do it easily in no time. It was bracing to be outside in the cold, crisp air and he needed the exercise. She didn't like it at all and kept an eye on him, but when she walked to the kitchen to shut off the stove and call him in to lunch he had collapsed and died.

She sobbed on Sunny's shoulder. "I was away from the window for only a minute. When I returned he was lying there in the snow. He was so still, not moving."

She had run to where he lay and tried in vain to revive him, then ran inside to call Randy. He came at once. He told her what she already knew but could not accept: that he had died immediately, that even if she had been at the window all the time Jonathan was shoveling snow she could not have prevented what happened. Randy assured her that she would only have seen him drop. Nevertheless, Holly felt she had failed him. She should never have let him take that shovel.

She looked at what she had written, the date of death of her husband, January 14, 1970. The numbers blurred. How impersonal they seemed. They couldn't begin to convey her feelings, the sorrow that consumed her. The comfortable, pleasant house held an emptiness that its new surroundings could not erase. How odd, how strange that a house that had once contained a sense of life and of living could so suddenly become so bereft. How lonely it was to roll over in bed and not feel his strong presence. He was gone. Despite their ages when they married, they had been husband and wife for 45 years, happy years because of Jonathan, who had made all the difference in her life. She was now a 76 year old widow, which in itself was not unusual, but she wasn't prepared for it. She doubted that any woman was.

She sighed and wiped her tears away. She closed the book and decided to not open it again for a long time. But she could remember each entry she had made. She pushed the book away and gathered up the thank you notes which Welters Funeral Home had provided. She must get up and mail them. Still, she didn't move. Everyone had been so good to her. At the funeral Sunny and Laurel took her under their wings, providing her with solace to sustain her. The funeral was larger than she had expected. The pastor of the Methodist Church gave a fine sermon, looking at Holly directly and at the assembled congregation in compassion, as he praised the good character of Jonathan Hoekstra and gave examples of his many deeds of kindness. Laurel had stayed with Holly that night and for two more days, helping her through the abrupt change in her life.

Holly sat still, thinking. She had been blessed with many loving friends. Laurel had been invaluable to her in her loss. She recalled an entry in her record book about Laurel, an entry made in 1967. She had come to see Holly one afternoon. Holly opened the door to find her with swollen eyes. She had been crying. Holly gave her a cup of coffee in the kitchen and Laurel sobbed out her story. Jennie had spoken to her about the frequency of Laurel's visits and telephone calls. She had been patient and tactful, but Laurel was hurt and could not understand her daughter's attitude.

"I only want to be of help," Laurel said in between sobs. "Jennie tires easily and I think her limp is getting worse. She says she manages just fine, but I think she's just telling me that so I won't worry. And I adore the children."

Holly listened sympathetically but said, "Surely Jennie would not hurt you intentionally, and aren't the children growing up?"

"Yes, but it's hard to stay away."

"I think you need something else to occupy your time, Laurel. Jennie and Bob and the kids are all right, aren't they? They have their own lives to live."

"I know, but ..."

"Laurel, have you thought about some volunteer work, perhaps at St. John's?"

She wiped her eyes and looked up in surprise.

"Why no, I've been taking care of my family."

"Laurel, your family doesn't need taking care of. It would do you good to use your spare time in another way. Sunny said that Randy enjoys doing work with the crippled children through therapy at the hospital and he could use some help. He donates his time and is very good with children. I know he'd be grateful for your help."

Holly continued to persuade and, although she was reluctant, Laurel knew that she was right, so upon inquiry of Randy she was enthusiastically accepted by him and St. John's Hospital. She quickly became involved and engrossed in the children, showering love and attention on them. They in turn loved her back. Her relationship with Jennie's family settled into a more normal one.

During her association with Randy and the hospital Laurel became indispensable, becoming Dr. Randall Thorne's spokesperson, giving talks and disseminating the findings and distributing brochures on his writings. She was influential in Huron and the surrounding towns and urged the importance of the immunization of infants and children against not only polio but all childhood diseases. Just because some diseases had supposedly been eradicated, she argued, was no reason to not immunize, at least not yet. Her selfless work and keen intellect earned her the honor of Woman of the Year. She was thrilled and overwhelmed by all the fuss, including an interview and her picture in The *Daily Plainsman*. Holly was gratified to know that it had worked out so well for everyone involved.

Time was ticking away as Holly reminisced. She wondered how Laurel was doing. She couldn't be at Jonathan's funeral as she lived in St. Paul, Minnesota, and the weather would not permit it. Jennie and her family had moved to St. Paul a few months previously. Bob had been transferred to the St. Paul Coast to Coast store as its new manager. Laurel followed them at their insistence and was soon busy at the Gillette School for Crippled children there. She was the same age as Holly, 76, but her active years with her grandchildren and children in the hospital had kept her young and had given her confidence and physical strength. She looked like a typical grandmother with white hair, a round smiling face and the ever present glasses on her nose which wouldn't stay put. She was happier than she had ever been and young Wendell was very proud of his mother. He was making arrangements to leave Huron and move to St. Paul to be with his family. Holly hoped they were all fine.

She glanced at the ticking clock and sighed. She roused herself and got up. She must get the thank you's to the post office by 5:00 o'clock.

The Viet Nam War dragged on, depressingly unwinable, until in 1973 the United States called it quits and pulled out. Veterans came home to a less than happy welcome, leaving bitterness on both sides. Wounds from the war and wounds from an unhappy populace would take years to heal, if they could be healed.

Huron College faced bankruptcy and was near collapse in 1976 when it was decided to disband fraternities and literary societies and place emphasis on integrating liberal arts and vocational technical courses. Holly was glad that Daisy had not seen that development after the many years she had been so totally involved in the college and Melvin's work and with faculty and students.

The drug culture made its way to Huron on the plains of South Dakota to the distress and anger of its citizens who had thought themselves immune to such degradations the rest of the country suffered from.

Then in 1977 a grave disagreement at St. John's Hospital occurred between the hospital staff and the Franciscan Sisters. The hospital was sold and its name was changed to the Huron Regional Medical Center. Plans were made to expand and improve its facilities.

Shortly thereafter in the fall of 1977 Holly received a Special Delivery letter from St. Paul. She opened it with anticipation. It was from Jennie and Holly's heart fell as she read.

> *Dear Aunt Holly,*
>
> *Mother died last night. It was her heart. She has always been well, but she had been working awfully hard and was getting on in years. Her heart just gave out.*
>
> *Bob and I and the kids will be bringing her back to Huron to be laid next to father. Thank goodness Wendell is still there. We are flying and I'll see you soon after you receive this letter.*
>
> *Please inform the others.*
>
> *Love, Jennie*

Tears began in reading Jennie's last line. The others. There were not many left of the others. But she made some telephone calls and, along with Sunny and Randy, met the plane to be with Wendell. It was a sad procession to Welters Funeral Home where they left another friend. An obituary had been placed in the *Daily Plainsman* so once again the Methodist Church was a meeting place for those who came to say goodbye. Older members of The Fortnightly were in attendance, as well as the few remaining friends of Laurel's family.

It had been several years since they had seen Jennie and the guests at the reception were impressed with how well she and her brother, Wendell, had taken care of the arrangements and of the courtesy they extended to those in attendance. Jennie had developed into an attractive, confident matronly woman. Her two children adored her and their father. She walked with comparative ease, even with the limp that was such a part of her and which no one took notice of any more. She came to Holly and Sunny with arms outstretched.

"Mother valued both of you so much. She often talked about the members of the original club and of how you had all known each other for so long. How wonderful to have such friendships."

She hugged and kissed them both. When she moved on to other mourners Sunny said, "What a fine woman she turned out to be. Laurel and

Wendell must have been so very proud. She's still so pretty. Remember when she was just a tot? She was such a doll."

Holly smiled and nodded.

The two of them stayed close all afternoon as though to be too far apart was to risk never to see the other again. Randy looked at the two women he had known so long and smiled with affection.

The following July in 1978 the Marvin Hughitt Hotel closed. The building was remodeled and converted to apartments on the upper floors, the marble ballroom floor was removed, and the building was renamed The Dakota Plaza, containing several businesses on the main floor with parking in the basement for tenants.

"Does nothing remain the same?" asked Holly in irritation. "What is the world coming to?"

Sunny replied, "Holly, we're just getting old."

Sunny and Holly, the last of the original nine

Chapter 27

A new era began in 1980. As with the beginning of each decade hopes were high that everyone's lives would steadily improve right up to the millennium. Talk had begun about the year 2000 and of approaching Armageddon. Those who had lived through most of the century stated the signs were clear to see and that mankind must make an about face and return to morality. The young, if they paid attention at all, dismissed such exhortations as mere rhetoric. Ronald Reagan had taken office as President of the United States and had captivated the country.

"Imagine!" said Holly. "A former movie star is our President. It's hard to comprehend, but he does have charisma."

"It could be just the actor in him," said Sunny.

They smiled. Both considered politics boring and more than a little corrupt and, at their advanced ages had abandoned any involvement in the political process.

They had settled into the routine of the elderly: relaxed and more secure, but slower in their movements, and enjoying the life that was left to them. They were having coffee in Sunny's big house, one of their regular routines. They were seated across from each other at a round marble topped table in front of the large picture window. The low ceilings and expanse of the rooms with an abundance of light coming through the big windows delighted Holly. She wished she could be as modern and up-to-date, although her own house had been updated. It wasn't the same and she had no intention of leaving her home, so she took great pleasure in her frequent visits with Sunny. And Sunny loved coffee at Holly's house, which evoked memories of an earlier time. Both houses had been built solidly and were in good shape to withstand the rigors of South Dakota's harsh weather.

The pleasant spring day was a tonic. They often gazed from the living room window onto the tree lined avenue. The lush trees, which had been mere seedlings when Sunny and Randy moved there, had grown tall and were of various hardy species, giving the neighborhood an aesthetic, tasteful sense. Many of the old elms in Huron that had arched over the streets so prettily for years had been thinned out due to Dutch Elm Disease. Elms and cottonwoods which once dotted the plains along river banks had been decimated. A few shelter belts of ancient, bent black trees were all that remained. In town residents planted ash, oak and maple, making the streets and avenues bright with color no matter what the season.

The sun-dappled landscape was quiet with only the sounds of birds coming through the open front door. There was little traffic in the afternoon and Holly had driven over. At the age of 87 she still drove the heavy 4-door Buick, the last car Jonathan had purchased. It was old but purred along nicely and required little maintenance. She surely didn't need such a big car, but it was there and she didn't drive much anymore. She sat erect and drove competently, but wondered about the old widows she would encounter driving in big cars that were their husbands, so small they could hardly see over the steering wheel. Some sat on cushions. She really should give up driving at all but to do so on occasion helped her to retain a sense of independence which, as she aged, was eroding.

Holly's hair was white and she had lines and wrinkles, as did Sunny. But, Holly noted, Sunny was far more attractive as an old woman. Her once thick blond hair was now thick white hair which she kept short, the better to manage it, and which framed her pretty face like a cloud. Holly just twisted her hair into a bun on top of her head. It was easier. The two women enjoyed a closeness that seemed to have lasted forever. There was a comfortable ease that didn't require constant conversation.

Despite the infirmities of old age, Holly felt very well. She was at peace with herself and her life, with no qualms about the end of it. As they sipped their coffee and looked out the window Randy's piano playing came softly from the den, adding a sense of serenity.

Sunny said, "I'm glad Randy resumed his playing. He had his training so long ago, but it never left him. Remember poor Miss Moselle? Such a waste of talent. Life is very strange."

Her freshly baked chocolate chip cookies arranged on a delicate china plate were set on the smooth surface of the coffee table. They always used their bone china when they met for their regular visits. It was a touch of elegance from the past and it would be a shame to not use it. They would comment on their afternoon teas with Violet and Mrs. Crane, tasting the clear liquid in her fragile cups. It was a time they cherished when they learned the genteel manners which they now took for granted and which affirmed their values, a barrier against the crudeness which was so prevalent.

They laughed as Randy swung into some boogie woogie, finishing with a flourish. As he strolled into the living room they applauded. He bowed slightly and murmured, "Thank you, thank you."

"Any cookies left," he asked mischievously as he scooped two from the plate and sat in a nearby chair.

"I love to hear you play," said Holly sincerely .

"It keeps my fingers limber and at my age it is definitely an achievement," he joked. He was in a particularly good mood and attributed it to the fine weather.

They gazed fondly at the man they loved and were content. Randy's tall frame was a bit stooped, but he was still a handsome man with a full head of silver hair. His glasses only enhanced his appearance. They spoke of the children. The two youngest had moved to Nebraska, but their brother, Scott, remained in Huron. He had become a doctor, now close to 50, and had formed a partnership with a younger man, had enlarged and modernized Randy's office and had a flourishing practice. Scott was the pride of his parents and absent brothers. On the times Holly caught a glimpse of Dr. Scott Thorne her heart jumped. He looked so much like his father. It was foolish of her to react in such a manner, but her heart gave a jump anyway. She would scold herself and consider the irony of the libido seeming never to die, and of the constancy of true love no matter what the age. She would tell herself that she did truly love Jonathan and that should be enough. She should not continue to think of Randy in that way every time she saw Scott. Such a fantasy! If all that reasoning didn't work she would look in the mirror and chide herself for such nonsense.

The time went by too quickly and Holly said she had to be getting home. She and Sunny made arrangements to go to the mall the next day and check out some new spring furnishings and maybe stop at Lewis Drug for some plantings. They stepped outside onto the long porch under the overhang, hating to part. Sunny gave her a hug. Randy did, too, and she let herself enjoy the feeling of his arms around her. No harm in that, not now. She stepped down onto the sidewalk and walked slowly to her car, turned and waved. She was refreshed. She wondered how many more pleasant afternoons they would enjoy.

In 1980 the population of Huron had dipped to around 13,000. People were more mobile those days and young folks tried their wings in other towns and other states. The Double H ice cream store was transformed into a barn-shaped structure, appropriately called The Barn, with a large seating capacity. Situated on the south edge of Huron on Highway 37 it was the first stop for a hungry traveler or a special stop for Huronites who wanted a delicious meal. The walls were decorated with pictures and western items and featured photographs of Cheryl Stoppelmoor Ladd, an aspiring actress from Huron, who later became one of Charlie's Angels on television and who achieved her goal as an actress in later years. Huron accepted it with pride and as par for the course for someone from the Midwest. Her periodic appearances in Huron to visit family were welcome proof she had not forgotten her roots.

In 1982 Huron boasted an Adult Day Care Center for the benefit of the aging population; the facility became the Huron Area Senior Center a few years later. Holly and Sunny joked about taking up residence there, to take advantage of the facilities, but there was a seriousness beneath the levity. They checked it out to satisfy their curiosity and decided against it because there were too many old people there. Each of them was all the other needed, and there was also Randy to meld them together.

But their trips to the mall or anywhere else that required extensive walking came to an end. Sunny became too tired to do it. It was necessary for her to sit down and catch her breath at frequent intervals. When Holly expressed concern she shrugged it off. "I'm just too old to walk much anymore. I'm all right. You have so much energy, Holly. Don't you ever get tired?"

She did, of course, but Sunny's chronic fatigue was becoming worrisome. Holly mentioned it to Randy one day when Sunny was in the kitchen getting refreshments.

"Yes, I have noticed it and I've made an appointment for her to see Dr. Engstrom in the office, at Scott's suggestion, for a long overdue check-up."

In the meantime, Holly and Sunny decided they should tender their resignations from The Fortnightly Club. They had been members for decades and had paid their dues without fail, whether they could be present for every meeting or not. But in recent years they agreed that they really had nothing to offer anymore and by their continued presence younger talented women were prevented from belonging. They made their resolve known, making way for invitations for two worthy women to join.

So in May, 1982, at the last meeting of the fiscal year, the club held a farewell tea of appreciation for them. Praise was given to two, loyal, contributing women to whom The Fortnightly was indebted and which would be the poorer with their absence. Holly and Sunny were overcome with all the unexpected attention. They were given a corsage, a spoken tribute, a plaque with their names and the years of service inscribed, along with many good wishes. It was with some sadness that they left the meeting for the last time, but with an exhilarating sense of accomplishment as well. It seemed ages ago when nine young women decided to meet and read and discuss in an effort to better themselves.

As they continued to read and discuss the newest books and magazines, which grew in profusion, Sunny laughed and said, "This is how we began." But some of their acquisitions of current best sellers left them appalled at what they found.

"Trash! Pure trash!" proclaimed Sunny. "Just look at what is in print nowadays — all this sex in graphic detail, and the violence! I just won't read this drivel. Besides, I consider it to be sinful."

"I don't know that it's sinful," replied Holly. "There is freedom of speech, remember."

"And that freedom carries with it responsibility. Why on earth would anyone write like that? Frankly, Holly, I don't know what this world is coming to — to repeat myself. And the movies are just as bad."

"Well, I have to agree with you there. The theaters are noisy, too. Maybe we should get one of those new-fangled gadgets, a VCR, I think they're called, and then we can pick and chose what we'd like to watch."

"Maybe someday, but I prefer to just play my records and read a good book. You can hardly find a vinyl record anymore either. Honestly! Thank goodness, the library is still intact."

Their generation was often criticized for being set in its ways. The older generation was quick to agree that they certainly were, and that those ways were mighty comfortable. They had lived long enough to settle into ways that fit them. Holly and Sunny were no exception and their golden years enveloped them in a protective cocoon with Randy at its center. On Sunday afternoons when the weather premitted Randy would take them for a drive around town on the deserted streets and out into the country to enjoy the air. They would treat themselves to ice cream cones from the Dairy Queen on the way home. They were compatible company which they did not want to lose; they took the days slowly, savoring what was left.

One Monday in October, after a particularly satisfactory Sunday outing the previous afternoon the telephone rang. It was late afternoon and Holly jumped at the sound, as she seldom had a telephone call from anyone but Sunny. It was Randy, His voice was choked with emotion as he told her that Sunny had collapsed and was in the Huron Regional Medical Center. With a lump in her throat and a pounding heart Holly got the car out and drove as quickly as she could to the hospital. Traffic was heavy at that time of day and school kids were everywhere in the pleasant weather. She chaffed at the delay.

It seemed to take forever to park and find Sunny's room. She opened the door with dread. She found Sunny lying motionless in the bed, pale and still, attached to a respirator. Randy was on one side and Scott on the other. They held her hands, but Sunny lay as though dead, with no response.

Holly stopped abruptly, her heart in her throat. "Randy," she whispered. "What's wrong with her?"

"The worst. A cerebral embolism."

Her heart sank.

Chapter 28

Sunny had had a stroke, a bad one. Randy and Scott remained at the bedside as she entered. Holly stayed with them.

She could not believe it, could not accept it, not her Sunny, her best friend in the whole world. She took a chair to one side, not wanting to intrude, and listened to the monitor as it recorded Sunny's irregular heartbeats. Randy laid his head down on the bed and his shoulders shook with his weeping. Scott sat staring at the prostrate form of his mother with his handsome face contorted in despair. Holly bent her head, not noticing the tears that fell onto her clasped hands.

She didn't know how much time elapsed, but was jolted alert by the sound of the monitor which suddenly emitted a steady pitch and the jagged line that had lurched across the screen flattened into a straight one. She went quickly to the bed. Randy leaped to his feet as a nurse rushed in. Scott commanded the nurse to do something, but knew it was useless. Valiant efforts to resuscitate Sunny were futile. They watched helplessly as the life supports were disconnected. An eery quiet filled the room. They were as motionless as the lifeless form on the bed.

Sunny was gone, her eyes closed in death. Scott sat beside his mother once more and put his arms across her body trying to keep her, not wanting to let her go. Randy and Holly stood side by side looking at Sunny's peaceful face through brimming eyes. Randy turned to her, his eyes full of pain and she held out her arms to him. They held each other and cried.

Wiping away the tears Holly walked to Scott, touched his shoulder and said softly, "Scott, your father needs you." Then she left the room and went to the nearby nurse's station to steady herself, leaving them with the wife and mother they had loved so dearly. Shortly the door opened and she had composed herself enough to go to them and offer her help.

She had no recollection of driving home, but it was dark when she found herself sitting in the car in the garage sobbing.

Arrangements for Sunny's funeral were made. Holly took on the sad task of notifying Randy's two sons in Nebraska and a cousin in Iowa. So few left to mourn.

Nevertheless the funeral was well attended by people who knew and respected Doctors Randall Thorne and Scott Thorne, not forgetting their selfless ministrations to the sick and dying. Various flower arrangements from Walker Florist were set around the casket and the altar at the Methodist Church. Beautiful music issued from the softly playing organ. As she stood there for one last time to look at her lifelong friend and etching the image forever into her brain, it took all of Holly's strength of will. Sunny was beautiful in every way, even in death. She could not stop the flow of tears and knew she could not bear it anymore. She gripped the side of the casket as a wave of dizziness swept over her. An usher appeared and led her gently to a pew at the back of the church. She was grateful to him and, although she was urged by Scott to join them and be with the family as they sat together, she refused and sank into herself as the music continued. She was filled with a sadness that was all-encompassing, the scent of the many flowers overpowered her senses, and sheer loneliness filled her being. As soon as it was over and before the pall bearers began their trip up the aisle to the back of the church, she fled out a side door. It was just too much.

She sat in her car and tried to pull herself together. She could not follow the line of cars to the cemetery, she just couldn't. But she couldn't go home either. She made a decision. She could at least do something useful. She drove to Randy's house and left a note on the door that she would be bringing the family their supper, in case they got home before she got there. Then she went to her home and busied herself with the preparations.

The three sons had wives and children and there would be many at the table. She plunged into her task with gusto, with a store of energy that rose to the surface, blocking out her sorrow, at least for a little while. She worked steadily and when she had finished she placed her succulent pork roast, baked potatoes, freshly sliced tomatoes and green beans in large containers. Thank goodness for Tupperware she thought. She drove carefully to Randy's house and let herself in with the key Sunny had given her years ago. She made several trips from the car to the house and was glad there was a wrought iron railing on each side of the few steps to the porch, as she gripped them firmly going up and down. She was breathing deeply from the steady exertion. Breaths came from deep down, purging her of grief and anger with every exhalation. The grief she understood, but even as she accepted it she didn't understand her anger. After all, Sunny was old, but Holly was as angry as she had ever been. But she mustn't dwell on it; she must just keep on moving until she had everything inside.

She got the food into the kitchen and sat down for a minute trying not to think. If she thought, she would cry, and she had cried until it hurt. She gave herself a good talking to and took a deep breath, then washed her hands and set the dining table. She had wrestled with the table leaves to make the table long enough. The rage within her gave her continued strength. But her eyes were dry as she found Sunny's linen table cloth and napkins and set the table with her best china and silver. She and Randy had entertained often and there was plenty of every piece to set a fine looking table. Then she turned to the kitchen and set the oven on low, transferred the roast and its savory juices to a large pan and placed it inside to keep warm, along with the potatoes. She was heating the beans when she heard them at the front door.

"Hello. Holly? We found your note," said Randy in a tired voice. "We missed you at the church."

She turned to face him. Her expression was grim and determined and he understood. He came to her and said, "Holly, my dear, dear friend, you certainly didn't have to make supper for us. But thanks." He had his arm around her waist and hugged her to him.

Randy's sons burst into the kitchen with appreciative comments on the wonderful aromas coming from the oven.

Scott said, "What a welcome home, Aunt Holly. We're all hungry. It was so hard to get through the church lunch and all the people there. I don't know how anyone is expected to eat and carry on a polite conversation after burying a loved one."

Holly began to relax with the friendly commotion. The knot in her stomach left her. She was pleased to see that all her work had borne the fruition she had hoped for. She was led into the living room where she greeted Randy's daughters-in-law and grandchildren of whom he was so proud and in whom he took such pleasure. She knew why. His sons had married fine women and the grandchildren had grown into intelligent, thoughtful adults. Holly basked in the warmth of the family and in Randy's presence. After a brief visit and getting them all settled at the table she put the dinner on with the welcome help of the women. Then, as a murmured prayer was said, she slipped quietly out the back door. She heard faintly, "Where is Aunt Holly going to sit?" But she had started her car and was gone before they realized it. She was suddenly exhausted. She drove home and went directly to bed where she sank into a dreamless sleep.

October continued warm and ablaze with the colors of the season. But its warmth could not penetrate Holly's being. Her heart felt cold and she experienced real loneliness for the first time in her long life. She had been lonesome now and then, but she had never before been so bereft of someone to be with or to turn to at any time. There was still Randy, but it was not her place to intrude unless asked by the family. She surely could not replace Sunny in their hearts.

Randy's sons and their families returned to Nebraska and Scott returned to his medical practice. He and his wife kept close watch on Randy who seemed to have suddenly aged years. He was more stooped and walked slowly, peering through his glasses. He was close to 90, but to Holly he was still a fine figure of a man whom she never stopped loving.

In late October Holly went out onto the porch to get her mail, hoping there might be something with a first class stamp on it, but she couldn't imagine who would be writing her a letter. After all, she reminded herself, everyone she had known had died. There was always junk mail, which made up most of her garbage, but she enjoyed leafing through the catalogs and marveling at what was considered fashion for a dandy price. She didn't need anything. Her wardrobe may have been dated, but her clothing was of good quality and in good taste. The wind was becoming quite brisk; the weather was definitely beginning to turn colder. She sighed as she lifted the flap of the mailbox. Nothing of interest. She turned to go back into the house when she stopped in surprise. There was Randy in the corner of the porch sitting on one of the old wicker chairs which she had not yet put into the garage for the winter.

"Randy, how long have you been sitting there? Why didn't you come in?"

He lifted his head and peered at her over his bifocals and said, "Hello, Holly. I haven't been here very long. I was just out walking and needed to sit down for a minute. I knew you wouldn't mind."

"Of course I wouldn't mind. Did you walk all the way from your place?"

He sheepishly admitted that he had. Holly took his hand and said, "For goodness sake, Randy, that is much too far to walk. You come right on inside and warm yourself. I'll make us some coffee." She scolded him all the way to the kitchen as he meekly followed her.

They sat at the kitchen table and were quiet for a few minutes as the coffee restored his spirits.

"Honestly, Randy, what will we all do with you? You can't just wander off like that."

"I didn't just wander off," he said testily. "I wanted to come to see you; it's a nice day so I just started out. I guess my old legs are giving out."

"Well, I am very glad to see you," she smiled. "But I could have come to get you. Or you could have driven over yourself."

"I told you it was a nice day and I wanted to walk," he said with his eyes snapping.

Holly began to laugh. "We sound like a couple of old codgers arguing over nothing."

"You're right. Sorry I raised my voice. I shouldn't yell at you."

"Forget it."

"It's lonesome in that big house. It's so empty now. I suppose I should move into an apartment — or a nursing home," he said grumpily .

"Nonsense. You are not ready for a nursing home. But it is true that that big house is plenty of room enough, with some left over. Maybe you could get someone to move in with you — you know, a housekeeper."

He snorted at that idea. "That house holds so many memories. Sunny made it a home and those memories surround me so completely sometimes that it is suffocating and I want to escape. Yet to sell the home we shared is a painful thought. I cannot imagine anyone else living there, not even a housekeeper."

"Take your time. There's no hurry. Come over here any time. And if you'd rather not drive I'll come and get you. So far, my driving hasn't caused any difficulty for me or the public."

He agreed and promised to call her if he needed her. She drove him home and walked with him up the steps. She told him she would be over the next day to fix him his supper. He said only if she would stay and share it with him.

The warmth of the fall was rapidly changing to the feel of approaching winter, but on pleasant days Randy and Holly would sit on her porch or on his porch and talk or simply sit quietly and watch the few people who passed by.

"Do you ever think about the days when we were children — all of us when we played in the vacant lot?" Holly asked one day.

"Yeah," he replied. "We did have fun, didn't we? Of course that Butch gave us a lot of grief. My antipathy for him turned to pity as grew older. He had a pretty miserable childhood."

"Yet most of us stayed right here in Huron, unusual," she said.

"Unusual according to the way things are today. It's different now; times change. But those days were something, a more innocent time," he nodded.

"Randy do you every wonder about Butch and his tragic life, and of Rose and Clarence dying the way they did?"

He didn't answer right away.

"As a matter of fact, yes, I gave it a lot of thought over time. We know what a villain Butch was and of the questionable people he associated with. Mind you, I never heard any explanation other than the official one that was given. But I did hear at one time that organized crime, as it's called, had something to do with the entire affair. And," he paused, "it is thought that the FBI was called in but had not been able to solve it to any satisfaction. As it turned out, they didn't have to act to get rid of Butch — neither the crime bosses nor the FBI — but Rose and Clarence knew too much and Rose was not shy about advertising it. Maybe the old brewery was purposely torched to set an example. Anyone who would really know the truth is long gone, dead and buried. It's probably just gossip. You know how people are. But, on the other hand, everyone involved was eliminated in one way or the other."

"It does make one wonder," she mused.

He stood up to leave, gripping the arms of the chair. "Well, we all had it much better with the people in our lives. You can't beat friendships that last like that. I miss everyone of them, too; we were one big family growing up together."

She gave a soft sigh. "And now they are all gone, except for you and me. I guess when we get this old it is inevitable that those we love will leave us. They die and we are alone."

"Yes, we are the ones left behind but our lives have been full," he said. He took her in his arms and held her closely as he said, "Holly, dear Holly, what would every last one of us have done without you? You are such a loving person."

He kissed her lips with a tenderness that made her young again and she smiled lovingly at the man she had loved all her life. His eyes showed a fondness for her. He spoke with undying friendship, but she responded with undying love.

With the darkness of late fall and oncoming winter they embraced the warmth and comfort of their time together. Holly would fix a meal in the kitchen while Randy set the table. They puttered around like an old couple who had been married for 50 years and more, two old friends comfortable with each other. When dishes were done they sat on the sofa and talked or watched a favorite television program. They particularly enjoyed Carol Burnett and chuckled at her antics. When she left his house to go home he left the set on for company until he fell asleep. Often as they sat closely together Randy held her hand. It seemed to comfort him. Thus, the two elderly people sustained each other, feeling that to let go would be to suffer another irretrievable loss. Oddly, Holly was happy, even knowing it could not last for a length of time.

In February the town was buffeted by a three-day blizzard. The telephone became their means of communication. Everyone was confined to their homes while the blizzard raged. When Randy began to cough and it became persistent he said he had better save his voice and would call her later. He had been saying this even before the blizzard hit and when she urged him to see Dr. Engstrom in Scott's office he told her that he was a doctor and that he'd soon be fit as a fiddle. As the temperature outside fell, the snow piled up and the windows frosted over she grew worried when she didn't hear from him. Then the tumult of wind and snow ceased. She hastily went to the telephone when it finally rang, it wasn't Randy, but Scott. He told her he was sorry, but Randy had died.

"When I couldn't get an answer to my telephone call I somehow managed to get over there. He was really sick and somehow Engstrom and I got him to the hospital. The medical report lists the cause of death as pneumonia, but he just faded away, Aunt Holly. Ever since mother died, he just seemed to be fading away. Except when he was with you and thank goodness for your constant help. Dad talked about you a lot and of how much you meant to him. We shall never forget that. I'll let you know about the arrangements. Aunt Holly ....?"

She dropped the receiver and sank into a chair. The emerging bright rays of sunshine that streamed through the windows, bouncing off the masses of brilliant snow, were a mockery.

Chapter 29

Holly was reading the *Huron Plainsman*, the name the daily had settled on by 1984. She always read it from front to back to keep up with what was happening. Time had marched inexorably on in the two years since Randy had died. She was alone. There were moments when she felt left out of the flow of life, that she had been left behind. After she had entered Randy's date of death in her memory book, as she called it, she had written:

> *"I am sad. I remember when we were all alive and vigorous and a part of things. But the years slip away and when I look around I find myself alone, solitary in a world that is foreign to me, with only my memories to remind me of my existence."*

She considered that morose commentary to be her last entry and saw no reason to add anything more. She felt there was no reason to even write it down, but in doing so she felt better.

Her routine gave her a reason to get up in the morning. She dusted the house every other day to get some exercise though it seldom needed it. The heavy vacuum cleaner gave her a challenge and kept her heart pumping. She employed a personable young man named Todd to keep the yard mowed, the snow shoveled, and to take her to Randall's where the bakery was superb. She enjoyed their conversations, but didn't understand his lack of concern when she expressed indignation when Huron College disassociated itself from the Presbyterian Church and concentrated on business courses. He was enrolled in business administration and didn't understand her point of view. But their clash of opinions didn't undermine the respect they had for each other. He expressed great admiration for her car and eventually she sold it to him. It was old, but the Buick ran perfectly. She no longer drove and he was thrilled to have a vintage automobile that worked fine.

As she perused the paper an item caught her eye. Gladys Pyle had entered the Huron Nursing Home. Gracious, she and Gladys had to be close to the same age. Holly had just turned 91. They had a lot in common except that Gladys had not married. She had also lived in the family home for a long time. Holly put down the paper and stared out the window where the sun was still ablaze. It was hot. She should have shut the house sooner, but she hated to move and the fan was giving off a gentle breeze. She became exasperated when her old bones refused her commands to move properly, which sometimes caused her to say aloud, "Darn it all anyway!" The epithet was as profane as Holly got.

She shook her head to ban the troublesome thoughts. If she let herself, she would sit too long pondering dark reveries. She turned to thinking of what she needed to do the next day. The new young pastor of The Methodist Church, a Reverend Charles Johnson, had called her, saying he was getting acquainted with his new parish and, in going over the roster of members, he saw that she had been a member for many years. He would like to stop in for a visit if it would be convenient. How about tomorrow at 2:00 o'clock? She decided to serve iced tea since it was so hot and she'd bake a cake, a small one, easy to make and so moist. Not one of those box cakes. She felt guilty whenever she used one, although some were quite tasty.

She picked up the paper again and read the comics, laughed at the Peanuts comic strip, then folded it neatly and added it to a stack of papers in the back entryway to be recycled. Land sakes, who'd have thought the country would someday run short of paper. As it was, the newspaper was getting mighty thin. Why, she remembered the satisfying sound of the rustle the paper made when Papa would fold it back to read the editorials. It was different now. Everything was different now, she thought irritably.

Early the next day she got out the ingredients for her vanilla cake, greased a small square pan, and looked at her old stained recipe card. She had often made the cake over the years when she and Sunny and Randy used to — she shook her head again and concentrated or the task at hand. She set the oven. The cake would be baked and the heat from the oven blown out the back door by her trusty fan before her guest arrived. Then she'd close up the house and turn the fan on high to keep the living room cool. She was used to living without air conditioning, but she realized that most people relied on it. Too late for that now at her age.

She turned on the radio in the kitchen to get some music and heard a country western fellow singing in a twangy voice 'You Took a Fine Time to Leave me Lucille.' She smiled at the lyrics, then laughed aloud. It must be one of those new comic songs. But the singer was dead serious, which made her chuckle even more. Maybe she could get the Aberdeen station. She finished mixing the batter and lifted the bowl to pour it into the pan when it slipped from her hand and broke into pieces, denting the pan in the process.

"Oh! Darn it all!"

She surveyed the mess caused by her carelessness and knew she had to throw it all out. She cleaned it up and deposited the broken bowl, the batter and pan in a paper grocery sack to take out to the garbage can later.

197

She didn't feel like starting over but she was piqued at having ruined her mother's baking pan, which had been used over and over. What should she do? she wondered what might be in the freezer compartment above the refrigerator. She opened the door and sighed as she found it full of plastic containers filled with bits of leftovers. She was positive she had some muffins or cookies in there somewhere. In her search small packages and old margarine tubs tumbled out and rolled all over the floor.

"Well,gee whiz!"

Laboriously she stooped over and picked them up and put them back, quickly shutting the freezer door before they fell out again. She considered her refreshments once more and decided she'd just serve cheese and crackers with the iced tea, which she remembered she had better do at once. She didn't like the prepared iced tea either, preferring to use tea bags, but it required a certain amount of refrigeration. She got it done, decided against having lunch after all the time in cleaning up after herself, and concluded that a nice cool bath would soothe her frazzled nerves.

She had closed off the upstairs rooms which she surely didn't need and used the downstairs bedroom and bath which were sufficient for her needs, except that the old claw-footed tub was too small for her long frame, but she adapted to it. The stairs were too hard to climb and there was no sense in heating the upper floor in winter with no one using it. She laid out a clean dress, one of her old lady dresses she called them, and dropped her others in the hamper. Laundry and ironing were getting difficult to do, too. But she didn't have time to think about it just then. She poured some Avon rose scented bubble bath into the tub as tepid water gradually filled it. It smelled nice and made the water soft. She stepped in and sat down, relaxing in the temperate water. The scent of the bubbles perked her up and she leaned back and soaked. Refreshed, she stood up and reached for the soft towel on the rack fastened to the wall, It slipped from her hand and fell into the water where she watched it slowly submerge.

"Well, if that doesn't get my goat!" she sputtered.

She climbed carefully from the tub, wiped her feet on the oval rug and walked to the linen closet in the corner where she took out another towel. She was getting a bit annoyed and hot in the process, but she dried herself and returned to the tub, letting the water run out. She picked up the sopping wet towel and wrung it out the best she could, muttering "Darned arthritis" and laying it along the rounded rim of the tub. It wouldn't take long to dry in the heat that promised to be worse than the day before. She had better get a move on if she was going to be ready when the pastor came. She dried her hands and arms and put on her light bathrobe, fastening it loosely with the belt. As she turned to go back into the bedroom she slipped on a patch of water left from her struggle with the bath towel..

There was no time to think as she fell and hit her head. All she was aware of was a sharp pain, then nothing.

She awoke confused. She wasn't sure if she had been asleep and just awakened and she didn't know where she was. Her eyes wouldn't focus, but she knew she had to get up and get busy. She was supposed to be doing something. She heard,

"Aunt Holly."

Her vision cleared a little and she saw Randy's face bent over hers. But no, it wasn't Randy. Her head ached.

"Aunt Holly, you are in the hospital." Replying to her perplexed expression he said, "You have a broken hip and a bump on your head. Reverend Johnson found you on the floor and called the hospital and they notified me. Dr. Engstrom and I arranged to have you admitted. The Reverend said you were expecting him but there was no answer to his knock. He heard the radio so he opened the door and found you, thank goodness."

That young pastor had discovered her on the floor in only her flimsy robe how awful! What would people think? She could only hope that she was fully covered. She tried to speak but couldn't.

"Don't try to talk just now. I've given you a shot for the pain. Just rest. You'll be well cared for. I'll look in on you later."

"Scott," she slurred the words, "how long —?"

"I'm afraid you'll need flat on your back bed rest for at least six weeks. You need to heal that hip." He patted her hand and smiled with compassion and left.

Six weeks. Impossible! She had never been a patient in a hospital in her life. For goodness sake she still had her appendix. Such a turn of events. And to think that young pastor had seen her looking like that. Why, she was practically — undressed. A fine state of affairs. Her brain was tired and she couldn't think anymore . She soon drifted off.

Holly slowly healed. During her hospitalization she did a lot of serious thinking about her future. She was very old and she had suffered a broken hip. It would probably never function properly again. She was glad her head had recovered swiftly, but she had a hard head so there couldn't be a problem there was her caustic remark to Scott. As time went on she came to a realization, and hated to admit it, but she needed someone to take care of her. She had been independent all of her long life and now she was totally dependent on strangers and would be for what time was remaining. She wanted to get well and go home. But what if she wasn't able to return to her home? What then? Oh, but I must go home, I want to go home.

Scott came to see her every day and she looked forward to it. He was a fine doctor and she loved his resemblance to his father. Scott was immensely pleased with how she was progressing.

"Aunt Holly, you are basically a strong, healthy woman." He looked at her somberly. "But we must think ahead about your plans when you are dismissed from the hospital."

Her heart sank at his expression. She knew what their discussion would entail. He pulled up a chair and they had a long talk. In the end they reached a conclusion and she knew it was for the best. She would admit herself to the Huron Nursing Home. How she dreaded it, but she simply could not remain alone in her home, not without help anyway, which was not easy to find. She required someone to live in and be with her. She had no family. Family and friends were all dead. What would she do if she fell again? What would she do when Todd could no longer take her on errands and keep up the yard work? What would she do if she ran out of groceries or the furnace didn't work? The answers frightened her and along with that fright was a different fear — she was no longer in control of her life.

She needed to talk to a lawyer. Gracious! Even her lawyer had passed on. But she found a new lawyer, a smart man in his early forties, who arranged everything. But first she had to go back home to dispose of some belongings and decide what to take with her to the home. Scott and his nurse took her. It was hard to have to be helped up the front steps and into the house because the hip wasn't yet back to normal. But she needed to return even though it would be the last time. It was so good to be home again, but tears came as they got to the chore of doing what they had come to do. How did one dispose of the belongings of a lifetime?

She had to be firm with herself. It was inevitable that she would reach this point in her life. She decided to donate her large library of books to the library to do with what they wished. She selected the nicest of her clothing, discarding the rest. After all, who would want her outdated clothes that would not fit anyone? She took the radio for company. It was decided that the house would be rented fully furnished with what was left. The money realized would supplement what Jonathan had left her. Before they left the house with the few items and a boxful of stationery, pens, a few toiletries and her memory book she paused and looked at her home, mentally saying goodbye. Scott took her arm and, with his nurse, led her out of the house and assisted her down the steps. She forced herself to not look back. She could not look forward to her life facing her, but she could accept it. There couldn't be much life left to her. She had just passed her 92nd birthday. When she was settled in the car Scott turned to her and asked, "Is there somewhere you'd like to go before we get to the ...."

She made one request which he gladly granted. Could they please stop at Osco Drug for just a minute? She wanted to make a small purchase.

Scott was eager to do anything for her. He wheeled her into the drug-store and she went directly to the perfume counter and bought a large bottle of Giorgio perfume. She explained, "I don't want to smell like an old woman while I'm there."

"Aunt Holly, you are the limit," said Scott in delight. "Is there anything else you'd like to do?"

"No, thank you, dear. I'm ready. Let's go before I change my mind."

Her sister Opal came to mind as they stopped in front of the nursing home. Her pitiful cries had wrenched at her heart. So Holly sat erect and smiled broadly as Scott wheeled her into the building where she was met with respectful greetings by cheerful young women who admitted her. She was shown into a room with two beds, both empty. The room was separated by a curtain. She was given the bed by the window and was pleased with the view, the green lawn, the trees and the sounds of the birds. Although she knew it would take some getting used to at what looked like very cramped quarters after having lived so long in a house, she endeavored to adjust without remourse. She didn't need much room and it surely wouldn't be for very long. She was prepared to meet her Maker at any time He chose.

She was soon settled in and adapting well to the routine. There were plenty of activities to keep residents occupied. She could listen to her radio and she read the *Huron Plainsman* every day to keep in touch with the outside world. She didn't need the wheelchair for very long and made it a point to walk around the area daily to build up her strength. The staff greeted her with cheer as they saw her on her daily walks and she responded in kind. She was enjoying the privacy of having the room entirely to herself but wondered how long it would last.

She didn't have long to wait. Soon an old woman named Ula was admitted and assigned the other bed, arriving making a loud fuss, weeping and wailing.

"I want to go home," she cried over and over. The nurse could not quiet her and the young woman who came with her tried in vain to persuade her that everything would be fine, that she would be well cared for, finally despairing and running from the room. Ula eventually quieted down and stared at Holly.

"Who are you?" she demanded.

"My name is Holly Hoekstra. I hope we shall enjoy being roommates."

They were roommates for years. Ula came to depend on Holly, who obligingly wheeled her in her chair all around the nursing home. They would watch television in the large lobby. Each afternoon there was something to do in the dining room, having coffee and cookies as they visited, playing cards or games. Ula had very little company, mainly the young woman who had been with her on Ula's admittance. She was Ula's niece and Ula caused her much distress with every visit as she entreated her to take her home. She would soon be in tears and one day explained to Holly that she was her only remaining relative and she could no longer take care of her. There was just no other solution than to put her in the nursing home. Holly assured her that she understood and that Ula was really just fine. She only liked to make a fuss to get attention. The niece seemed relieved to hear it. Eventually, she moved away and Ula had no visitors except for an occasional delegation from her church on their regular visitations.

The years went slowly by and Holly continued her active participation in any event offered by the nursing home. She needed to keep busy and keep the blood flowing. She would not even take a nap, claimed she slept much better if she didn't. Besides, there was plenty to keep her brain working in the daytime. She walked the halls every day, often pushing Ula. She tried to ignore the sounds of the old people and to maintain a sense of humor and not be any trouble. Her supply of Giorgio perfume was replenished from time to time by Scott's thoughtful nurse. Holly was grateful to use it to mask the sometimes unpleasant odors emanating from some of the rooms. Then Scott had a new nurse and she didn't have the heart to ask her to run the small errand for her. However, at Christmas one year and for the few Christmases thereafter Holly's gift from Jennie was a beautifully wrapped set of Yardley lavender scented soaps. She grew to love the smell and knew it was much more appropriate for a woman her age.

The staff liked Mrs. Hoekstra who was such a contrast to many of their residents. Holly fervently wished, though, that the nurses would not shout when addressing her. She could hear perfectly, but they evidently did not believe her and continued to yell. Holly knew that many of the people there were hard of hearing. Some of the residents refused to hear, shutting out everyone and their surroundings. Holly did plenty of reading from material supplied by the library cart which was pushed by volunteers. She was very pleased to find one of her donated books now and then, but most of the books were in large print for those whose eyesight was not good.

Each passing year Holly appeared to grow shorter, having become more stooped, and her legs refused to walk as far as they used to. Her mended hip flared up every once in awhile when the weather changed. She rarely got any mail, except on her birthdays. There would always be a birthday card from The Huron Fortnightly. They never forgot. Holly was sure they wondered how many more birthday cards they would be sending to old Mrs. Hoekstra.

She read the newspaper thoroughly and was pleased to read the big spread it contained when the Crossroads Hotel and Convention Center opened downtown on May 30, 1987. It was a large building containing meeting rooms, a large lobby, and a fine restaurant aptly called The Library with actual books adorning shelves along the wall. On the grounds of the center stood a beautiful 9 foot statue of a prairie woman. The $50,000 sculpture was cast in bronze by a talented young man, Dale Lamphere, and appropriately called Spirit of Dakota. Holly hoped that she could see this work on one of the monthly outings set aside for the residents. She took advantage of every opportunity to get outside when it was offered, especially enjoying lunch at The Barn. She loved feeling a part of civilization again.

Holly was 97 years old in 1990, once again pondering the beginning of a new decade. She knew she wouldn't see the end of it, probably wouldn't even survive 1990. But she did. Ula continued her erratic outbursts and drove the nurses frantic when she would turn up the volume on her radio's religious station and sing along. She would be admonished to keep her radio turned down and if the lowered decibels lulled her to sleep everyone was happy. Ula could drift off to sleep anywhere and anytime. Holly used these times to read in peace.

One day in 1991 while reading the paper Holly uttered, "Well, if that doesn't beat all!" She was chagrined to note that Huron College had been sold to the Japanese. Imagine! She was outraged. Of all things! What on earth did the Japanese want with a college on the plains of South Dakota! If Daisy were still alive she would have plenty to say about that.

When Holly awoke on July 31, 1993, she suddenly realized that she was 100 years old. Her birthday had already been observed, as it was customary to observe a day each month to celebrate all the birthdays in that month. Everyone looked forward to the cake and ice cream. Holly considered her birthday to be over. She groaned. One hundred years old; it was a fact.

"Holly, you OK?" came from Ula on the other side of the curtain.

"Yes, of course; my old bones ache, that's all."

A nurse entered the room with a helium balloon with Happy Birthday emblazoned on it and some mail in her hand. She presented the envelopes to Holly with a broad smile.

"Open this one first, Holly." she said.

It was from President Clinton. "My goodness," exclaimed Holly. There was the usual greeting from The Huron Fortnightly and one from Jennie. Holly remembered her as a perennially beautiful young woman, but who undoubtedly must be aging and graying herself by now. Scott stepped into the room and gave her the biggest card decorated with flowers and birds and a verse that made tears come. He kissed her and she was aware of his aging as well. When formerly young people began to look old to her she knew she really was 100 years old.

Scott smiled and said, "Happy birthday, Aunt Holly. What a feat to have lived 100 years. I'm very proud of you. You are still as bright and full of love as you have always been. Did you know that Willard Scott wished you a happy birthday this morning?"

"Who is Willard Scott?"

He laughed and replied, "He's the weather man on NBC's TODAY show, the morning news program. He's been wishing a happy birthday to people observing their 100th birthdays for years. You were on national television this morning. Just think of that."

Holly smiled at him in affection. Goodness gracious, what a fuss. Lots of folks reached the age of 100 these days. She added to herself that she clearly didn't know why, for what purpose. Most of them were pretty helpless. But she was still around and grateful for her good health. She enjoyed the day in spite of herself.

When they told her that someone from the *Huron Plainsman* was coming to interview her and take her picture she was unprepared.

"Whatever for?" was her remark.

"Because you have turned 100 and that is still news," they explained.

On the designated day Holly rose, bathed and dressed as usual. After lunch she was all ready and sitting on the bed waiting for the person who would be talking to her. They told her the appointment was for 2:00 o'clock, but it was after 2:00. Oh, well, what else would she be doing? Patience was a virtue she had long cultivated. Ula was taking a nap and Holly wished she wouldn't snore so loudly. What would this person think?

She heard, "Hello?" and then a pretty young woman came into the room and walked to her bed.

Chapter 30

After two weeks of being interviewed by that nice Karen Williams Holly felt strange. It was nothing she had ever experienced. It had not been all her talking that had tired her; in fact, it had proved to be exhilarating.

She was tired, but in spite of it there was a compelling urgency to relate more. With an effort she leaned over and pushed the record button on Karen's machine which was set on Holly's memory book to keep it steady. Then she laid back on her pillow, wearily closed her eyes and heard herself speak into the recording machine. Or were the words merely thoughts in her fevered brain?

She continued on and on and hoped that the tape would contain all she needed to say. She began to feel better. She was not as dizzy as before. Then she was wonderfully refreshed and a sublime contentment filled her being. At last she was finished. She breathed a deep sigh and smilingly opened her eyes. With surprise she found herself bathed in a brilliant light and experienced an enveloping unconditional love and a peace that was not of her world.

Karen entered the nursing home with a spring in her step. She carried a framed photograph of Mrs. Hoekstra as a gift from herself. She had all the information she needed from Holly and all she had to do was pick up her tape recorder and hasten to the office to put the finishing touches on her article, which was taking shape nicely. She had really enjoyed the assignment, which she had dreaded that first day when she came to interview Mrs. Holly Hoekstra. She also had a far different view of old people, saw them in a different light. They were not all senile, nodding in their wheelchairs. They embodied wisdom and experience and had so much to pass on to younger generations, if only someone took the time to listen. Well, they would listen when they read her article.

She waved her usual greeting to the woman at the desk, ignoring the efforts to catch her attention, and walked down the hall to Holly's room. The door was unexpectedly closed, so she knocked and opened the door slightly. She smiled and said hello to Ula and walked in, then stopped abruptly. The curtain dividing the room was drawn back as far as it would go and a nurse's aide was packing a few items of clothing into a box. The bed had been stripped of its linen. Karen looked wide-eyed at Ula who sat in her wheelchair, watching intently. In answer to Karen's unspoken question she said, "Holly died. I get the place by the window now."

In a shocked voice Karen asked the aide, "Is it true? Did Mrs. Hoekstra die?"

The young woman turned to her and said matter-of-factly, "Yes, it's true. Holly died sometime last night. Are you a relative? We have to dispose of her things."

"No. No, I'm not a relative, just a friend. I just spoke to her yesterday," she protested. "In fact, I've spoken to her several times in the past two weeks. I know she was elderly, but she seemed fine, except that yesterday she wasn't quite herself."

The aide was moving competently around the room removing the birthday cards from the window sill and packing miscellaneous items into the box. She stepped around Karen.

"Excuse me, but I have to get this space ready as soon as possible. We have a waiting list you know. I wonder what I should do with these plants. They're looking a mite poorly."

The woman from the front desk rushed into the room and said, "I'm sorry but I tried to stop you when you came in."

"I get the place next to the window. Holly said I could," wailed Ula.

She was ignored and sank into her private mumbles.

Karen was driven to tears. Why am I crying? I scarcely knew the woman. But the stripping away of the last bestige of a person's life was so cold and impersonal, not at all like the warm woman Karen had come to know and respect.

The aide continued, "She died peacefully in her sleep. There was nothing to indicate any stress when we found her this morning. In fact, she had a really sweet smile on her face. She was a nice old lady, no trouble at all. Oh well, I guess it's the best way to go, wouldn't you say?"

Karen didn't hear the apologetic woman from the desk say, "I'm truly sorry, Miss Williams, but I just couldn't catch your attention."

"I've come for my tape recorder," she said as she reached for it. On impulse, she snatched up the memory book and, still clutching the framed photograph, she turned and fled. Tears blurred her vision. How quickly and silently one could die. Maybe she had tired her. She had caused Holly to dredge up some painful memories. But no, that wasn't it. Mrs. Hoekstra was an old woman alone in the world. Karen couldn't face it if she might have hastened her death.

Quickly she left the building. The early autumn wind stirred the dust in the driveway into tiny funnels as she got into her car and returned to the office. She stopped in the ladies' room and rinsed her face, blotting it dry with a paper towel. She stared into the mirror and wondered what she would look like when she got old, wondered how old she would live to be, and what the whole thing was about anyway. You were born, you lived a life that was often unsatisfactory, and then you died alone in a nursing home with no one to mourn your passing — or to care.

"What's the matter with you?" asked Mr. Stern as he stopped at her desk where Karen sat staring at her computer.

"I just got back from the nursing home. Mrs. Hoekstra ...."

"Well, I hope you can finish the article on that Mrs. what's-her-name, because I'm losing interest."

She shot him a look that made him wonder, but he said "Get on with it and we'll still get in the Sunday edition." She began to type:

> "A venerable lady died last night. Mrs. Holly Hoekstra, a resident of the Huron Nursing Home since 1984, died in her sleep after a long, productive life. Mrs. Hoekstra celebrated her 100th birthday a few weeks before her death. This reporter was privileged to interview her and a full report will appear in Sunday's edition of the *Huron Plainsman*. Mrs. Hoekstra left no survivors. Funeral arrangements are pending."

Karen set to work on her article which contained a large photograph of Mrs. Holly Hoekstra sitting on her bed smiling brightly. Then she turned her attention to her notes and the tape recorder and leafed through the book she had picked up as she fled the nursing home. The tape contained some indistinct remarks that made no sense but she let it run to the end, when Holly's frail voice was heard.

> *"We girls were bound together in love, connected in friendship and in spirit. True friends are truly a blessing. How fortunate we were."*

Fortunate indeed. She opened the book to the first entry which said: Today I turned 60. The book consisted mainly of the names and dates of birth and death of family and friends plus some comments that augmented her notes. The last entry was a poem in Holly's precise handwriting. Karen had what she needed, easily completed her article and presented it to Mr. Stern, who was pleased with the finished result. It would be featured in the PRIDE AROUND TOWN section of the paper.

The day of the funeral Karen entered the Welter Funeral Home, signed the guest book with its short list of names and approached the casket. On each side stood a small floral arrangement provided by the funeral home. Karen looked down at Holly's face, so serene in repose, yet the strength and resolve with which she had conducted her life were there. They had dressed her in a pink frock with a white collar which complemented her white hair which was set in a neat bun on the top of her head. Somehow

Karen was filled with an inspiration which no one had ever conveyed to her. What a nice feeling. Maybe that was a part of what life was all about.

Her sadness was gone and she took a seat behind the few who had come to bid Holly goodbye. She had not attended many funerals in her young life, but she was sure they were better attended than this one. It was the smallest gathering she had ever seen. She stared at the six pallbearers, then glanced at the folder containing information about the deceased. The pallbearers listed were not the familiar names she had come to know. They obviously were not descendants of Holly's friends. She rightly surmised that the distinguished silver-haired, bespectacled gentleman was Dr. Scott Thorne seated beside a younger man who looked like a lawyer. A lone representative from the nursing home was there and that was all except for herself. The others present were looking at her with as much curiosity.

Recorded music was playing old hymns — 'Nearer My God to Thee' and 'Abide With Me.' It was very quiet. The service was brief. The Reverend Charles Johnson spoke of his regrets at not having known Mrs. Holly Hoekstra, but he had been made aware of her exemplary life and mentioned the tribute to be published in a forthcoming article of the *Huron Plainsman*. Karen was proud of what she had written and, if such things were possible, she trusted that Holly herself would also approve. The sermon ended with a prayer, the closing music began and the casket was closed.

Karen roused from her musing, feeling oddly euphoric. How could it be possible to be so uplifted at a funeral? Then came the thought: It was not a person's death, it was the life that mattered.

She must talk to her boyfriend, Jack. She left the funeral home with a light heart. She had a new resolve and hope for her future and she knew it would last her a lifetime. She got into her car and drove off to give Jack her answer.

THE END